# THE STRAW MEN

Being the Twelfth of the Sorrowful Mysteries of
Brother Athelstan

## Paul Doherty

CRÈME de la CRIME

This first world edition published 2012
in Great Britain and the USA by
Crème de la Crime, an imprint of
SEVERN HOUSE PUBLISHERS LTD of
19 Cedar Road, Sutton, Surrey, England, SM2 5DA.
Trade paperback edition first published
in Great Britain and the USA 2012 by
SEVERN HOUSE PUBLISHERS LTD.

British Library Cataloguing in Publication Data

Doherty, P. C.
  The Straw Men.
  1. Athelstan, Brother (Fictitious character)–Fiction.
  2. John, of Gaunt, Duke of Lancaster, 1340–1399–Fiction.
  3. Tyler, Wat, d. 1381–Fiction. 4. Great Britain–
  History–Richard II, 1377-1399–Fiction. 5. Murder–
  Investigation–Fiction. 6. Detective and mystery stories.
  I. Title
  823.9'2-dc23

ISBN-13:  978-1-78029-037-9 (cased)
ISBN-13:  978-1-78029-536-7 (trade paper)

*All Severn House titles are printed on acid-free paper.*

Severn House Publishers support The Forest Stewardship Council [FSC],
the leading international forest certification organisation. All our titles that
are printed on Greenpeace-approved FSC-certified paper carry the FSC logo.

Typeset by Palimpsest Book Production Ltd.,
Falkirk, Stirlingshire, Scotland.
Printed and bound in Great Britain by
TJ International Ltd, Padstow, Cornwall.

To our first and most beloved grandaughter, Lila May Doherty,
known to us all as 'Princess Yum Yum'.

# HISTORICAL NOTE

Edward II: King 1307–1327, deposed by his wife Isabella and his own eldest son. Allegedly murdered at Berkeley Castle in September, 1327.

Edward III: The Warrior King. Launched the Hundred Years' War by claiming the throne of France through his mother. He reigned 1327–1376; married to Philippa of Hainault.

Edward the Black Prince: Eldest son and heir of Edward III, he died before his father.

Richard of Bordeaux: The Black Prince's son and heir. Richard II succeeded to the throne on the death of his grandfather. A minor, Richard was managed by his uncle, John of Gaunt, the Black Prince's younger brother.

# PART ONE

## *'Febris synocha: hectic fever'*

Sir John Cranston, swathed in cloak, muffler and beaver hat, dug in his spurs and coaxed the great destrier, his old war horse Bayonne, closer to the scaffold, which rose like a black shadow against the snowbound countryside around St John's Priory in Clerkenwell.

'Do you recognize one of your friends, Sir John?' A member of his escort, similarly garbed against the cold, called out.

'I have no friends,' Cranston replied over his shoulder. 'At least, not here,' he whispered to himself. He pushed Bayonne, who began to snort and paw the ground, nearer to the high-branched gallows. 'I know, I know,' Sir John soothed. 'But at least there is no smell.' Cranston lifted his considerable bulk up in the stirrups and stared at the frozen, decomposed cadaver, its head slightly awry, the thick, hempen rope strangling the scrawny throat like some malignant necklace. Crows and ravens had done their work, pecking out the eyes and all the other tender bits, nose, ears and lips. The corpse's face was nothing but an icy-white, frozen mask with black holes; the rest of the shrivelled corpse had merged with the shabby tunic the felon had been hanged in. Cranston glimpsed the scrap of leather pinned just beneath the man's shoulder. No one had bothered to remove it. Cranston did. He unrolled the stiffened leather scrap even as Bayonne, shaking its head in protest, backed away snorting, the hot breath rising like clouds in the freezing morning air.

'Yes, yes,' Cranston whispered, 'we have seen worse, old friend. Remember that row of stakes at Poitiers . . .?'

'Now, what do we have here?' Cranston peered down at the execution clerk's bold but faded script. 'Edmund Cuttler, felon, nip and foist, caught six times, branded twice, hanged once.' Cranston smiled at the gallows humour, then stared at the pathetic remains of Edmund Cuttler. 'Nip, foist, bum-tailor, pickpocket – poor old

butterfingers caught at last.' Cranston squinted down at the scrap
of parchment and studied the date. Cuttler had been hanged four
days before Christmas.

'Well,' he murmured, 'just in time to join the angels, if he
didn't steal their haloes.' Cranston crossed himself, pattered a
prayer for the faithful departed, pinned the execution docket back
and turned his horse's head. Once again Cranston stared along
the winding path which snaked north of the old city walls. A
cloying river fog had swept in, thickening the dense mist which
swirled over Moorfields. A heavy pall of freezing whiteness had
descended, smothering sight and sound. Somewhere deep in the
fog the bells of Clerkenwell Priory boomed out the summons to
divine office, calling the faithful to prayer on this the ninth of
January, the Year of our Lord 1381 in the Octave of the Epiphany.
Christmas, Yuletide and the Feast of the Kings were long past.
No more revelry, Cranston ruefully thought. The green holly with
its blood-red berries had withered. No more Christmas feasting
on a juice-packed goose or brawn of beef in mustard sauce. The
jugs of claret had been filled and emptied. Cranston had danced
a merry jig with his lady wife Maude, his twin sons, the poppets,
dancing beside him, and Gog and Magog, his two great mastiffs,
throwing their heads back to carol their own deep-voiced hymn.
No, the feast and the festivities were certainly over. Soon it would
be the Feast of St Hilary and the courts would open. Cranston
would return to the Guildhall to sit, listen and judge over a long
litany of human weakness and mistakes, as well as downright
depravity and wickedness. 'How Master Clumshaw did feloniously beat upon Matilda Luckshim and did cause her death other
than by natural means . . .'

Bayonne abruptly skidded on a piece of ice. Cranston broke
from his brooding. He stared around the bleak-white wilderness
then back at his own retinue, an entire convoy of mounted men-
at-arms wearing the city livery under heavy serge cloaks. They
sat, horses close together, quietly cursing why they had to be
here. Cranston gripped the reins of his own horse, his fingers
going beneath his cloak to stroke the pommel of his sword. When
he first arrived here he'd found it boring, freezing cold, highly
uncomfortable . . . but now . . .? The mist abruptly shifted and
parted to reveal ruins which, some claimed, dated back to the

days of Caesar. The Lord Coroner blinked, straining both eyes and ears. Had he glimpsed movement? Had he heard the clink of metal? Bayonne also became agitated, as if the old war horse could smell the approach of battle, see the lowered lance, hear the scrape of sword and dagger, the creak of harness and the ominous clatter of war bows being strung and arrows notched. Cranston quietened the destrier, fumbled beneath his cloak and brought out the miraculous wine skin, which never seemed to empty, took a deep gulp of the blood-red claret and sighed in pleasure. He pushed the stopper back even as he wondered what Brother Athelstan, his *secretarius* and closest friend, would be doing on a morning like this. 'Probably preaching to his parishioners about the common good,' Cranston whispered to himself. He breathed out noisily. Athelstan's parishioners! Were they, or people like them, responsible for bringing him and the rest to wait by a frozen gibbet at a desolate, ice-bound crossroads for a delegation travelling as fast and as furious as they could from Dover? Was an ambush being planned, devised and carried out by the Upright Men?

'My Lord Coroner.'

Cranston whirled around. The serjeant of the men-at-arms had pushed his horse forward.

'Sir John, with all due respect, we have been here long enough to recite a rosary.'

'And we'll stay here for ten more,' Cranston snarled, then shook his head in exasperation at his own cutting reply.

'Come, come,' Cranston lowered his muffler with his frost-laced gauntlet. 'We are here,' he stared at the ruddy-faced serjeant, 'because His Grace, the self-styled Regent John of Gaunt, uncle of our beloved King, may God bless what hangs both between his ears and between his legs, is arriving with his agents the Meisters Oudernardes and their retinue. They are fresh out of Flanders. As you may know, they will be escorted by Master Thibault, My Lord of Gaunt's Magister Secretorum, Master of Secrets and his mailed clerk, Lascelles.'

'Sir John, what are they bringing – treasure?'

'I don't know; all I have been told is to wait for them here and escort them to the Tower of London.'

'But they have enough guards themselves, surely?'

'I thought that,' Cranston replied, 'but they apparently need more.' Cranston stroked his horse's neck. 'What's your name?'

'Martin, Sir John. Martin Flyford.'

'Well, Martin Flyford, what's the poison in the boil?' Cranston gestured in the direction of the city. 'London seethes with discontent. The Great Community of the Realm plots to root up the past and build a New Jerusalem by the Thames; their leaders, the Upright Men, are devising great mischief.'

'Sir John, they have been doing that for years.'

'This is different . . .' Cranston broke off at a harsh carrying call from some bird sheltering among the ruins. Was that a marauding jay, he wondered, or something else? Bayonne was certainly nervous, while the other horses had become noticeably agitated.

'They could be approaching, Sir John. I just wish I knew why we are really here?'

'Because My Lord of Gaunt wants it that way.' Cranston turned his horse, flinching at the whipping cold. 'The Oudernardes are bringing something important, God knows what. Gaunt certainly doesn't want them to go into London. We are to meet them here and escort them along this lonely track to the Tower.' Cranston paused at a clink of harness. 'Let us pray to God and all his saints that they come soon before our backsides freeze to our saddles.' Cranston felt beneath his cloak and drew out his wine skin. He took a gulp, offered it to the serjeant then took it over to the huddle of men-at-arms, who also gratefully accepted. Mufflers were lowered, chain-mail coifs loosened, eyes gleaming in cold, pinched faces. They shared out the wine, laughing and joking.

'Look, a lantern!' one of them cried. Cranston turned in a creak of saddle. Out of the icy mist loomed a hooded rider with a lantern box attached to the rod he carried. Other figures emerged like a line of ghostly monks, cloaks and cowls, hiding everything except for the occasional glint of steel and chain-mail. Cranston touched the hilt of his sword then relaxed as the outriders approached and he glimpsed the stiffened pennants boasting the golden, snarling leopards of England against their vivid blue and blood-red background. The entire cavalcade now broke free of the mist, fifty riders in all, Cranston quickly calculated. He saw the Flemings' frozen faces shrouded in ermine-lined hoods; the rest were veteran archers from the Tower, master bowmen, who had signed an indenture to serve the Crown after years of fighting in France. Each man was hand-picked and wore the insignia of a chained white hart emblazoned on his cloak. Cranston knew their captain, Rosselyn, both by name and reputation – a hard-eyed slaughterer who'd amassed a petty fortune from ransoms in France. Cranston spurred his horse forward, pushing back his cowl, calling out Rosselyn's name. The barest courtesies were exchanged. Cranston grasped Rosselyn's hand and asked how the journey from Dover had been. Rosselyn's answer was to turn, hawk and spit.

'Very eloquent,' Cranston murmured. 'There was no trouble?'

'Not yet.' Rosselyn stared up through the mist. 'But then His Grace still believes we might be attacked close to London and within bowshot of the Tower. Treason and treachery press in from every side.'

'What are you guarding?' Cranston asked. Rosselyn's light blue, popping eyes never blinked. He just gestured with his head to behind him, where the escort of archers had parted as they relaxed. Cranston glimpsed a woman, he was sure of that, from her lithe form and the way she sat slumped in the saddle, holding her reins. Her head was covered by a deep hood, her face completely masked with only slits for the eyes, nose and mouth. The sumpter pony behind her had an escort of four archers; she herself was flanked either side by three master bowmen. Leather straps had been tied around her waist and wrists; the ends of them were held by her escort.

'No questions,' Rosselyn whispered.

'Therefore no lies,' Cranston retorted. The coroner pulled up his muffler, lifted his hand and turned his horse into the flurry of snowflakes now beginning to fall. Cranston and Rosselyn rode knee to knee in silence. Cranston kept peering to the right and left; the silence around them was increasingly unsettling.

'Reminds me of Aix in France,' Rosselyn murmured. 'Remember Philip Turbot – Gentleman Jakes as we called him, leader of a gang of freebooters? Well,' Rosselyn continued, not waiting for a reply, 'the Jacquerie did for his coven, impaled them all on stakes. Turbot was reduced to robbing a church. He was caught in a snow storm and, so thick did it lie, the Jacquerie couldn't take him out of the gates to the town gallows.' Rosselyn indicated with his head to the one they'd just left. 'So they hanged him from a tavern window bar and buried him in the city ditch.'

'I remember Turbot,' Cranston broke in. 'He claimed to be a warlock. He boasted how he'd climbed to the top of Saint Paul's steeple, even though it is crammed with holy relics. Turbot said he held a burning glass – this caught the power of the sun and cast its light with such force on a monk walking below that it struck him dead, a bolt more violent than lightening.'

'Yes, that's the same Turbot.' Rosselyn was enjoying himself. 'Anyway, they thrust his corpse into the city ditch. During the night, however, a company of wolves came, tore him out of his grave and ate him up.'

'And?'

'His was the only corpse they devoured to fill their bellies.'

'Well, no wolves prowl here.' Cranston made to grasp his wine skin when hunting horns brayed loudly to his left and right. The coroner gazed in surprise as the snowy wasteland all around them seemed to erupt into life. Figures garbed in white rose out of the earth. The first ranks, armed with arbalests and war bows, loosed a volley of hissing shafts while others, armed with pikes, swords and daggers, streamed into the horsemen, deepening and widening the confusion as archers struck by shafts slumped in their saddles or horses, similarly hurt, plunged and reared, striking out with flailing hooves. Cranston drew his own sword, the freezing cold now forgotten as a figure, masked and garbed in white, came at him with a pike. Cranston urged Bayonne forward; his enemy faltered, lowering the pike, and the war horse crashed into him. Cranston turned swiftly, striking with his sword, cleaving his opponent's head with such force the blood shot up in a fountain. Cranston stared around. The entire cavalcade was now under attack – white-clothed assailants swarmed everywhere. Cranston recognized the tactics. More pikemen were massing to hem the horsemen in while others turned and twisted, striking at leg and fetlock to maim and cripple. The archers' bows were useless here – they didn't have the time or space to notch and loose. The main brunt of the attack was against the Flemings in the centre, as if the enemy wished to seize the mysterious prisoner and her pack pony. Cranston urged his horse alongside that of Rosselyn; the captain was busy hacking furiously at an attacker already soaked in blood.

'For God's sake,' Cranston shouted, 'break off! We are mounted. We cannot be trapped here!'

Rosselyn drew a mailed foot from his stirrup and kicked his assailant away while pulling down his muffler, his face now flecked with bloody frost and sweat.

'Sweet tits,' he agreed, staring breathlessly over his shoulder. 'Sir John, you are right, they will hem us in.' The fighting was now furious around the centre, a swirling mass of men lunging, stabbing and cutting, churning the ground into a bloody, slushy mess. Rosselyn grabbed his hunting horn and blew three piercing blasts. At first the signal had no effect. Rosselyn repeated it and the cavalcade slowly began to push its way forward out of the throng away from the flailing sword, the jabbing pike and thrusting dagger. City men-at-arms and royal archers massed closer together, using both horse and weapon to break free of their oppressors. Bodies still tumbled out of saddles yet Cranston, who had been virtually ignored as the attack seethed around the centre, breathed a sigh of relief. The cavalcade broke through, horsemen spurred their mounts into a gallop across the frozen waste, arrows and bolts whipped the air, but at last they were completely free. The horde of horsemen thundered forward past the church of All Hallows in the London Wall, on to the main thoroughfare, glistening with ice, which stretched past Aldgate and down to the Tower.

Athelstan, parish priest of St Erconwald's in Southwark, stared despairingly at his congregation gathered before the rood screen in the sanctuary of their parish church. They were all grouped together, cloistered like angry sparrows, he thought, on this the feast of St Hilary, the thirteenth of January in the year of our Lord 1381. The parish church was freezing cold despite Athelstan's best efforts. He had brought in braziers crammed with charcoal fiery as the embers of Hell, or so Moleskin the boatman had described them. Nevertheless, the early morning mist had seeped like some wraith under the door, through any gaps in the horn-filled windows and across the ancient paving stones to freeze them all. Athelstan had decided to wait. He would not continue the Mass. He had recited the consecration, offered the Kiss of Peace then the trouble had surfaced – one incident among many. The source of conflict lay with a separate group to Athelstan's right, close to the sacristy door: Humphrey Warde, his wife Katherine, their big, strapping son Laurence, Margaret, their daughter and little Odo, a mere babe swaddled in thick cloths now held so protectively by his mother. The Wardes were spicers who had moved into a shop in Rickett Lane, a short walk from the parish church. They had, according to Humphrey, withdrawn from the fierce competition in Cheapside to do more prosperous trade in Southwark, raise sufficient revenue then return to Cheapside, or even move out to a city such as Lincoln or Norwich. A simple humdrum tale, until Watkin the dung collector, Pike the ditcher and Ranulf the rat catcher, together with other luminaries of his parish council, had intervened. They only had to level one accusation against the Wardes – traitors! Athelstan took a deep breath; perhaps that issue would have to wait, along with the other business which had surfaced during the Mass. Despite his involvement in the ritual, Athelstan had seen the narrow-faced rat catcher, as slippery as one of the ferrets he carried in his box, dart under the rood screen to whisper heatedly with Watkin and Pike. Some mischief was afoot! Athelstan glanced expectantly at the lovely face of Benedicta the widow woman, but she could only stare pitiably back. Athelstan searched for another ally, a newcomer to the parish – Giles of Sempringham, the anchorite, otherwise called the Hangman of Rochester, a strange, eerie figure garbed completely in black, his straw-coloured hair framing a ghostly white cadaver's face. The anchorite, who also worked as an itinerant painter, had recently moved from his cell at the Benedictine abbey of St Fulcher-on-Thames to St Erconwald's. Athelstan had secured the appropriate licences from both his superiors at Blackfriars as well as the Bishop of London. The anchorite, who had moneys from his grisly task as the dispenser of royal justice as well as revenue from painting church walls, had financed the construction of a cell here at St Erconwald's, turning the disused chantry chapel of St Alphege into an anker hold. The anchorite now sat next to Benedicta, one hand clawing his hair, the other sifting Ave beads through his fingers.

Athelstan glanced quickly at Pike and Watkin; they had lost some of their stubborn obduracy, openly agitated by Ranulf's news.

'Father,' Crim the altar boy, kneeling on the steps beside him hissed. 'Father, we should continue the Mass.'

'Aye, we should!' Athelstan's strong declaration rang like a challenge across the sanctuary. He left the altar and strode over to Katherine Warde, holding his hands out for the baby.

'Please?' he whispered, ignoring the surprised murmuring from the rest of his parishioners.

Pernel the mad Fleming woman sprang to her feet, her thick, matted hair dyed with brilliant streaks of deep red and green. Ursula the pig woman also got up, as did her great lumbering sow; ears flapping, fleshy flanks quivering, the beast followed her everywhere, even into church. Both women were staring at their parish priest as if he had introduced some new rite into the Mass.

'Please?' Athelstan smiled at Katherine. 'I need Odo now.' He turned. 'Ursula, Pernel, don't get agitated, sit down.' The mother handed the baby over. Athelstan hugged the warm little body, kissed him on the brow, then went over to confront his parishioners. 'Our Mass will now continue,' he declared loudly. Then, holding up the baby instead of the host and chalice as expected, Athelstan intoned, 'Behold the Lamb of God, behold Him who takes away the sins of the world.'

'He's not the Lamb of God,' Pike the ditcher's sour-faced wife Imelda rasped, eyes glittering with malice, mouth twisted in scorn.

'Yes, he is!' Athelstan replied fiercely. 'Behold the Lamb of God. Behold Him who takes away the sins of the world! If you,' he continued hotly, 'cannot see Christ in this little child, then do not look for him under the appearances of bread and wine. You are wasting your time, my time and, more importantly, God's time. So get out of my church!' Ursula and Pernel immediately sat down, as awestruck as the rest at the fierce temper of their usually serene parish priest. This little friar with his olive skin, dark, gentle eyes and eccentric ways now throbbed with anger. 'If you cannot share the kiss of peace with your neighbour,' Athelstan handed the baby back, thanking the mother with his eyes, 'you are not welcome here.' Athelstan moved back to the altar and stood there, his back to his parishioners. He heard movement. A stool scraped, a leaning rod clattered against the wall. When he turned round, Benedicta had risen and was sharing the kiss of peace with the Wardes. Others followed, including Ursula's sow. The pig sniffed at the baby and then decided to bolt through the rood screen, lumbering down the nave to the front door, now flung open, the great bulk of Sir John Cranston, Lord Coroner of London, blocking the light. Athelstan murmured a prayer of thanks. Cranston slammed the door shut and strode up the nave, kicking aside the great sow, who always regarded the coroner as a close friend. Behind Cranston padded another self-appointed friend, Bonaventure, Athelstan's sturdy, one-eyed tom cat, who always seemed to know when Mass was finishing and possible morsels were available from visiting parishioners.

'Lord,' Athelstan murmured, 'give me patience!' He nodded at Cranston, who stood just inside the rood screen, and continued with the Mass. He paused before the final blessing to announce that the parish council would not meet that morning but possibly tonight, once Mauger the bell clerk and council secretary had pealed the hour of Vespers. Athelstan then sketched the final blessing, declared the Mass over and swept into the sacristy. He divested, swiftly aware of Cranston standing behind him.

'Good morrow, Sir John,' he declared without turning. 'You walk into my church like the Angel of the Second Coming. I am needed, yes? We are needed?' Athelstan corrected himself. He turned and smiled at the white, bewhiskered face of the coroner, who just stared back, his great blue eyes full of sadness.

'Happy feast day, Sir John. Saint Hilary bless us all. What is the matter?'

'You are.' Cranston clasped the friar's outstretched hand. 'I sense you are upset, Brother. The business of the Wardes, that new family? I received your message. I have whispered to the sheriffs and their underlings but they know little about them. I also approached Magister Thibault, Master of My Lord of Gaunt's secret matters. He neither said "yea" or "nay".' Cranston clapped his gauntleted hands together. 'The Great Community of the Realm plots; its leaders the Upright Men prepare for what they call the Day of the Great Slaughter; they promise a new Jerusalem here in Southwark and elsewhere. The storm is coming, Athelstan, mark my words. Some of your parishioners are deep in the councils of the Upright Men.' Cranston shrugged. 'But, in the end, it will be your hangman who will be the busiest of them all. He will be kicking them from the scaffold in their hundreds.' Cranston sighed noisily. 'You're needed.' He beckoned. 'Master Thibault wants you, so collect your cloak and writing satchel.' Cranston gestured where the friar had laid these over a small trestle table. 'Tell the widow woman and the rest to look after your church. A bloody business awaits us.'

'What, Sir John?' Athelstan's stomach lurched. He recollected how most of his parishioners had attended Mass except for Ranulf the rat catcher, who'd burst in so unexpectedly.

'We will talk as we walk,' the coroner smiled, 'or at least try to.'

They re-entered the deserted sanctuary. Benedicta was lighting a taper in the Lady Chapel. Athelstan quickly whispered to her that she and Crim look after the church and the priest's house, for God only knew at what hour he would return.

'Be careful, Father.' The widow woman's lovely face creased with worry. Her anxious eyes held those of this celibate priest whom she loved so much, she had to be shriven at another church in the city. After all, how could she confess her most secret thoughts to the man who was the very cause and root of such thoughts?

'Be careful, Athelstan, please.'

'What, Benedicta . . .'

She grasped his hand in her mittened fingers. 'Father?' She looked over her shoulder at Cranston standing further down the church, admiring Huddle the painter's most recent offering, ably assisted by the Anchorite, a vivid warning against pride.

'Benedicta?'

'Father, I have heard rumours. They have trapped some Upright Men in the Roundhoop, a tavern near the Tower . . .'

'Brother Athelstan!' Cranston was marching towards the door. The friar squeezed Benedicta's hand, raised his eyes heavenwards and hurried after him. Cranston was standing on the top step outside the church, glaring across at Watkin, Pike, Ranulf and others huddled together like the conspirators they were.

'Keep well away from the Roundhoop!' Cranston roared. 'I

do not want to see any of you fine fellows across the bridge. Do
you understand?' Watkin detached himself from the group as if
to challenge the coroner, who went down the steps, hand resting
on the hilt of his sword.

'Watkin!' Athelstan warned, coming out of the church, shifting
the strap of his writing satchel more comfortably around his neck.

'Watkin,' he repeated, 'go into God's Acre. Make sure Godbless
has enough to keep himself and Thaddeus warm and fed.'
Athelstan forced a smile at the thought of that omnivorous goat
ever going hungry. 'Merrylegs!' Athelstan beckoned at the
pie-shop owner. 'I will need two of your pies by the time I return.
Huddle, you are being given money to finish the Fall of Pride.
Ask the anchorite for his advice.' Athelstan walked down the
steps, calling each parishioner by name, giving them either work
or advice. The group broke up. Athelstan crossed himself in
gratitude. He must not lose his temper. He closed his eyes and
whispered the prayer he always did after the Eucharist.

'Jesus Lord, welcome thou me
In form of bread as I see thee
Jesus, for thy holy name,
Shield me today from sin and shame.'

He opened his eyes. Cranston, despite his bulk and swagger,
had come quietly up beside him and was now staring at him
curiously.

'Sir John, I am ready.'

They left the enclosure, going up the alleyway to the main
lane leading down to London Bridge. Flaxwith, Cranston's
principal bailiff, together with his mastiff, which Athelstan
secretly considered to have the ugliest face in London after its
owner, were waiting, swaddled in their heavy cloaks. Flaxwith,
along with other members of Cranston's *comitatus*, had cornered
a relic-seller, who bleatingly introduced himself as 'John of
Burgundy', more popularly known as 'Bearded John'. This
counterfeit man owned a little fosser of blue and black satin
holding what he proclaimed to be the most holy relics, including
a finger of one of the Holy Innocents and a bone of one of the
Eleven Thousand Virgin Martyrs of Cologne, as well as a piece
of rock from where God met Moses. The relic-seller, eyes bright
in his chapped face, babbled like a babe. Cranston heard his

patter then thrust the fosser back into the man's trembling hands.

'John of Burgundy, be gone,' the coroner whispered, pushing him away. 'Today, we hunt greater prey.'

'I did hear . . .' Bearded John babbled.

'Yes, yes, I'm sure you did.' Cranston thrust him out of the way and continued on. Athelstan had to hurry to keep up. He felt like reminding the coroner how he would like to know what was happening but the noise and bustle of the streets made that impossible. The snow clouds had broken and a weak sun had brought out the crowds. For the last few days the grey, icy frostiness had stifled trade and imprisoned people in their chambers and garrets. Now, even this mild change in the weather had enticed them out. Everybody wanted to trade, sale, buy, beg or steal, not to mention visit the cook shops, wine booths, alehouses and taverns. An enterprising leech had set up shop close to Sweet Apple Court, a name Athelstan considered to be the most blatant lie in Southwark as the enclosure was as filthy and stinking as any piggery. Nevertheless, in spite of the reeking odours, the leech had gathered a crowd, assuring all and sundry that if they adjourned to his chambers in nearby Firkin alley, he would examine their urine and let a little blood. Afterwards he would provide them with his miraculous elixir, the cheapest sort containing cloves, nutmeg, mace and similar ingredients; the more expensive, 'for the more discerning', would be made up of ambergris, juniper and white frankincense. Athelstan, bemused, shook his head, constantly surprised at the sheer gullibility of the human heart. He walked on cautiously. The ground underfoot was frozen, the rutted ice covering the filthy slops and congealed mud. Athelstan murmured a prayer for safety to St Christopher as he dodged sumpter ponies, high-wheeled carts and lumbering oxen. A stiff river breeze blew a cauldron of smells and odours, a rich stew of fish, spices, fried meat and freshly baked bread along with the stench of animal dung and human waste. The ever pervasive, bitter tang of saltpetre made Athelstan gag. The saltpetre was thrown along the lanes to mask rank odours till the lay stalls, crammed with frozen refuse, were emptied by the dung carts. The scavengers who manned these were now busying to clear the mess left to rot during the previous week's snow storms. Beadles patrolled the streets, screaming at householders not to empty jakes' pots. One beadle had been rewarded for his efforts by receiving the entire contents of two night jars over him, and now he and his colleagues were battering at the door of the citizen responsible, determined on punishment.

The dead were also being buried. The break in the weather meant requiems could be sung, graves hacked out of the iron-hard ground and mourners allowed to provide their beloved departed with the appropriate religious farewell. Coffins bobbed on shoulders or bounced in hand carts as mourners, preceded by a priest pattering the psalms, led funeral processions to this chapel or that cemetery amidst the fiery glow of candles, lantern boxes and torches. Gusts of incense sweetened the air. The throng of citizens divided to allow the dead to pass before the crowds closed again, surging in every direction. Athelstan could only murmur his own prayers and keep his hands, freezing cold despite the woollen mittens, tightly on his writing satchel. The tribe of filchers, nips and foists were out, eager for plunder, hunting the swinging purse or loosely hung wallet. Cranston was recognized. Insults were hurled when the 'parishioners of the devil', as the coroner called them, fled up alleyways and runnels. At last they approached the bridge, though this was fast becoming a battleground involving a group of scavengers clearing the dirt. They had clashed with street hawkers, hucksters and chapmen who insisted on taking up their position with their baskets of eggs, butter, cheese, brushwood and heather 'fresh from the countryside'. A group of fish wives from Billingsgate, their thick leather aprons encrusted with blood, had joined the fray equally determined to sell their eel tarts, fish pies, oysters and mussels. The air was riven with curses and obscenities hurled backwards and forwards. The tumult had blocked the approach to the bridge. Cranston barked out an order. Flaxwith brought out a hunting horn from beneath his cloak and blew strident blasts before bellowing at the top of his voice that everyone was to keep the King's peace and step aside for the Lord High Coroner. The tumult subsided. As the brawlers dispersed into the shadow of the overhanging houses, Cranston swept on. Once he had passed, the tumult began again. Athelstan heaved a sigh of relief as he glimpsed the bridge's high gates and towers as well as the cornices, sills and steeple of the Priory of St Mary Overy. They had to pause for a while as an execution party made its way down to the gallows – three wolfsheads who'd escaped from sanctuary at the priory and been wounded during the affray. Each had been summarily tried, condemned and loaded into wheelbarrows, commonly used to collect dung, and were now being taken from the Compter Clink to the riverside gallows. Athelstan blessed each of the groaning men then passed on to the bridge through the cavernous gate, its curving rim spiked with the boiled heads of traitors.

They made their way along the narrow lane between the houses and shops, which rose above them, leaning over to block out the sky. Beneath them echoed the thunderous roar of the river as it crashed against the starlings protecting the pillars of the bridge. Athelstan was sure the bridge was moving; as always, he tried to distract himself while keeping a wary eye on the ground beneath. A cluster of eel stalls stood at the near end of the thoroughfare and the discarded skins made the lane more slippery than ice. Athelstan glanced to his left and right. He was always fascinated by the apparent wealth displayed by the stalls and shops along the bridge. Some of the costliest items in London could be purchased here. Cloths and fabrics from Constance, Tournai and Rouen. Canvas from Westphalia and silver thread from Cologne were sold alongside amber and bone beads, ivory combs, silk girdles, brass rings, leather hats and hand mirrors of steel, crystal and jasper. Apprentice boys loudly proclaimed the virtues of buckram, silk, sarcanet, lawn and dyed wool. Jewellers and goldsmiths offered diamond necklaces, buckles and girdles, precious stone paternosters, mazer cups, silver gilt goblets and salt cellars, as well as spoons of every precious kind studded with gems or embroidered with gold or silver tracery. Another stall, manned by three clerks, 'learned in the halls, schools and Inns of Court,' offered to write or copy letters, deeds, leases, memoranda or bills of exchange. Between life-size statues of St Catherine the Virgin and St Nicholas of Colenso, the haberdashers of the hat, haberdashers of the small wares and ironmongers offered kerchiefs embroidered with religious devices, pyxes or kissing boxes, night-time laces, pepper mills, girdles and pouches, the latter adorned and embroidered with silver clasps. At Becket's shrine in the centre of the bridge, merchants met bankers before going into the chapel either to seal documents at the altar or pass money over. All this was recorded by the chapel's clerks in a leather-bound book of debts kept in an iron chest beneath the relic stone; this made repayment a matter of faith not just business. In the stocks next to the chapel, a vintner, found guilty of mixing cobbler's wax with the dregs of his wine, was sitting with his legs firmly clasped. The disgraced merchant was being forced to drink a draught of his own adulterated beverage. A market beadle slowly emptied another jug over the unfortunate man's head while a second beadle loudly proclaimed, 'That Richard Pemrose, vintner, could do no further trade in wine or any other commodity for a year and a day'. Beside Pemrose sat an imprisoned cook's apprentice from a nearby pie stall. He had sold pies and patties stuffed with the flesh of hen, goose, duck, lark and fish, but he'd also plucked at the costly gowns of passers-by and so, as the notice around his neck proclaimed, 'damaged their clothes with hands dirtied and fouled'. Cranston paused to take a drink from his wine skin. He offered this to Athelstan, who refused even as he shook off the grasp of a chapman eager to sell him a trinket.

'It will change now, little friar.' Cranston gestured to the near-end of the bridge. 'The hustle and bustle will fade and,' he nodded at the spikes above the gate leading into the city, 'there will be fresh offerings on them tomorrow morning.'

They left the bridge, turning right up the lane leading to St Magnus Church. Men-at-arms had sealed the streets. Chains had been pulled across. Carts closed over the entrance to the twisting alleys and lanes. Knights in chain-mail stood by their war horses. Mounted hobelars, swords drawn, clustered nearby. The air reeked of sweat, leather and horse. Cranston had to leave Flaxwith and the bailiffs at one of the barriers; only he and Athelstan were allowed up the lane to where the Roundhoop stood behind its high curtain wall. Athelstan had visited the tavern before, a strange building, circular in shape, of harsh grey stone with a sloping red-tiled roof. Once it had been a barbican or weapons' tower until some enterprising ale-master had bought it and reopened its great doors as a hostelry. The main gates to the tavern hung loose, and on either side along the wall stood men-at-arms and archers. Cranston recognized Rossleyn; now and again the captain would edge forward, peer round the open gate then hastily withdraw. On the other side of the gates clustered a group of men, heads together in heated discussion. These broke off as Cranston and Athelstan approached. The friar immediately recognized Thibault, Master of Secrets, the senior clerk of John of Gaunt's chancery. A born plotter, an inveterate schemer, Thibault dabbled in all the dark, sinister affairs which flowed around his master. Thibault was also a cleric who nursed secret ambitions of a bishopric. Cranston had mocked this, claiming Thibault would make a fine shepherd as long as his flock produced a rich fleece. 'A man who would merrily give you the shirt off your back,' the coroner had added. Thibault's looks belied such barbs: small and plump, his round, smiling shaven face glistened with oil and good living. A fastidious man, Thibault's corn-coloured hair was neatly cropped in strict accordance with Canon Law to show his tonsure. Master Thibault dressed ever so modestly in a dark fustian cotheardie over a white cambric shirt and Lincoln-green leggings pushed into the finest leather boots from Cordova. Thibault's blue eyes creased in good humour as he clasped Athelstan's hand and welcomed him to what he termed 'this delicate affair'. Other introductions were made. Athelstan nodded at Lascelles, Thibault's man-at-arms dressed completely in black leather, his dark hair swept back and tied in a queue. Lascelles always reminded Athelstan of a raven with his sallow-pitted skin, pointed face and a nose as sharp as a hook above thin, bloodless lips. A strange soul, Athelstan considered, Lascelles was Thibault's dagger man and enjoyed the most unsavoury reputation. The Flemings were only known to Athelstan by common rumour. The red-faced Oudernardes, father and son, were Gaunt's agents in Ghent – powerful merchants, they looked the part with their heavy-jowled features, luxuriant beards and moustaches. Both were dressed soberly although costly in beaver hats, ermine-lined mantles and cloaks of the purest wool. Lettenhove, their man at arms, was a hardbitten veteran, his narrow face and close-cropped head marked with old wounds and cuts. Cornelius, their secretary, was small and round as a dumpling with narrow, blackcurrant eyes which almost disappeared into the folds of his pasty white face. Cornelius' hand shake was soft and limp, his voice lisping like a girl's, yet Athelstan caught his shifty, haughty look; how

Cornelius' lips pursed in a smirk as he surveyed Athelstan from head to toe. He then turned away, nodding to himself as if he'd weighed the Dominican in the balance and found him wanting. Athelstan bit back his temper. Cranston coughed and clapped his hands.

'No movement?' the coroner barked louder than he intended. 'Rosselyn, what is happening here?' The captain of archers on the other side of the entrance edged forward; he stooped and raced across the entrance to the tavern yard. He'd hardly reached the other side when an arrow whipped through the air to clatter further down the lane.

'In God's name!' Athelstan exclaimed.

'Peer round the gate, Brother,' Cranston urged, 'but stoop, be quick!'

Athelstan did so. The cobbled stable yard glistened with bloody, melted slush. The outhouses on either side, the storerooms, smithy and stables looked deserted, though Athelstan heard the whinnying of horses in their stalls. He edged further and gasped. Two corpses hung by their necks from the bars of an upper window, its shutters flung back. The men just dangled there, hands tied behind their backs, booted feet swaying, necks twisted, heads slightly back, faces frozen in a horrid death. Closer to the main tavern door two huge mastiffs were sprawled in a pool of freezing blood; arrow shafts pierced their throats and flanks. One of the shutters in the grey-rounded wall moved. Athelstan drew back as another shaft sped through the air.

'Sir John, Master Thibault,' Athelstan demanded, 'what is going on? Why have I been brought here?'

'They have asked for you.' Cranston took a swig from his wine skin.

'Who have? Sir John, please, what is happening?' Though remembering Ranulf's interruption of Mass, Athelstan began to suspect the worst. Cranston leaned against the wall, the others grouped around him. Athelstan sensed there was something very wrong. The coroner would not look him in the eye. He was about to speak when a shout echoed from the Roundhoop.

'We have glimpsed a black and white robe. Is Athelstan the Dominican here?'

'Yes!' Athelstan shouted back before anyone could stop him.

'Yes, I am. What do you want with me?'

'To talk.'

Athelstan turned to Cranston. 'Why,' he demanded fiercely, 'am I here?'

'Four days ago,' Thibault answered, 'we were attacked on our way to the Tower.'

'Yes, I'd heard about that – the entire city did.'

'Our assailants were despatched by the Upright Men, leaders of the so-called "Great Community of the Realm".'

'And?'

'We heard,' Cranston replied, gesturing at Thibault, 'how some of the Upright Men were meeting at the Roundhoop. Minehost here, Simon Goodmayes, is known to be sympathetic to their cause.'

'In other words,' Athelstan replied abruptly, 'Master Simon does not want his tavern burnt to the ground when the Day of Judgement arrives; that is what they call it, yes?'

'True.' Cranston smiled at the little friar so uncharacteristically angry. 'Master Thibault has spies among the Upright Men; they alerted us to this meeting.'

'We surrounded the Roundhoop,' Thibault declared. 'The tavern stands behind a square stone wall with a garden at the back. We now have it sealed. Believe me, Brother, escape is impossible.'

'The Upright Men realized they'd been betrayed,' Cranston declared. 'They hanged two of the tavern servants and slaughtered Master Simon's mastiffs. Everyone else has fled, faster than rabbits under the hawk. The Upright Men now have Master Simon and a few customers held to ransom.'

'How many Upright Men are there?' Athelstan asked.

'Perhaps ten in all,' Thibault replied. 'We arrived and they acted swiftly. Doors were barred; two of the servants apparently tried to escape and were summarily hanged. The mastiffs turned nasty; they realized their master was in danger, so they were killed.'

'And why are you here, sirs?' Athelstan turned to the two Flemings.

'Because, Brother,' Pieter Oudernarde lowered the muffler from around his mouth, 'we believe these same outlaws organized the attack on us four days ago. We are certain our possessions were stolen.' The Fleming caught Thibault's eye; he coughed and pulled a face. 'We would also like to see justice done.'

'And your property returned?'

'Yes, Brother,' Cornelius piped up, his reedy voice uncomfortable on the ear. 'To see our property – certain items – returned.'

'And yet I ask again,' Athelstan insisted, 'why am I here? What do you want me to do?'

'The Upright Men want to negotiate,' Cranston murmured, holding the friar's gaze, warning him with his eyes that all was not what it appeared to be.

'To negotiate? Why me?'

'You are well known, Brother,' Cranston again replied, gesturing at the others to remain silent.

'Will he talk?' a voice bellowed from the tavern.

'What do they want?'

'Safe passage, probably by river.'

'And if not?'

'They will kill the hostages and fight to the death!' Cranston declared brusquely. 'Look at the Roundhoop, Brother – built of stone like a castle tower. We cannot burn them out.'

Athelstan ignored the deep unease tugging at his soul. Cranston could say more but this was neither the time nor the place.

'I will go in,' Athelstan said wearily. 'Let us hear what they have to say.' A bunch of evergreen was brought from a nearby garden lashed to a pole. Athelstan threw this into the gateway.

'*Pax et Bonum*,' he called. 'I will speak.'

'*Tu solus frater*,' a voice sang out in Latin. 'You alone, Brother.' Athelstan, fingering the wooden cross on the cord around his neck, stepped around the gateway. He walked slowly across the cobbles, quietly murmuring the prayers for the dead, trying not to think of himself but the two corpses dangling by their necks, young men hurled violently into eternity with neither prayer nor blessing. The great wooden doors of the tavern swung open though no one appeared.

'Enter!' a voice called. Athelstan paused.

'Enter!'

'Cut down the hanged men,' Athelstan retorted. 'Cut them

down now. Let me pray over them. God knows their souls may
not have left their bodies. Judgement could still await.'

'Enter!' the voice screamed. Athelstan took a deep breath. He
knelt down on the cobbles, head bowed, ignoring the repeated
shouts to enter. Silence fell. A window opened and the two
dangling corpses were cut from their ropes to tumble on to the
ground. Ignoring the faces frozen in hideous death, Athelstan
administered the last rites to both victims. He blessed their
corpses, rose to his feet and walked up the steps into the circular
tap room, a murky place of shifting shadows. All the windows
were shuttered, the only light thrown by squat tallow candles
and narrow lantern horns. A figure loomed out of the gloom,
head covered by a pointed hood, a red mask hiding his face, his
heavy, draping cloak hung loose to reveal a war belt with sword
and dagger sheaths. Other shapes stepped into the pools of light,
dressed all the same, sinister phantasms of the night, armed and
menacing. Athelstan stared round. Minehost Simon lay badly
wounded, along with two servants. A Friar of the Sack and a fat,
painted whore, a bushy orange wig almost hiding her face, sat
like terrified children on a bench against the wall. They gazed
owl-eyed at Athelstan, except for the whore, who put her face
in her hands and began to sob.

'Well,' the friar asked, 'what now?'

'We trust you, Athelstan. The earthworms say you are not one
of us yet you are sympathetic.' The voice of the masked figure
confronting him scarcely rose above a whisper.

'The earthworms?' Athelstan retorted. 'You mean my poor
parishioners who, according to you, will spin Fortune's wheel
and change the power of Heaven.' Athelstan shook his head.
'Gaunt will burn this city before he allows that to happen.'

'We shall burn it for him – an easy enough task.'

'Gallows and gibbets are just as easily erected.'

The masked figure laughed softly.

'Why did you hang those two poor unfortunates – aren't they
earthworms too?'

'They tried to escape; that can only mean they were either
spies or intent on raising the alarm. They had to be punished; a
warning to the rest.'

Athelstan stared around the gloomy tap room. He glimpsed

about six Upright Men – others, he reasoned, must be in the galleries above. He also noticed their war belts and quivers, the arbalests, maces and clubs and, in his secret dread, Athelstan sensed this would end in bloodshed.

'So what must I do now?' Athelstan tried to keep his voice calm.

'We are near the river.' The Upright Man went on to demand, 'We want one of the royal war barges from the Tower. We—' He abruptly paused. Athelstan heard a whooshing sound followed by a scream in the galleries above; something hot and fiery smashed into the shutters of the Roundhoop. The Upright Man drew his sword. Athelstan gestured at the hostages.

'Run!' he screamed. 'Run!' He hastened over and dragged the friar and the whore to their feet. She kept her face down, her voice squeaky, muttering curses in the patois of the London slums. Athelstan pushed them both towards the door. He glanced swiftly around; more fiery missiles smashed into the wooden shutters. Smoke billowed down the stairs. Athelstan hurried towards the door. An Upright Man emerged out of the murk, pulling the red mask from his bearded face. He gazed wild-eyed at the friar and raised his sword threateningly, moving sideways as Athelstan tried to avoid him. More missiles smashed into the walls. Thick smoke curled. The air was shattered by screams and yells. The Upright Man lowered his sword, an almost beseeching look in his eyes.

'I didn't know!' Athelstan yelled at him. The whore close to the door collapsed to her knees, sobbing in terror.

'I didn't know,' Athelstan repeated.

The young man let his sword arm droop then abruptly lurched forward, mouth open. He tried to speak but gagged on his words. He staggered towards Athelstan before collapsing to the floor; the yard-long shaft had pierced him deep in the back between his shoulder blades. The stricken man rolled to one side, stretching his head back as if searching for someone. Athelstan knelt beside him as royal archers and men-at-arms surged through the door, knocking aside Athelstan and the other hostages in their rush to engage the Upright Men. The smoke was thickening, reducing individuals to mere shapes. More soldiers charged in. Swords and daggers flashed in the light. Blood snaked across the floor, trickling over the green supple rushes. The friar and the whore, on all fours, crept out on to the steps. Athelstan was tempted to follow but he could still feel the Upright Man's body warm against his shaking hand. He turned the man over on to his side; he was dying, the fluttering eyes dulling, blood bubbling out of nose and mouth.

'Thank you,' Athelstan whispered. 'You did not strike. God be my witness, I did not know the attack would be launched.'

'Father, shrive me of all my sins.' The dying man tried to speak but the blood gathering at the back of his throat choked him. Athelstan whispered the words of absolution even as he watched the life light die in the stricken man's eyes. He gave a gasp summoning up his last energy, what Aquinas called the 'last leap of the soul' before it left the body. He grasped Athelstan's hand.

'Your name?' the friar asked gently.

'No name.' The dying man sighed. 'Tell my beloved to continue gleaning.'

'Gleaning?' Athelstan leaned over the man. 'What do you mean?'

The Upright Man tried to rise and twist his head as if searching for someone or something. 'Tell her to glean; I won't see her.' His grasp on Athelstan's hand tightened and relaxed. He sighed out his soul, body trembling; he coughed blood then lay still. Athelstan sketched a blessing and rose to his feet. The attack was now deep in the tavern, the Upright Men retreating into the upper galleries. The tap room was like a battlefield across which echoed screams and yells, the strident screech and scrape of sword on sword yet the struggling shapes, the fire licking at the shutters and the noise of battle seemed eerily distant as if muffled by a sound like that of pounding waves in a storm. Athelstan stared around, trying to make sense of the confusion. The smoke was now thinning, drifting out through the main door. The Friar of the Sack and his whore had disappeared. Minehost Simon and his two servants lay stretched out on the cobbles, corpses stiffening, their throats slit, a mess of blood congealing at neck and chest. Athelstan went out and administered the last rites but he fumbled and forgot the words. He paused, took a deep breath and began again. He whispered the words of forgiveness and that final petition to the Lords of Light to go out and greet all these souls: 'Lest they fall into the power of the enemy.' He felt a hand on his shoulder. Cranston stood there, holding his chancery satchel. Athelstan had never seen the coroner look so sad; his ruddy face was pale and those glaring blue eyes dimmed. Even the glorious white whiskers seemed to droop.

'By Mary and the Mass,' Cranston breathed. 'Athelstan, I swear, I did not realize this was going to happen and yet, as you know,' he blinked, 'from the moment we arrived I smelt treachery. I was asked to accompany the Flemings around the wall to the back of the tavern. When I got there, the mangonels released their first shots, fiery, pitch-coated bundles of bracken and old cloth. Only then did I realize what was about to take place. I hastened back but the assault had already begun. Athelstan . . .' The Dominican simply shrugged off the coroner's hand, grasped his chancery satchel and strode over to the gate where Thibault stood, legs apart, hands on his hips, head slightly back as he watched his archers drag out the corpses from the Roundhoop. The Master of Secrets narrowed his eyes, lips twisted in a smirk as the Dominican confronted him.

'Brother, I gave them no promises except one!' Thibault held up a hand. 'They wanted to speak to you and so they did. They were traitors, rebels, taken in arms plotting against the Crown. They were murderers and ravagers. Now they are dead and their heads will provide further decoration for London Bridge.' He leaned forward, the smirk replaced by false concern. 'Brother?'

'Once a scorpion asked a wolf to take him across a fast-flowing river. The wolf,' Athelstan held Thibault's gaze, 'at first refused. "You will sting me and we shall both die". The scorpion denied this, promising all would be well so the wolf allowed the scorpion to stand on his head as he braved the waters.'

'And?' Thibault drew his head back, glancing over his shoulder at his archers now kicking and abusing the corpses.

'The scorpion stung the wolf, who protested, saying the scorpion had given him his word and now they would both die, so why had he stung him? You know the scorpion's response?'

'No, Brother, I don't.'

'The scorpion replied, "Because it is in my nature". Good day, Master Thibault.' Athelstan stepped around him and, clutching his chancery satchel, strode down the lane, ignoring Thibault's cry of 'Very good, very good!' as well as Cranston's shouts to wait awhile. Athelstan walked on through the cordon of men-at-arms now fighting to keep back the gathering crowd, whose mood was turning ugly. Athelstan glimpsed faces he recognized: the pious fraud, the Sanctus Man, with his tray of religious artefacts; Mudfog, a member of Moleskins' Guild of St Peter; and Shrimp and Castoff, two members of the Fisher of Men's company, that strange individual who made his living by gathering corpses from the Thames. Athelstan did not pause but passed on, taking the path down to London Bridge. His mind was in turmoil, angry at what he had witnessed yet relieved to be free though still deeply anxious about the doings of some of his parishioners. Would they also be trapped to be cut down or hanged? He recalled the dying Upright Man's last words about asking a woman to glean. What did that mean? What had that unfortunate man been looking for?

# PART TWO
## 'Mulcator: Despoiler'

A thelstan crossed on to the bridge, coughing and spluttering at the thick smoke and fumes wafting up from the nearby tanneries. He made his way around the potholes, choked with rank weeds and coarse grass which thrived in the sluggish ooze and slush left by the ebb and flow of the river. So lost in his own thoughts, he was across the bridge before he knew it. Athelstan paused, took a deep breath and made his way up towards St Erconwald's. Now and again the friar paused to exchange a few words with those he met, especially the Brotherhood of the Cloak. Athelstan always liked to find out what mischief they were plotting. The Brotherhood was really a group of beggars who sometimes used the nave of his parish church for what they called 'Conclaves of their Pastoral Councils'. The leading light of the Brotherhood was Freelove, a buxom young woman with jet-black hair and cheeky eyes, who was always accompanied by her group of admirers – men who rejoiced in the names of Littlerobin, Rentabut, Eatbread and Godshelf. His brief encounter with these colourful characters calmed Athelstan's mind, though he told them off roundly when they confessed that they planned to cross the bridge to beg in the city under the guise of poor pilgrims to Jerusalem and elsewhere. To deepen their deception, the Brotherhood had fixed fraudulent scallop shells, sprigs of greenery and small pilgrim medals to their tattered cloaks.

Further up the lane, Athelstan found to his dismay Matilda Milksop, scarcely a gospel greeter at St Erconwald's, though one who considered herself a member of his parish. Matilda was fastened by her neck and wrists in the stocks. The notice pinned next to her proclaimed, 'How Matilda Milksop, through her malicious words and abuse, had greatly molested and annoyed her neighbours, sowing envy, discord and ill-will, and oft times defamed and back-bitten many of the same neighbours, so she must be punished as a common scold'. Matilda was crying from the pain and the freezing cold. The bailiff, seated on a stool beside her, chewing one of Merrylegs' pies with a brimming blackjack of ale from the nearby Piebald tavern, ignored her pleas. Athelstan, having produced a coin and mentioned Cranston's name more than once, secured Matilda's release. Once she could stand upright, he helped the woman into the dark, warm stuffiness of the Piebald tavern with strict instructions to Joscelyn, its owner, the one-armed former river pirate, to give her good sustenance. By the time he reached the lychgate of St Erconwald's, Athelstan felt much better, slightly regretting his treatment of Sir John. He stood just beyond the entrance and stared out over the hard, frozen ground. The ancient headstones and crosses glittered in the frost light, and a small column of smoke curled between the shutters of the death house.

'Godbless,' Athelstan shouted, 'you are well?'

'God bless you too, Brother,' the beggar replied. 'God bless your trousers and all you have in them. Thaddeus and I are warm and snug. Mistress Benedicta gave me a bowl of stewed pottage and a jug of ale. We are as merry as robins.' Athelstan smiled and went up the path through the main door of the church. A strong flutter of torch light further up the northern transept showed only Huddle, ably assisted by the anchorite, busy in what both proclaimed to be their 'Magnum Opus', an eye-catching, vivid portrayal of the Seven Deadly Sins. Huddle had finished Greed and was now busy on Pride, 'that great snare of the devil', as Huddle had written in the scrolled tag at the bottom of the painting.

Both artists acknowledged Athelstan as he walked over to them, but they were really lost in their creation, almost impervious to his presence. Athelstan stopped to admire the work. Huddle had taken as his theme for Pride the fall of Lucifer from Paradise. The painting depicted fanged, clawed and cloven-hoofed demons as well as bat-winged, sooty hobgoblins, the usual citizens of Hell. Lucifer, however, was totally different. Still an archangel, he fell from Paradise in a thick ream of golden stars while the rebel angels he had seduced flowed after him like brilliant tongues of fire. Lucifer was no creature of the dark pit but a beautiful young man, blond curls framed a face of serious sweet youthfulness; his body glowed white and pure as the driven snow; his limbs were perfectly proportioned. Athelstan was tempted to ask how Huddle had devised such an original treatment but he and the anchorite were locked in deep discussion about the mixing of paints, so he left them to it and returned to the priest's house. He first checked that Philomel the old war horse was, as Crim the altar boy declared, 'still breathing'. He certainly was, chewing slowly on a bundle of sweetened hay. Athelstan patted and blessed him and crossed to the priest's house. He found the secret place where Benedicta had left the key, unlocked the door and walked into the cold, stone-flagged kitchen.

Athelstan moved quickly, building up the fire so the flames flared up, licking the cauldron dangling from its hook; this soon exuded a delicious smell of onions, cooked meats and sprinkled herbs. Bonaventure appeared like a ghost to sit beside the fire before joining the Dominican at the great table. Athelstan took yesterday's loaf and a pot of butter, filled a tankard of ale from a small barrel in the buttery, washed his hands at the *lavarium* and blessed both himself and Bonaventure; he sat at the table sipping from his horn spoon, every mouthful being carefully watched by Bonaventure, who always stayed to lick the bowl really clean. Athelstan ate slowly, reflecting on what he had seen, felt and heard. What should he do? Undoubtedly there was a very tangled tale behind the Roundhoop incident but that would take time to unravel. Or would it? Athelstan sensed an evil was gathering like poison in a wound, surging in a boil of pus and filthy matter. His stomach tingled with excitement. He should confess that and yet, he stared into the fire, God forgive him, he loved the tangled maze of mystery. Deep in his soul Athelstan sensed he had reached the meadows of murder; soon he would be through the gate walking that crooked path into the House of Cain. The pursuit would begin. One soul hunting another, like God did the first assassin. Only this would be different: Athelstan would have to wait for the murderer to strike. The friar pushed the bowl away and watched Bonaventure lick it clean. He climbed the steps to his neatly prepared bed loft and lay down on the palliasse, staring up into the darkness.

'Who will you be?' he murmured. 'When will you come? How will you strike?' Athelstan's mind drifted back to the

Roundhoop – the arrows slicing the air, the screams and yells, that young man bubbling his life blood, his mind all a wander. The orange-wigged whore. Master Simon lying with his throat cut. Thibault's face, smirking. Bonaventure came up and decided to lie on the other side of him.

'When it comes, I must act like you, my terror of the alleyways,' Athelstan whispered. 'Swift and deadly.' He was promising to do that when he drifted into a deep sleep, only woken by Bonaventure scratching at the door to get out. Athelstan scrambled down the ladder, opened the door and watched the tom cat disappear into the freezing night. Rubbing his arms, Athelstan went to build up the fire. He peered across at the hour candle on its iron stand. Two rings had burnt – late afternoon, it was time he acted. He doused the candles and lanterns, swung his cloak around him and hurried up the lane to Merrylegs' pastry shop to find its garrulous owner was absent on business.

'Father said it was very important.' Little Merrylegs piped up, serving the friar, handing over the linen-wrapped pies and pastries.

'You mean he is at the Piebald tavern with the rest of his coven?'

'Undoubtedly.' Large Merrylegs, the eldest of the cook's brood, agreed from where he knelt coaxing the ovens either side of the great hearth. Athelstan made to pay but Little Merrylegs pushed the coins back. 'Father always tells us . . .'

'Thank you.' Athelstan smiled, tapping a coin back. 'But this father would like you to take a message to the Piebald. Tell those two worthies, Watkin and Pike, that I wish to see them within the hour at the priest's house.' Little Merrylegs solemnly promised he would. Athelstan walked back into the lane. The houses on either side lay silent and dark. Athelstan felt a tingling along the back of his neck and drew a deep breath against the gathering terrors. No candlelight peeped out between shutters. The lantern boxes which glowed when he came down here now hung empty. Athelstan continued on, his sandal-clad feet crunching on the frozen dirt, head bent against the nipping breeze. He walked slowly and, as he did, became aware of two shapes like shadows flitting either side of him. Athelstan stopped and so did they. He turned to his right and glimpsed a man, head cowled, face blackened. Athelstan glanced over his shoulder; others were merging out of the murk like hell-borne wraiths.

'Benedicite?' Athelstan whispered. 'Blessings on you, brothers! What do you want with a poor friar?'

'Vengeance.'

'Haven't you read, Brother?' Athelstan replied. '"Vengeance is mine, says the Lord, I will repay"?'

'The Roundhoop,' the voice grated.

'I was used, you know that?'

'How do we know?'

'On reflection,' Athelstan retorted, 'that Friar of the Sack was no more a friar than you are, Brother.'

The man laughed a merry sound which lessened the tension. 'Why do you say that?' he asked.

'Because, allegedly, he belongs to a strict order dedicated to the dying, yet he was more interested in getting out of that tavern than I was. Men were dying violently; never once did he stay to offer the *consolamentum*. He must have been one of yours; he told you about what happened.'

'True,' the voice whispered. 'He was still a priest, a friar just terrified of being caught both in our company,' he laughed, 'as well as that of a common whore.'

'Brother.' Athelstan walked on, clutching his linen parcel. 'My pies are getting cold. I am hungry and very tired. Why lurk in the shadows? Come and join me at the table. I could even hear your confession, shrive you, forgive your sins before you also die.'

'When the Apocalypse comes, the Day of Great Slaughter and the strongholds fall, which side will you be on, Athelstan?'

'I will do my duty to my parishioners. I will say my prayers.'

'You will not be on the side of God?'

'God has no sides.'

'What about justice, right?'

'Micah chapter six, verse three,' Athelstan retorted. '"Three things I ask of you, Son of Man, and only these three. To love justly, to act tenderly and to walk humbly with your God."'

'We want you to join us.'

'I will pray for you.' Athelstan heard the scrape of steel from a scabbard; he stopped, his mouth dry.

'*Pax et Bonum,*' the voice whispered. 'Fear not, little friar. We are near the end of the lane and we don't want to be surprised by your fat friend the coroner.'

'He is my friend and a good one. He does not draw steel on a poor friar or worse, make his supper grow cold.'

'We know that. Now listen, just ask Sir John who is the prisoner the Flemings brought to the Tower? Oh, and tell Sir John to be more prudent. He should not walk so bold; most of his masters are both bought and sold.'

'What do you mean?'

'This is the hour of Judas, Friar. Darkness is falling. The poor earthworms stir and the hawk lords survey the field and wonder how all this might end.'

'What is that to him?'

'Tell him the tribes of Edom, Moab, Philistia and Egypt are already plotting to divide the spoils.'

'I do not know . . .'

'He will, Brother, but now, a word of warning to you and yours.' The voice became a hiss. 'Among your parishioners, those who serve the Upright Men, walks a true-arch priest Judas – for him there will be no mercy or compassion. The business at the Roundhoop was this Judas' work. Keep an eye on your flock, Brother. We certainly shall. If necessary we shall impose the ban.'

'The ban?' Athelstan felt a deep chill, half suspecting what he meant.

'You quote scripture, Brother, so do I . . .'

'So did Satan,' Athelstan retorted, 'when he tempted Christ.'

Again, the laugh. 'Consult the Book of Samuel, Brother.' The figure drew closer and, before Athelstan could react, grasped the friar's hand and pressed in a small pouch of coins. 'For the poor. You gave the last rites to one of our comrades at the Roundhoop. What did he say?'

'You know I cannot tell you what he confessed but he babbled about gleaning; he was searching for someone.'

'Aren't we all?' came the sardonic reply. 'Farewell, Brother, for now.' The shadows receded. Athelstan looked back down the alleyway: lantern horns had been lit; candles glowed from upstairs windows. Athelstan shook his head at the power and influence of the Upright Men. This secret war, he reasoned, fought in flitting shadows and murky chambers, would soon erupt and what then?

He reached the priest's house, went in, put the pies in the small oven built into the side of the small hearth and waited. His two guests arrived shortly afterwards, shuffling into the kitchen in their mud-caked boots. Both Watkin and Pike looked flushed with ale.

Athelstan pointed at the *lavarium* and told them to wash their hands as he placed three tranchers on the scrubbed kitchen table and served the pies. Athelstan waited till they had eaten then picked up his psalter. He found the verse he was looking for and fought to hide the fear spurting within him. He closed the book. 'Well, gentlemen,' Athelstan forced a smile, 'and so it is written that the prophet Samuel placed Agag and the Amalekites under the ban, to be smitten hip and thigh, no quarter to be shown to man, woman, child or beast. Now tell me,' Athelstan's voice thundered, 'who among us would do what the Prophet Samuel did?' He paused. 'Examine yourselves before your priest. Remember, as Christ does, your misdeeds. Make no secret of your sins even though your wickedness might be difficult to confess.' Athelstan breathed in. 'To cut to the quick, in a word, I ask you in God's name, has the ban been imposed on our parish . . .?'

The leaders of the Upright Men: Wat Tyler, Jack Straw, John Ball the preacher, Simon Grindcobbe and others, disguised in the robes of Friars of the Sack, stood before the gates to the entrance of London Bridge on the city side of the Thames. Capped candles were carried before them. They had, in their pretended role as preachers, permission from the Guardian of the Gates and Keeper of the Heads, Master Burdon, to pray for those slain during the furious bloody affray at the Roundhoop. They all stared up at the heads of their dead comrades now poled on staves jutting above the gate. They were unrecognizable; the crows had already been busy with their eyes, while the heads had been boiled and tarred before being displayed.

'How many?' Grindcobbe whispered.

'All of them,' came the murmured reply. 'Most were killed in the assault. Three were sorely wounded and lowered by chains into the river to slowly drown as the tide changed.'

'By whom?'

'A creature called Laughing Jack, a grotesque with a gargoyle face. He and two others are Thibault's hangmen. They now rejoice, spending their earnings in the Paradise of Purgatory tavern near the house of the Crutched Friars.'

'Kill them,' Grindcobbe whispered over his shoulder. 'Kill them when their bellies are bloated with wine. I do not want them to hear the bells of vespers tomorrow.' Grindcobbe stared at the row of severed heads: their hair had been combed before they'd been spiked, a truly gruesome sight in the dancing flames of the cresset torches beneath. John Ball the preacher intoned the requiem and the others joined in; a few, including Grindcobbe, just waited for the words to peter out.

'And the traitor?' Tyler's broad Kentish accent did nothing to diminish the menace in his voice. 'Our comrades were betrayed. Gaunt was informed.'

'We have our suspicions,' Grindcobbe murmured. 'The parish of Saint Erconwald's may nurse a traitor; their priest Athelstan has been warned.'

'But he is innocent.' Jack Straw pulled his cowl further over his head. 'Magister Thibault, that devil in flesh, just used him. Our brothers,' he sighed, 'should have been more vigilant.'

'Thibault was furious about what we seized,' Tyler remarked.

'Perhaps it's time we returned his property.' Grindcobbe laughed. 'But this mysterious prisoner. Who is she? Why does Gaunt place such a value on her? For now that must wait. Oh, yes, it shall, as will why our spy in Thibault's stronghold failed to inform us that an attack on the Roundhoop was being planned.'

'Perhaps he did not know.'

'Or perhaps he did not wish to expose himself further. But one day he will have to – perhaps sooner than he thinks.' Grindcobbe stared up, watching the tendrils of mist curl round the spiked heads. 'I wonder who our traitor is?' Grindcobbe spoke as if to himself. 'But come.'

They moved from the gateway, making their way up East Cheap. The night was quiet. The Upright Men walked, hoods pulled forward, hands up the voluminous sleeves of their gowns.

They were not afraid or wary; their henchmen, weapons at the ready, went before them. To the casual observer they appeared to be a group of friars, yet no beggar or footpad lurking in the slime-filled, dirt-coated doorways dared approach them. Only once did they stop, to allow a group of mounted men-at-arms to ride by. Ball the preacher simply lifted a hand and intoned a blessing which he immediately followed with a curse once they had passed. They turned off into Crooked Lane, flitting like dark shadows past St Michael's Church and into the Babylon, a decayed tavern with as many entrances, doorways and windows as holes in a rabbit warren. They went up the staircase just within the doorway and along the gallery which reeked of urine, rotting vegetables and human sweat. Rats squeaked and scuttled in corners as a mangy alley cat padded like any soft-footed assassin across the creaking floorboards. A man hooded and masked stood by a doorway. He bowed to the Upright Men, opened the door and ushered them into what once was the tavern's principal bedroom, now just a square dirty chamber, empty except for one long table with benches down one side and a stool on the other.

The Upright Men sat on the benches, pulled back their hoods and donned their masks before re-covering their heads.

'The basilisk,' Grindcobbe ordered.

The guard left and a short while later pushed the basilisk, also cloaked and hooded, into the chamber, where he had to assist as the basilisk's eyes were blindfolded. Once his guest, as Grindcobbe described their visitor, was seated on the stool, the guard withdrew.

'Announce yourself to my comrades. What is your name?' Grindcobbe demanded.

'Basilisk!' came the whispered reply.

'Why?'

'Because the basilisk is a creature which lies in ambush before it strikes.'

'You have taken the oath to live and die with us; you have helped us before, but now you are sworn.'

'I am.'

'You accept us as your liege lords?'

'I do.'

'You will wage war and kill on our behalf?'

'I will.'

'Treachery will be punished.'

'I know.'

'By the ban?'

'I know.'

'Which means what?'

'The total annihilation of me and mine.'

'And if you are captured and unmasked, Basilisk, clever and subtle though you may be, we can do little to assist you against Gaunt and his minions.' Grindcobbe paused at a strident screech from the alleyway below as some night predator caught its prey. Grindcobbe's tone lightened. 'A warning indeed! Gaunt and his henchmen, Thibault in particular, will be ruthless, you understand that?'

'Yes.'

'And your task,' Grindcobbe leaned across the table, 'is to wage war by fire and sword against our enemies, to fight the good fight, to kill, to terrify. Do you understand?'

'I do.'

'Not only among Gaunt and his coven but the Straw Men.'

'I understand.'

'Once you enter the Tower, everything will be provided. You will not be alone – we have one friend there. He will reveal himself to you – do not be surprised. We have made it very clear that he is to do exactly what you say; otherwise he, too, will be marked down.' Grindcobbe raised a hand. 'He will, in particular, help you with a certain sack which the guard outside will give to you before you leave the Babylon. Do not be shocked at its contents, grue-some though they are. I believe you may suspect their origin.'

'How will I recognize this so-called friend?' The basilisk's voice betrayed contempt.

Grindcobbe dug into his purse and took out a scrap of parch-ment. 'He will give you this.' Grindcobbe pulled the candle closer so he could read the script:

'When Adam delved and Eve span,
Who was then the gentleman?
Now the world is ours and ours alone,
To cut the lords to heart and bone.'

Grindcobbe smiled behind his mask. 'A doggerel verse but,

as you know, many of those we lead do not read or write. They certainly understand what this means.' He pushed the scrap across the table, grasping Basilisk's outstretched hand. 'Don't fail us,' he warned. Grindcobbe rose. 'Your escort will see you safely back. As I said, we will supply whatever you need for your first act of terror. Farewell. We may not meet again but go, rejoicing that you do with the full blessing and support of the Upright Men.'

Athelstan sat on the stool close to the inglenook of Cranston's favourite tavern, The Holy Lamb of God which fronted Cheapside. He pulled off his mittens and unbuttoned his cloak, smiling at Mistress Rohesia, its jolly-faced owner who came bustling across.

'I will wait for Sir John,' he assured her. 'He will not be long.'

Mistress Rohesia, snow-white, apron all fresh, soft napkins over her arm, returned to the kitchens even as she loudly chanted what was on offer. 'Chicken with cherries, pike in doucettes, beef rissoles, roast coney, and a selection of the sweetest, hottest and softest pies.' Athelstan half heard her out. He had broken his fast immediately after his dawn Mass attended by a very few. He'd then changed, left the keys with Benedicta and hurried across the frozen bridge to meet Sir John here before the Nones bell rang.

Cranston had sent Flaxwith late the previous evening, about an hour after Watkin and Pike had left. Flaxwith offered his master's apologies over what had happened at the Roundhoop and asked Athelstan to meet the coroner here in his favourite tavern, which stood directly opposite the Guildhall. Athelstan wondered about his own agitation over what he had learnt the previous evening. Danger certainly pressed on every side. He stared around. The tap room, so clean and welcoming with its host of delicious smells, was fairly empty. A harpist sat in the far corner reciting a poem about 'the Lord of the Ravens'. Two chapmen sifted through their trays in preparation for another day's bustling trade along Cheapside. A slaughterer from St Nicholas' shambles bit greedily into an eel pie, his hands and arms stained to the elbow in dried blood. A herald enjoyed a pot of ale while three raggedy scholars from St Paul's loudly conjugated 'Mensa' and 'Cursus' before they met their Latin master. They rose, still chanting, to pick food from the horse-saddle table, a few boards placed across trestles and covered with linen cloths on which Minehostess had laid tranchers and pewter dishes piled high with blood-red sausages, cutlets of pork and sliced white bread. For a few coins every morning, customers could fill a platter with these meats, sops of bread and collect a blackjack of ale from the young tapster.

'Good morrow, Friar.' Silent as a ghost, despite his breadth and size, Cranston slid on to the stool opposite Athelstan.

'Once again, my friend.' Cranston pulled down the muffler and doffed his beaver hat. 'I had no knowledge about what Thibault intended at the Roundhoop.'

'I know.' Athelstan leaned across the table and grabbed Cranston's gauntleted hand.

'I heard what you said about the scorpion.' Cranston chuckled, tossing his cloak and hat on to the empty stool beside him. 'Brother, I owe you an explanation.' Cranston paused to order a capon pastry, a pot of vegetables and a goblet of Bordeaux's best. He waited until Mistress Rohesia served this, whiling the time away by carefully scrutinizing the rest of the customers. 'You can never be too careful, especially in this vale of tears.' He sniffed. 'Life is becoming dangerous, Brother. The Lady Maude, the two poppets, my wolf hounds, not to mention steward Blaskett are all, thank God, in the best of health and safe. Lord knows, I've lit enough tapers before the Virgin at Saint Mary-le-Bow in thanks for this. However, once the weather breaks and spring begins to green everything, I'll send them off to our small manor at Overton.'

'Matters are so bad?'

'No, but they will be.' Cranston thanked Mistress Rohesia for the food and wine, blew her a kiss and lifted the goblet in toast to Athelstan, who declined yet again Mistress Rohesia's litany of mouth-watering delicacies.

'You should eat, Brother.'

'Brother has eaten and drunk enough for the day.'

'True, and you will feast tonight.'

'What!'

'Not for the moment.' Cranston took a generous bite. Athelstan glanced away; he was fasting and the smell of hot, juicy chicken in a spice sauce might prove to be a temptation too much.

'Now,' Cranston dabbed his mouth with his napkin, 'let me be brief for the hour will soon be upon us. First, you and I know this city bubbles like a bucket of oil over a fire. Secondly, the day will come when the oil and fire meet. The angels be my witness, London will burn. Thirdly, our king, the noble Richard, is only a child. True power lies with his dear uncle, our self-styled Regent John of Gaunt, Duke of Lancaster etc., etc.' Cranston waved his hand. 'Gaunt is also preparing for the evil day. He has brought across his agents in Flanders, powerful Ghent merchants – the city Gaunt was born in – Pieter Oudernarde and his father Guido.' Cranston pulled a face. 'The rest are just minions, household henchmen. On the ninth of January last I was told to meet them north of the old city wall near Saint John's in Clerkenwell. The Upright Men launched an attack. Now,' Cranston took a sip of his claret, 'the Upright Men could have easily discovered something was afoot. Many of them are old soldiers; they disguised themselves in white sheets in order to blend in with the snow, an old trick used many times in France.' Cranston paused. 'Anyway, the attack was launched but beaten off – there's the rub. At first, I thought they were trying to kill the Oudernardes – they weren't. The Flemings had brought a prisoner, I'm sure it was a woman, cloaked, cowled and strictly guarded. The fiercest fighting took place around her and certain bundles on the sumpter ponies. The prisoner was kept safe but some of the baggage was plundered and taken.'

'And the prisoner?'

'Escorted down to the Tower. I and my men-at-arms parted company with them at the Lion gate. Rosselyn, captain of archers, together with Lascelles, Thibault's henchman, were very strict on that. The prisoner, the sumpter ponies and their escort disappeared swiftly inside.' Cranston pulled a face. 'More than that I do not know. And you?'

Athelstan told him about his parish, the troubles faced by Spicer Warde and Athelstan's own eerie meeting with the envoys from the Upright Men the previous evening.

'I confronted Watkin and Pike,' Athelstan declared. 'Sir John, what I tell you now is what you already suspect. Both are members of the Great Community of the Realm. Pike certainly sits high on the councils of the Upright Men.' Athelstan sighed. 'They know all about the Roundhoop affair. They'd been instructed once that meeting was over to receive the Upright Men in Southwark and arrange safe passage back into the southern shires.' Athelstan crossed himself. 'Of course, all the Upright Men were killed.'

'Because Gaunt and Thibault knew about the meeting.'

'According to Pike, this information may well have come from the Community of the Realm's cell-house, as they call it, the parish of Saint Erconwald's. In other words, one of my parishioners, while acting as a fervent supporter of the Community of the Realm, could be one of Gaunt's informants.'

'And so we come to Agag and the Amalekites,' Cranston murmured.

'In the book of Samuel, Agag and his tribe were defeated by the Israelites. The prophet Samuel put them under the ban; he ordered King Saul to slaughter them all.'

Cranston scratched his forehead. 'I have heard of this,' he whispered fiercely. 'Anyone who betrays the Great Community of the Realm will not only be punished, but all those related to them will be also. Something like that happened near King's Langley in Hertfordshire. A small hamlet was put to both torch and sword. Ostensibly the work of outlaws, common rumour has it that the hamlet housed a traitor who informed the lords of the shire at Hertford about the doings of the local Upright Men. Very few survived. Men, women, children and animals were killed.' Cranston grasped Athelstan's hand. 'Brother, I say this in all honesty: the same could happen in Saint Erconwald's. Houses, shops, taverns and alehouses all burnt, people slaughtered. It will be put down to river pirates or wolfsheads from the forests to the south; in truth it will be the Upright Men enforcing their will. Believe me, Brother, if there is a traitor and you discover him, hand him over. The Upright Men are ruthless!'

Athelstan stared across the tavern at the harpist, his long hair hanging over his face.

'Oh, don't worry about him,' Cranston whispered. 'That's the Troubadour.' Athelstan raised his eyebrows.

'One of my little swallows,' Cranston tapped the side of his nose, 'who swoops through the alleys of London collecting all

sorts of juicy morsels of information, my spy brother! He watches
to see who watches us. Now,' Cranston leaned across the table,
'as for the treachery of the hawk lords, I do wonder how many
of my so-called masters have been both bought and sold?'
Cranston took a sip of his claret as the harpist ran his fingers
smoothly across the harp strings, a beautifully melancholic sound.
Cranston grinned. 'All is safe, Brother. Now, my masters and the
so-called tribes of Edom and Moab?' Cranston rearranged his
platter and goblet on the table. 'Brother,' he grasped the platter,
'My Lord of Gaunt.' He tapped the goblet. 'The Upright Men.'
Cranston moved the knife. 'In between these, the Lords of
London: Walbrook, Legge, Horne and the other hawks. These
control the so-called tribes of rifflers, the gangs who lurk in the
shadows of Whitefriars, Newgate and even Southwark. Now these
knight errants of Hell organize themselves into tribes after the
ancient people of the Bible: Edomites, Philistines, Moabites and
so on. Their captains assume fantastic titles such as the Duke of
Acre or the Earl of Caesarea. Believe me, Brother, there is nothing
fantastical about them. They are the brothers and sisters of the
knife, garrotte and the club. They swarm like flies over a turd;
they wait for Lucifer's watchman to blow his horn.' Cranston
gulped from his goblet.

'In a word, Sir John, when the Day of the Great Slaughter
breaks, these tribes will rise to revel in murder and mayhem.'

'Correct, Brother, but worse. Some of our leading citizens,
whom the tribes serve, may well go over to the rebels. Then we
shall truly see the Apocalypse. No one will be spared – king,
earl, duke or commoner.' Cranston glanced towards the harpist.
'Blood will run ankle-deep in Cheapside. For the moment we
can only watch and wait. Yet, I assure you, my friend, the arrival
of the Oudernardes and their mysterious prisoner, the attacks
near the Tower, the bloody affray at the Roundhoop are all part
of the gathering storm. But,' Cranston rose and went to peer at
the hour candle; he came back looking rather shamefaced. 'I'm
afraid, Brother, you must come with me.'

'Must, Sir John?'

'No less a person than His Grace the Regent,' Cranston ignored
Athelstan's groan, 'has insisted on your presence at the third
hour in the afternoon.' Cranston was now grinning at the friar's

surprise. 'In the Chapel of Saint John the Evangelist at the White Tower,' Cranston leaned down, 'His Grace's own troupe of mummers, the Straw Men, are staging a small masque or mystery play for the delight of His Grace and his special guests. One of whom,' Cranston pressed his fat forefinger gently against the friar's slender nose, 'is you. This will be followed by a collation of juicy meats and the best wine. Brother, all I can say is that I am delighted I will not be supping alone.'

Athelstan crossed himself, murmured *Jesu Miserere* and followed the coroner out into the icy thoroughfare of Cheapside. He pestered Sir John about why he had been invited and swiftly learnt that the Regent may have been helped in the invitation by Cranston himself, who, as he kept chortling, would not have to suffer alone. The coroner truly hated such occasions and was only too grateful for Athelstan's company. The friar decided that cheerful compliance was the best course of action and followed the coroner's great bulk as they turned by the Cross near the Standard, down towards Bread Street. The streets and alleyways, despite the harsh weather, were thronged with traders and hawkers who competed with the many funerals being carried out. The smell of pinewood and rosemary, in which the long-dead corpses had been drenched, mingled with the sweet smells of pastries, bread and grilled meats. Thankfully the hard ice under foot had frozen the ordure and waste and provided some grip. Nevertheless, Athelstan remained wary of the sheets of puddle ice, not to mention the legion of Trojans, as Athelstan called the petty cheats and cozeners who scurried fast as ferrets from the mouths of alleyways and lanes. The apprentice boys were also busy, darting like sparrows from beneath their master's stalls to offer, 'cloth of Liege, tin pots from Cornwall, pepper mixers and boxes of cloves'. Prisoners manacled together, shuffled like one monstrous being; recently released from the debtors' house at the Marshalsea, they begged for alms while moaning at the freezing cold which had turned their bare feet purple. A group of whores caught soliciting on the steps of All Hallows were being marched up to the stocks. They were forced to hold their skirts over their heads, revealing dirty-grey flabby buttocks, so they could be thrashed with white split canes by the escorting beadles. Every so often these officials made their prisoners stop at a horse trough to receive a drenching from buckets of icy water. Athelstan closed his eyes at the sheer misery. Head down, cowl pulled close, the friar wondered at the evil which throbbed inside every soul and expressed itself in such cruelty. He felt Cranston clutch his arm. They had stopped outside St Mary-Le-Bow. A dispute had broken out over a corpse sprawled out on a coffin-stretcher, its left eye still open. Passers-by had glimpsed this and were demanding that such a sign of ill-luck be covered, the eye pressed down with a coin. A fresh disturbance distracted the mob as a group of flagellants, naked except for loin cloths and hoods daubed with a huge red cross, pushed their way through, flailing their backs with three-thonged whips, each of the knots pierced with a sharp needle. The whips went backwards and forwards, splashing blood and staining the padded paltocks, close-buttoned hoods and long-toed Cracow shoes of a group of fops. These loudly objected but the flagellants ignored them, whipping themselves even more fiercely as they chanted a hymn and followed their cross-bearing leader. They moved in a shower of blood which splattered and streaked everyone. The court fops became belligerent; daggers and swords were loosened. Cranston pushed Athelstan aside when abruptly a horn sounded: a powerful wailing blast and horsemen burst out of nearby Weasel Lane. Cloaked and hooded, faces blackened, the horsemen cantered down, scattering the crowd to rein in at the bottom of the steps of St Mary-Le-Bow. Hooves clattering, the horses snorted and reared in a creak of harness and steel. The intruders carried small hand arbalests, already primed. The horsemen moved backwards and forwards. Three naked corpses, skin all blotched, throats gaping in a dark, bloody slit, eyes staring, were slung across the saddle horn of some of the horses. These were tipped down to sprawl at the foot of the church steps. Cranston made to go forward. Athelstan grabbed him by the arm and pulled him back.

'Peace, Sir John,' he whispered. 'Think of the Lady Maude, the two poppets; this is not your fight. Not yet, anyway.'

'Hear ye!'

One of the riders surged forward on his grey-black warhorse; the destrier, head shaking, snorting furiously, clattered iron-shod hooves against the cobbles. The rider, like Satan's own henchman, tall and black in the saddle, cloak billowing out like the wings of some fearsome bird, raised a leather gauntleted hand.

'So die all traitors to the Great Cause,' he shouted, pointing at the corpses. 'Death to all who offend the Upright Men!' Then the horsemen were gone, clattering back into the darkness of the alleyway as the crowd surged forwards to view the corpses. Cranston bellowed at them to stand aside. Athelstan knelt at the bottom step and, opening his chancery bag, swiftly administered the rites of the dead, closing his mind to everything except the ritual, the anointing and the blessing. As he did so, Cranston turned the corpses over. All three were fairly elderly men with sagging bellies, fat thighs and vein-streaked legs, their faces unshaven, hair unkempt. Athelstan flinched. One of the dead men's faces was hideous, not just due to the cruel wound inflicted deep into his left side where the dagger had pierced his heart, but his features were distorted by an older, earlier wound across his mouth so his lips seemed to stretch the entire length of that narrow face.

'Laughing Jack, Thibault's man.' Cranston tapped the corpse. 'Executioner in Billingsgate, from the bridge to the Tower. These are his two assistants, Sinister and Dexter, literally his left and right hand. I wager they were responsible for severing the heads of those slaughtered at the Roundhoop and their poling on London Bridge.' Cranston sighed, got to his feet and shouted at a group of gathering bailiffs to take care of the corpses.

'Come, Brother,' he urged. 'Our noble Prince, against whom all this is directed, awaits us . . .'

The Upright Men's assassin, the basilisk, had been very busy. The meeting at the Babylon had ended amicably and the basilisk had prepared. The traitor in Gaunt's circle had revealed himself, a startling surprise swiftly swept aside by the need for preparations following a heated discussion in the dark recesses of the Chapel of St Peter ad Vincula. The basilisk had been insistent. Assassination would take place. Weapons had been demanded and prepared, including that leather sack with its grisly contents. They had clasped hands in what both knew to be a deadly contract. They would stand or fall by each other. Now, gowned and hooded, carrying a special pass impressed with the Regent's purple wax seal, the basilisk had already surveyed the sprawling fortress of the Tower from the Lion Gate through past St Thomas' Tower, along Red Gulley and under the dark shadow of Bell Tower, with its massive wooden casing on top housing the great bell which marked the passing hours and sounded the tocsin. The assassin noted that and passed on into the inner bailey, clearly marking out the different towers – especially Beauchamp – close to the parish church of St Peter ad Vincula. Only then did the basilisk approach the great White Tower, the central donjon or keep, its soaring walls of Kentish grey ragstone all whitewashed and gleaming in the harsh frost of the winter's day. Once again the basilisk stared back at Beauchamp Tower, where the mysterious prisoner brought from Flanders was lodged. It was best not to go too close to its approaches, closely guarded by archers and men-at-arms. What, the basilisk wondered, did Gaunt want with such a prisoner? Why all the mystery and secrecy? Who was that woman? Even the traitor in Thibault's circle knew very little. Why were the Upright Men so keen to seize her? What was the true connection between the prisoner and the leather sack the Upright Men had entrusted to her? Yet the politics of this place were of little concern – vengeance was!

The basilisk shifted and stared at the black-timbered and white-plastered guest house which stood in its own neat square garden, the shrubs and plants held fast in the iron grip of a savage hoar frost. Oh, yes, the basilisk promised, those who sheltered there – the mystery players – would also be visited by Murder. The Regent's acting troupe, the Straw Men, Master Samuel and his companions, were nothing more than a coven of treacherous Judas people. They, too, would chew on the bitter bread of pain and sup deeply from the poisoned chalice of the rankest wormwood. The basilisk, however, had to be careful. The Tower thronged with Gaunt's retainers, henchmen, armoured knights, archers, mailed clerks and household minions, all busy scurrying to do their infernal master's bidding. The basilisk glimpsed the small dovecote near St Peter's and smiled; they'd all hasten even faster when the hawk appeared above the doves. What was being planned was only just and right. How did the verse of one of the Upright Men's songs run? 'God is deaf nowadays. He will not hear us and, for their guilt, grinds good men to dust.' God needed a little help!

The basilisk looked up at the grey, lowering sky and recalled a recent story, now common gossip in Gaunt's household. How the Regent had gone hawking in the wastelands east of Aldgate. Ever so proud of his new snow-white falcon, Gaunt had released this against an old heron which frequented a misty, tree-fringed mere. The falcon, superb and swift, had climbed above its prey then plunged for the kill but the old heron, desperate in its flight, had turned on the wing and speared the falcon with his dagger-like bill. The story was seen as a possible prophecy and augury of how the hunter could become the hunted. Well, that was one prophecy which would soon come to fruition. Clutching the leather sack, the basilisk moved across the icy bailey, wary of the frozen, slippery cobbles. The guards at the bottom of the wooden staircase acknowledged the pass sealed by Rosselyn, captain of archers. The basilisk continued up and entered the crypt of St John's Chapel, a long, dark chamber lit by pools of light thrown by the wall torches and warmed by braziers crammed with fiery charcoal. Despite the light and fire, the crypt, which stood on the first floor of the White Tower, was cold and dark. The basilisk peered through the murk at the chink of light from the far window; the crypt was empty except for benches and tables, as well as battered chests and aumbries to store clothing. The basilisk nodded – all was well here, and returned to the narrow spiral staircase. The ingenuity of its builder was fascinating. The staircase constantly twisted so the defenders could use their right arm while attackers would be forced to wield swords with their left. The basilisk promised to remember this in case flight became the only path to take.

Breathing heavily, the assassin emerged through a narrow doorway and into the full glare of the Chapel of St John the Evangelist, pausing just within the entrance. The basilisk stood, studying the ancient Norman chapel intently – not for the first time, but this was different. The real drama to be staged here would be subtle murder; the chance to strike Gaunt at the heart of his power, to wreak vengeance on those who had brought about the hideous slaughter at the Roundhoop. The basilisk drew a deep breath: that would never be forgotten! This place would be where the dish of vengeance was served. Built so its apse projected out of the south-east corner of the White Tower, the chapel was oval shaped with a recess just close to the door. Here the King could sit enthroned directly opposite the elaborately decorated rood screen depicting the crucified Christ. Above its doorway stood life-sized figures of the Virgin and St John painted in brilliant colours of gold, red, blue and silver. The actual entrance to the rood screen was now filled by a grotesque Hell's mouth carved in the likeness of the gaping jaws of a fearsome dragon's head. The face was blood red, its eyes large black pools, the irises a sickly yellow, the parted heavy lips smeared purple, a leather tongue jutting out between sharp white teeth. The basilisk thought this piece of scenery very fitting; a nightmare picture which would dominate the drama played out in front of it. The aisles either side of this rood screen had been curtained off with heavy, silver-powdered damask cloths. The nave of the chapel had been set out with elegant leather-backed chairs; those in the front for Gaunt and his special guests had quilted arm rests. Along either side of the chapel ranged six pillars to represent the twelve apostles with narrow galleries or transepts between these and the outside walls. The gaps between each pillar were now tastefully screened by tapestries of eye-catching colours celebrating the legends of St John and the devotion of the royal family to Christ's beloved disciple. The figures on the tapestry were all clothed in priestly vestments: rose-coloured chasubles, brilliant blue dalmatics and mauvy-pink amices. The basilisk had seen all this before yet the arrogance of the Plantagenet royal family remained truly breathtaking. The figures were all blond-haired and blue-eyed. St John had been painted likewise as if Gaunt was claiming that the great evangelist was a member of the Plantagenet family. These gorgeous tapestries hung half down; just beneath them stood supper tables, covered in shimmering white damask and groaning under pure gold and silver platters heaped high with deliciously savoury collations for the Regent's guests. The air, already sweetened with the fragrance from a myriad of beeswax candles and smoking herb pots, was made even richer by the mouth-watering odours of gelatine pie, coras sauce, swan-neck pudding, minced chicken and loach fried in roses and almonds. The basilisk surveyed the scene for the last time watching the servants in their blue, scarlet and gold livery, the knight bannerets, the men-at-arms, the archers, all busy. None of them gave the basilisk a second glance, totally unaware of how this splendid chamber would soon become a place of slaughter. A royal chapel where the power of the Crown would be truly shaken.

Athelstan closed his eyes in sheer pleasure then opened them and stared around the glorious chapel of St John: the entire place blazed with glory. The eye-catching colours delighted the eye, be it the gold, silver, reds, blues and greens on the tapestries hanging between the pillars or the small walnut tables, legs polished to a shine, bearing cups, goblets, bowls and mazers of the most precious metals studded with dazzling stones. Gaunt and his guests looked similarly magnificent in their houppelands and gowns of many colours, powdered with silver and gold. Finger rings, bracelets, collars and pectorals dazzled in the shimmering light of countless tongues of candle flame. The air was beautifully fragranced, warm and sweet. Such a contrast, Athelstan reflected, to their freezing cold, sombre journey by barge along the north bank of the Thames, the mist curling around the shoreline gallows heavy with the crumbling corpses of river pirates. They had shot through the thunderous water passage under London Bridge then docked at the Tower quayside. They'd entered the mighty fortress and the sheer bleakness of this house of war dulled the spirit with its sinister, silent donjons and fogbound cobbled baileys. Now and again the murky river mist would shift to reveal the great engines of war: mangonels, catapults and battering rams. A place of evil repute was how Athelstan's parishioners described the Tower, and the friar could only agree. A place of ominous silence broken only by the clatter of weapons, the clanging from its many smithies or the heart-chilling roars and growls from the royal menagerie which, according to Cranston, on a hot day made the fortress reek. Athelstan had glimpsed the long enclosure with the cages on either side where the leopards and lions prowled, gifts from rulers in Outremer. Cranston had even told him about a huge snow bear kept in a special chamber cage close to the moat in which the bear was allowed to swim. Athelstan had rejected the story as fanciful. Cranston had assured him that the animal was a recent gift from the King of Norway, almost three yards high and kept on a long chain which allowed him to swim in the nearby water. Athelstan had quietly promised himself to view such a magnificent spectacle.

The Tower was certainly grim. Athelstan turned on his chair, yet this chapel was an island of beautiful serenity in the fear-filled fortress. He and Cranston had been ushered in and served belly-warming, mouth-sweetening cups of hippocras and slices of spiced toast coated with almond sauce. Gaunt with the face of an angel, his extraordinary blue eyes crinkling in good humour, had welcomed all his guests. He had stood before the brilliant rood screen dressed in cloth of silver and lavished them with his charm. Light danced along the golden 'SS' collar of Lancaster around the Regent's neck while the gorgeous finger rings made every elegant gesture of his hands shimmer in the glow. Gaunt wore cream-coloured, Spanish leather riding boots, and every time he moved the jewelled spurs on the heels jingled like the soft ringing of the sacring bell. He had personally welcomed Cranston and Athelstan, thanking for them for their work at the Roundhoop. The Regent then passed them on to Master Thibault who, dressed in a houppeland and shoulder cape of dark blue murrey brushed with silver, ushered them to their seats. The other guests included a few important clerics, Walbrook the mayor and other leading citizens. Lascelles, garbed as usual like a raven, looked after the Flemings, resplendent in their silver brocaded cloaks. Athelstan noticed how Lettenhove, their bodyguard, seemed ill at ease, plucking at his dagger hilt and staring suspiciously around the luxuriously furnished chapel.

All of this had been swept aside by the drama. Gaunt's mummers, the Straw Men, appeared from around the rood screen to present themselves – seven in all. Master Samuel, their florid-faced, grey-bearded leader, explained how he and his troupe had no personal names but took those from ancient scripture. He was Samuel; the four young men of varying heights and descriptions were called after the heroes of Israel: Gideon, Barak, Samson and Eli. Two young women were also members of the troupe. Judith, called after Israel's great heroine who resisted a tyrant, was small, dark and rather plump, her raven-black hair cropped close around an impish face. The woman's dancing eyes and merry mouth reminded Athelstan of one of his parishioners, Cecily the courtesan. The second woman was young and slim; her pointed, snow-white face only emphasized her tumbling, gorgeous fiery-red hair; she was Rachael of Galilee, named after the woman who had mourned the innocents slaughtered by Herod the tyrant. Cranston chuckled quietly at this and, as he whispered to Athelstan, hoped that John of Gaunt would not be offended. The Straw Men bowed at the applause and then reappeared masked and gowned. They staged the Laon play about Herod's confrontation with the Magi. Athelstan watched, fascinated. The drama swirled vigorously, the mummers changing masks and gowns as they played out the confrontation before Hell's mouth. This piece of scenery intrigued Athelstan with its sheer ugly vigour and eye-catching carvings and colours, especially the huge, extended jaws through which Herod came and went. Athelstan quietly calculated how much was in the parish chest of St Erconwald's and wondered if he could hire the Straw Men to stage a similar drama in his own church.

Once the play had finished with Herod disappearing forever into the gaping mouth of Hell to the flourish of a trumpet, Athelstan remained seated while Cranston, hungry and thirsty as ever, went hunting for refreshment. The friar asked a servant if he could speak to Master Samuel and sat waiting expectantly as the rest of Gaunt's guests rose and moved about, selecting food and wine from the hovering servants. One of these asked Athelstan if he wished to have something to eat. The friar courteously refused and, when he turned back, Rachael of Galilee was kneeling on the chair in front of him, her red hair now tied back. She was staring at him and Athelstan smiled at the look of tenderness in her face, then she grinned, her green eyes bright with excitement.

'Brother Athelstan?'

'Yes?'

'Master Samuel will see you now.'

Athelstan followed the young woman under the curtain which hung to the right of the rood screen and into the sanctuary, behind where the rest of the troupe were hastily storing all the paraphernalia from their play. Master Samuel greeted Athelstan warmly, ushering him to the sanctuary chair and, much to the friar's embarrassment, the troupe gathered like disciples to sit at his feet. Master Samuel introduced them all again and, in a voice betraying a West Country burr, explained how the 'Brotherhood', as he described his colleagues, were foundlings or orphans whom he had taken in, educated and trained.

'Why the names from scripture?' Athelstan asked.

'Why not?' Judith teased back, her dark eyes full of mischief.

'We are one missing,' Gideon declared. 'Boaz has disappeared.'

'But that's our rule,' Samuel observed. 'Each of us is free to come and to go as they wish. Now, Brother, what is it you want?'

Athelstan told them, describing his parish and church. The Straw Men listened, obviously touched by this little friar's enthusiasm. Samuel replied how they would reflect, discuss and vote on it but, he added smilingly, they would be only too willing to help.

Athelstan was about to question them further when Rosselyn, garbed in a heavy military cloak, appeared, soft and silent as shadow shifting along the wall. He clapped his hands and declared that His Grace awaited them all. Master Samuel pulled a face, but they all followed the captain of archers back into the chapel nave. Athelstan delayed a while to examine the magnificent Hell's mouth with its pulleys and levers. As soon as he had joined the rest, ushered in by Rosselyn, Athelstan took a platter of diced chicken and a goblet of wine. He watched as the Straw Men were formally thanked by Gaunt and congratulated by the guests, who raised their goblets and showered the Straw Men with coins. Once this was finished, the feasting continued. In the recess near the door a group of minstrels played sweet music, the heart-tugging strings of a harp echoing clearly. Athelstan, intrigued, walked down the chapel, nodding and smiling at the guests, though scant acknowledgement was given to the small friar, who was dismissed as Cranston's clerk.

The coroner himself was holding forth to Walbrook and a group of leading aldermen about his plans to improve the city water supply through the Conduit in Cheapside. He caught Athelstan's gaze and winked; the friar peered round, stared into the recess and smiled. He was correct in recognizing the same harpist who'd played in the Holy Lamb of God. Athelstan turned, searching for Master Samuel or Rachael, when a small explosion occurred and smoke poured out from one of the braziers. Gaunt's guests turned in alarm as the same happened in another brazier on the other side of the chapel. The silence was broken by shouts and exclamations. Gaunt's household hurried towards their master. Athelstan jumped at a scream. He glanced to his right. Lettenhove was swaying on his feet, staring in disbelief at the crossbow bolt embedded deep in his chest. Shouts and yells rang out. People hurried instinctively towards the door. Another sharp scream shrilled as Guido Oudernarde on the other side of the chapel staggered away, one arm up, his face contorted in pain as he turned, trying to free the crossbow bolt which had struck him high in his back. The old Fleming, gagging at the pain, collapsed to his knees. Gaunt, sword in hand, was shouting at his household knights who hurried across to form a protective ring around their master and his fallen guest. The rest of the company, however, now panicked, jostling and pushing to leave the chapel. Athelstan was knocked aside, forced to clutch one of the great drum-like pillars as the chapel swiftly emptied. He glimpsed Eli taking refuge beneath one of the food tables in the transepts. The rest of the troupe had apparently fled with the rest. Cranston's audience had also melted away but the coroner stood his ground, dagger drawn, his back to one of the pillars. Athelstan waited for the crush of bodies near the narrow entrance to dissipate before hurrying to join him. Cranston clutched the friar's arm, kicking aside chairs to where a Tower leech knelt before the fallen Lettenhove. The Fleming, however, was beyond all human help. Athelstan went to kneel as the dying man jerked in his final agony, blood seeping out of his mouth and nose, only to be pushed aside by Cornelius.

'I am a priest,' he murmured in Latin. 'I will shrive him.'

Athelstan rose and glanced across the chapel. Gaunt's henchmen now ringed their master with kite-shaped shields while Lascelles tried to restore order, ushering people towards the door. Athelstan started at a man's high-pitched yell. Eli, hiding under a table, had pushed back the heavy covering cloth and was pointing at the rood screen. Athelstan followed the direction and stifled his own exclamation. Two severed heads lay either side of Hell's mouth. He hastened across, knelt and turned both over; they were very similar to those master Burdon poled on London Bridge. Both heads had seemingly been severed some time ago, the dirty-grey skin and the jagged remains of the neck were as dry as leather. Their features were all shrunken and shrivelled, the hair on both very brittle, the eyes sunk deep in their sockets, almost hidden by the crumpled lids.

'Sweet Lord of Heaven!' Cranston breathed as he crouched beside Athelstan. 'In God's name, where have they come from?' He broke off as Athelstan plucked a scrap of parchment from one of the dead mouths. He unfolded this and whispered what was scrawled there.

'When Adam delved and Eve span
Who was then the gentleman?
Now the world is ours and ours alone
To cut the Lords to heart and bone.'

'Brother!' Thibault stood behind them, 'Brother!' The Master of Secrets' usual smiling face was pale, taut with anger. 'Brother, Sir John. I must ask you to go.' He forced a wintry smile. 'For the moment leave those heads where they are.' He plucked the scrap of parchment from Athelstan's hand. 'Lascelles will see you to a comfortable chamber. You can . . .'

'Master Thibault!' An archer stood in the doorway. 'Master Thibault, the assassin has been found!'

'What is this?' Gaunt shouted, breaking free of the encircling knights.

'My Lord.' Thibault stretched out his hand and pointed to the grisly human remains on the exquisitely tiled floor. 'My Lord, I beg you stay here.'

Thibault turned back, snapping his fingers at Cranston. 'Sir John, I think you'd best come. You too, Brother Athelstan.'

All three left the chapel; outside the freezing darkness was falling. Archers carrying cresset torches moved about, shepherding those guests who'd fled the chapel to the great hall in the nearby royal lodgings. Officers of the Tower could only stand by and watch helplessly.

'Master Thibault,' Cranston whispered, 'will not be interfered with. Royal palace or not, the King's fortress of the Tower is now firmly under his control. Mark my words, dear friar, this will certainly end in bloodshed.' Athelstan did not reply but pulled his cowl more firmly against the cutting cold as they followed the archer around the keep. The friar glanced up at the light flaring from the Chapel of St John above them. In the distance he could see a pool of flame where men clustered near the north-east corner of the Tower. Athelstan glimpsed a lantern box burning from a window, its shutters flung wide open, and reckoned this must be a window to the crypt. As they reached the circle of flame, the archer stepped back to allow them closer to where Rosselyn knelt by a crumpled corpse, its face ghoulish white, eyes popping. Blood from the head, which lay strangely twisted, had oozed out to create a sticky puddle. A young man dressed in jerkin, hose and hooded cloak, Athelstan peered closer and recognized Barak, one of the Straw Men. He glanced up the side of the Tower where the end of an oiled hempen rope swung in the evening breeze. A short distance away from the corpse lay a small hand arbalest or crossbow. Athelstan gently moved the twisted cloak, found the man's belt and touched the stout leather case containing two barbed bolts.

'You said he was the assassin?' Athelstan asked over his shoulder at the archer who had led them here.

'It must be,' Rosselyn replied as he turned the corpse over on to its back. Athelstan flinched at the way the head flopped and the horrid wound which disfigured the entire right side of Barak's face. Rosselyn, swift and nimble as any foist, searched the corpse. He emptied the belt purse – a few coins, a medal and two scraps of parchment. Athelstan sensed what was written and quoted the lines he had just read in the chapel. Rosselyn simply stared dead-eyed at him and handed the scripts to Thibault who plucked at the friar's sleeve as a sign to withdraw. Athelstan chose to ignore him and recited the rite of absolution.

'If you are finished, Brother,' Thibault crouched beside him. 'The night is so cold, and my master awaits.'

'For whom?' Athelstan held the sinister clerk's hard stare.

'Oh, for you, my dear friar and you, Sir John.' Thibault moved his head from side to side as if assessing some complex problem. 'Oh, yes, Brother Athelstan, my master and I certainly need words with you but until then . . .'

A short while later Athelstan and Cranston were ushered into the Tower guest house which stood close to the church of St Peter ad Vincula. This two-storey building, fronted with snow-white plaster and brown beams, boasted a great hall, kitchen and buttery on the ground floor, its upper storey being reserved for guest chambers. The hall was pleasant enough, the paved floor covered with tough rope matting. A great, hooded hearth housed a merry, spluttering fire, while braziers stacked with blazing coals and strewn with herbs provided more warmth and fragrance. They walked into a barn-like room with black rafters, the lime-washed walls covered with heavy painted canvasses which described the legends of the Tower, how it was founded by Trojan exiles and strengthened by the great Caesar. The long communal tables down either side gave the impression of a monastic refectory, a likeness heightened by the great black cross nailed to the far wall and the tall *pulpitum* opposite the hearth. The Straw Men were there, clustering in a frightened huddle on stools around the fire. They had been provided with stoups of ale and platters of food which now stood on one of the tables, and hardly stirred as Cranston and Athelstan entered, though Master Samuel recalled his manners and hurriedly fetched two stools from a recess near the buttery door. Athelstan sketched a blessing and glanced back over his shoulder. Thibault had disappeared as soon as they had entered the hall but he had left a cluster of archers close to the entrance. One of these became busy, walking around the refectory, ensuring the window shutters were firmly clasped before taking up guard near the buttery door.

'I suspect we are the Regent's guests,' Cranston whispered, 'whether we like it or not.' They sat down on the stools placed before the fire. Cranston gazed around at the assembled company and, fumbling beneath his cloak, brought out the miraculous wine skin. He offered it around and, when no one accepted, took a generous swig and placed it between his feet.

'We have heard the news.' Samuel's face and voice were bitter, no longer the bonhomie or gracious courtesy of a few hours earlier. 'They say Barak is the assassin, that he was killed while escaping.'

Athelstan held his gaze, staring at that ruddy face, the neatly clipped moustache and beard. A resolute, determined man, Athelstan thought, well educated and skilled. A former soldier, perhaps a mailed clerk?

*It was built for William I, who lodged at Barking Abbey until it was ready. The opinion of the nuns is not recorded.*

'Is that true, Brother?' Rachael, even more pale-faced, her fiery red hair now hidden beneath the hood of her gown, stretched out her hands to the fire.

'Those heads,' Eli whispered, repressing a shiver, 'where did those grotesques come from? Brother Athelstan, they were severed heads.' He pulled a face. 'Real heads, no mummers' trickery, no subtle device.'

'God have mercy on them, whoever they were,' Athelstan replied slowly. 'They were the heads of two unfortunates. I suspect they were severed some time ago, washed, soaked in heavy brine and left to dry.' He shrugged at their cries and exclamations. 'Possibly the work of the Upright Men.' Athelstan blew his lips out. 'They must be; they were left as a warning, weren't they, for our noble Regent?'

'When I first saw them,' Eli declared, 'I really did think they were part of our wardrobe – masks we'd left unpacked.' He laughed, shaking his head. 'Foolish lad I am! Brother, Rachael stitches and embroiders our costumes, paints and cuts most of our scenery, yet I'd never seen them before. They were not Rachael's work. I stared again and realized they were real.'

'How long before you noticed them there?' Athelstan asked.

'Oh, only a few heart beats before I yelled.'

'And nobody saw them being placed there?' Cranston asked.

'We saw nothing,' Rachael replied. 'I was eating some food, there were those explosions from the braziers, then Lettenhove was struck and almost immediately Oudernarde on the other side of the chapel. We fled.'

'It's true, it's true,' Samuel murmured. The rest of the company quietly agreed.

'Brother Athelstan,' Gideon, his blond hair so heavily oiled it seemed pressed down and held by a net, half rose; Samuel gripped him by the shoulder and forced him back on to the stool. 'You claim this is the work of the Upright Men?'

'You know who they are?' Athelstan demanded.

'Of course,' Samson and Eli answered as one. 'Who hasn't heard of them?'

'Are you saying,' Samson accused, 'that we are their retainers, members of their coven? Is that why we have been brought here, to be questioned?'

'Hush now,' Samuel intervened, 'Brother Athelstan, I'm sorry, but this is . . .?' He gestured at Cranston.

'Sir John Cranston,' Athelstan finished the sentence. 'My friend, also Lord Coroner of London, the King's law officer.' Athelstan stared around. 'Sir John is no retainer or lackey of this lord or that lord but the keeper of the King's peace. Nevertheless, he, like me, like you, has little knowledge about what is truly happening here.' Athelstan paused as a snow-white cat slipped through the buttery door and padded softly down the hall. Athelstan wondered how his constant companion, the one-eyed Bonaventure was faring.

'Brother Athelstan is correct,' Cranston, basking in the heat from the fire, stirred and stared round the semicircle of anxious faces. 'Yes,' he breathed, still jovial and benevolent after the claret he'd supped. 'We truly are in the kingdom of mayhem and mystery.' He smiled at his description taken from Athelstan. 'Though some things are becoming clearer.' He pointed at the fire. 'Those explosions before the two men were struck were caused by cannon powder, I suspect – small leather pouches wedged between the charcoal.'

Athelstan nodded in agreement.

'Now,' Cranston smacked his lips and straightened up, 'I am the Lord Coroner. Murder has been committed.'

'Is this an *inquisicio*?' Samuel protested.

'Yes and no,' Cranston retorted. 'Let us at least determine where we were. Brother Athelstan and I stayed in the chapel. What happened to you?'

'When the second man was struck,' Judith replied, screwing up her eyes as she peered at the coroner, 'we all fled. We were frightened.' Her voice broke. Samson went to stroke her arm and she shrugged him off, a look of distaste on her face. Rachael leaned over, murmuring comfortingly.

'We ran down the steps with the rest,' Judith continued in a rush, 'out into the snow.'

'Do you all know where you were?' Athelstan asked.

'Brother,' Rachael replied, 'we were terrified. We all fled. I cannot remember who was where.'

Athelstan nodded in agreement. He realized it would be futile to ask anybody where they had been. All was confused. Everyone would describe not so much what happened but how they perceived it. The assassin would certainly not betray himself. Moreover, there were others, such as the leading citizens, whom he could never question. 'Asking people where they were, when and what they were doing is not helpful,' Athelstan conceded. He stared down at the floor, tapping his sandal-clad feet. 'We do not even know when the severed heads were placed. Before or after the explosions? During the attacks, before or after?' He shook his head.

'Did anyone see Barak leave?'

'Brother,' Judith retorted, 'we've told you. We fled. God knows who went where.'

A sharp discussion broke out about what happened after the two attacks. The more he listened, the more convinced Athelstan became that establishing the whereabouts of anyone was a fairly fruitless path to follow. The Straw Men grew increasingly vociferous about who was where and when.

'Except you!' Athelstan pointed at Eli. 'You stayed. You hid beneath one of the tables?'

'I was terrified,' the mummer replied. 'True, I hid beneath a table, behind its drape. I then decided to move out. I lifted the cloth and saw the heads.'

'And nobody else?'

'No, Brother.'

Athelstan, just for a moment, caught a fleeting look, a glance as if Eli was hiding something, then the rest joined in, talking vigorously about their perception of events.

'My friends,' Athelstan intervened, 'we, like you, are detained here. God knows how long we will have to dance attendance upon our masters.' Athelstan held his hands up. 'Remember that the questions we ask, others undoubtedly will, eventually.' He paused. 'Barak? Was he a supporter of the Upright Men? Did he plot rebellion? Come now,' he urged, 'you travel the length and breadth of both the Kingdom and this city. You see and hear things. You are patronized by no less a person than Lord John of Gaunt . . .'

'Barak.' Rachael cast off Eli's restraining hand. 'Barak,' she repeated, 'lived only for the play, the mummery, the masks. He had no time or inclination to meddle in such matters. He was absorbed in his lines. He lived for the performance.'

'And the poor,' Eli added. 'Come, sister, we know that. He often declaimed against the popinjays, the city fops, the court gallants in their gold-encrusted paltocks, their multicoloured hose, Cracow shoes and ridiculously long liripipes, men in woman's clothing.' Eli scoffed. 'Nor did the lords of the manor escape his judgement.'

'And His Grace the Regent?'

'A dog does not bite the hand that feeds it,' Samuel swiftly retorted. 'Barak neither said yea or nay against him.'

'Yet according to the evidence,' Athelstan insisted, 'Barak was an assassin hand-in-glove with the Upright Men.' Athelstan then described the scraps of parchment found in the mouth of one of the severed heads as well as in Barak's wallet purse. They heard him out in silence, clearly disbelieving what they were hearing.

'Those heads?' Judith asked, 'why did they contain such a message?'

'Mistress,' Athelstan sighed, 'I cannot really say. I suspect they were severed some time ago then carefully preserved. One, I suspect, was that of a youngish man and the other belonged to an older woman but,' Athelstan shrugged, 'I cannot be precise. Now, Barak, was he skilled in the use of the crossbow?'

'Very skilled,' Samuel agreed. 'We are all for battle as any man-at-arms – that includes Rachael and Judith. We have no choice. We must protect ourselves. We travel lonely roads and we carry money and provisions, clothing and jewellery. Wolfheads, outlaws, the so-called men of the Greenwood, approach us. Every one of us here, whatever else we do, is skilled in the war bow, the arbalest, the pike, the sword and dagger. Usually we are unmolested but these are desperate times and they produce desperate men.

'And your company has an armoury?' Cranston asked sleepily.

'Of course – swords, daggers, bucklers and maces.'

'And small hand-held arbalests?'

'Yes, Sir John.'

'And today?' Athelstan asked. 'Did Barak act any differently?'

'No,' Samuel replied. 'As Rachael said, Barak lived and breathed for the masque and the miracle play. He was no different today. I've asked the rest. He fled from the Chapel of St John.

Nobody saw him do anything untoward. Why should he? He was happy, contented.' Master Samuel drew his brows together. 'He didn't act as if . . .'

'He was planning murder?'

'No, no, he didn't. He was excited about us staging a great play at the Cross in Cheapside. He urged me to indenture a new mummer. I mean, ever since Boaz left—'

'Boaz?' Athelstan asked. 'You have mentioned him before.'

'A member of our company,' Eli spoke up, 'very skilled in learning lines and painting. He helped us decorate the dragon's head – Hell's mouth.'

'A magnificent sight,' Athelstan agreed. 'Truly magnificent.'

'Boaz left us just after we visited Castle Acre in Norfolk around the Feast of All Hallows,' Rachael declared. 'God knows why. We woke one morning and he was gone but,' she blew her cheeks out, 'we have our rules – liberty is one of them. We are not bonded to the company.'

'What are you then?' Cranston asked. 'Come.' He offered the miraculous wine skin; this time it was gratefully accepted.

'The hour is late but we must wait,' Sir John insisted, 'so why not chat. Just who are you?'

Master Samuel, after taking a generous gulp of the fine claret, described how the Straw Men were his company. An Oxford clerk ordained to minor orders, he had studied the Quadrivium and Trivium, then stumbled on to the plays of Plautus and Terence. He began earning a few coins reciting their lines at the Carfax in Oxford or on the steps of St Mary the Virgin Church. The authorities were not impressed. Time and again the proctors of the university as well as the mayor's bailiffs had warned him off. On at least three occasions they even forced him to stand in the stocks and recite his lines for free. Eventually Samuel – he claimed to have forgotten his real name – had fled to serve in the commission of array in France, where he had entered Gaunt's household as a troubadour. On his journeys Samuel became acquainted with the Laon and Montpellier mystery plays. Gaunt had presented him with a fine copy of *The Castle of Perseverance*, the Lincoln miracle play, peopled by characters such as Bad Angel, Plain Folly and Backbiter. Samuel had immediately fallen in love with both the themes and the verse and so, using the money he had acquired, founded the Straw Men.

'Why that title?' Athelstan asked.

'Because, Brother,' Samuel laughed sharply, 'we bend and change with every breeze. You want us to be Herod or perhaps Pilate, or may be Saint John or,' he pulled an arrogant face, 'Pride.' He relaxed. 'Or Sloth.' Athelstan laughed at Samuel's swift change of expression, listening carefully as the others gave their story. Judith, who had been a bear-tamer's daughter, worked as their travelling apothecary and cook. Rachael, who had been in the care of the good nuns at Godstow, was costume mistress. Samson, a former soldier, burly-faced, thickset and lugubrious, could act the jester or Master Tom-Fool. Eli, an orphan, was as slim as a beanpole, with an impudent, freckled face and who, Samuel assured them, could mimic anyone or anything. Eli promptly did, springing to his feet to perform the mincing walk of a courtier before changing swiftly to that of a pompous cleric. Gideon, with his blond hair and pretty, girlish face, openly admitted to mimicking women and, despite the gloom, made Cranston and Athelstan laugh as he imitated a court maiden playing cat's cradle to Samson's burly knight.

'Do you really think,' Rachael's voice stilled the merriment, 'that Barak was an assassin?' Athelstan held those anxious green eyes. He recalled Barak's corpse, the arbalest lying nearby.

'Was Barak left- or right-handed?' he asked.

'Right-handed, like myself,' Rachael replied. 'Why?'

'I don't know,' Athelstan murmured. 'Mistress, I truly don't.'

'*Pax et Bonum!*' They all whirled round. Thibault stood at the doorway, his thick coat glistening with freshly fallen snow. Behind him was an old woman grasping the hand of a small girl. Rosselyn, Lascelles and a group of archers also came through the doorway, armed as if for battle. Thibault, quiet as a cat, crossed the hall. Cranston lumbered to his feet; the rest followed. Thibault stopped in front of them and gave a small bow. Athelstan couldn't decide whether he was being courteous, mocking or both. Thibault brought his hands from beneath his cloak and allowed the velvety skinned ferret, its lithe body rippling with muscle, to scramble up the folds of his gown before catching it, nursing it in the crook of his arm as he gently stroked it with one satin-gloved finger.

'Father!' the little girl broke free of her stern-faced,

grey-gowned nurse and began to leap up and down, trying to take the ferret. 'Father, please let me have Galahad.' Thibault knelt and carefully handed the ferret over before grasping his daughter by her arms, pulling her close and kissing her tenderly on cheek and brow. Athelstan watched this viper in human flesh, as Cranston had once described him, stroke his daughter's hair, a look of pure adoration on his smiling face.

'It's yours, Isabella,' he lisped, 'but promise me – prayers then bed, yes?' Thibault turned back, his hooded eyes watchful, as if noticing them for the first time. 'Master Samuel,' he beckoned. 'Rosselyn will provide you and your companions with comfortable chambers.' He smiled. 'Each of you will have a room in one of the towers where,' he waved a hand, 'you will be more safe and secure than here.' He clapped his hands. 'Sir John, Brother Athelstan, His Grace awaits us.'

Gaunt was sitting in the great sanctuary chair, which had been brought around the rood screen to stand before Hell's mouth. At any other time Athelstan would have been amused at how close this subtle, cunning prince was to Hell. Gaunt's face was devoid of all graciousness and humour. He sat enthroned, wrapped in a thick, dark blue gown of pure wool which emphasized his beautiful but sharp face, his eyes no longer amused but glass-like. He glared at Athelstan before fixing on Cranston as they were both ushered to stools before him. Gaunt gestured at them to sit then picked up the long-stemmed, jewel-encrusted goblet and sipped carefully. Master Thibault stood close to his right while on a quilted bench to the Regent's left sat the younger Oudernarde and his secretary, the bland-faced Cornelius.

'Your Grace,' Thibault's voice was scarcely above a whisper, 'I have said goodnight to Isabella. She sends you her love. Captain Rosselyn will see to the Straw Men; they will be given chambers and forbidden to leave the Tower on pain of death.'

'Not together,' Gaunt declared brusquely. 'They must be kept apart.'

'Of course, Your Grace. They have been provided with separate quarters throughout the Tower. Barak's possessions have been searched; nothing untoward was discovered.' Athelstan was sure Gaunt whispered, 'Traitor!' For a while the Regent just sat on his chair, cradling his wine. He rocked slightly backwards and forwards while staring at a point above their heads, his face muscles rippled. Now and again he blinked furiously, as he fought what Cranston knew to be a savage temper. The silence in the chapel grew oppressive. Athelstan pushed his hands up the sleeves of his gown and stared calmly at this brother of the Black Prince, uncle and protector of the young King Richard, Duke of Lancaster, possible heir to the throne of Castile, patron of the arts and of religion, even if it meant favouring heretics like Wycliffe, builder of this palace and that, and fervent enemy of both the Commons and London. Gaunt was truly a formidable opponent. The Regent broke from his reverie, lifting a satin-gloved hand.

Thibault stepped forward, clearing his throat. 'Sir John, Brother Athelstan – you saw how much I love my daughter, Isabella?'

Neither replied.

'Before I took minor orders,' Thibault explained, 'her mother died in childbirth. Do you love the Lady Maude, Sir John, your twin sons?'

'Of course.'

'And Brother Athelstan, whom do you love? You, a priest who is supposed to love everybody – do you love anybody?' He raised his eyebrows. 'The good widow Benedicta, perhaps?'

'Aye,' Athelstan replied calmly, 'as I love you, Brother Thibault. Isn't that what Christ commanded?'

Gaunt smiled bleakly.

'Very good, very good.' Thibault took a step forward. 'And His Grace dearly loves Meister Oudernarde who, thanks be to God, is recovering, although he still lies gravely wounded. He will be moved to the hospital at Saint Bartholomew's for more special care. Lettenhove, however, is dead, sheeted cold in his coffin. The Regent's guests, Brother Athelstan, Sir John, were grievously attacked in this hallowed place. Those guests were sacred. His Grace the Regent was cruelly mocked; he grieves for what has happened.'

'For all of this,' Athelstan turned to the strong-faced Fleming, 'both Sir John and I are truly sorry.' Oudernarde bowed his head slightly in thanks.

'We want you,' Thibault continued, 'Brother Athelstan and

you, Sir John, to examine most closely what truly happened here today.'

'The assassin lies dead, does he not?'

'To examine most closely, Brother Athelstan, what happened here today,' Thibault repeated. 'Captain Rosselyn will provide you with comfortable quarters.'

'I have other duties,' Athelstan replied.

'*Voluntas principis*,' Thibault leaned down, '*habet vigorem legis*', or so Justinian says. 'The will of the prince has force of law.'

'*Et quod omnes tangit*,' Athelstan quoted back, '*ab omnibus approbetur*.' You have read your Bracton, Master Thibault? What affects all should be approved by all.'

The Master of Secrets was about to reply when a savage roaring and growling echoed through the chapel.

'The keepers are feeding the King's lions,' Thibault whispered. 'You must visit them, Brother, during your stay here.'

'My parishioners?' Athelstan ignored Cranston's quick intake of breath.

'Oh, yes,' Thibault smiled, 'your parishioners! You heard about the murder of my hangmen, Laughing Jack and his two minions. Perhaps, Brother, their assassins might be hiding among your parishioners – His Grace's enemies, the Upright Men, who can be hanged out of hand.' Thibault pursed his lips. 'Yes, that would be justice. We could hire that strange anchorite you shelter, the Hangman of Rochester. We could set up a gallows outside your church. I could have your parishioners' filthy, mean hovels searched and ransacked. And who shall we begin with? Watkin? Yes, I'm sure it's Watkin, the shit collector? And his great friend, the grubby-faced ditcher? We could search their shabby houses. Rosselyn could bring them here for questioning in certain chambers beneath this tower.'

Athelstan repressed a shiver. Now he was certain. There was a spy among his parishioners. This Master of Secrets knew too much.

'Of course,' Thibault smiled, 'your parishioners will miss you. But, if you stay and do my master's bidding, there will be no need for the search or the gallows.' He wagged a finger like some master in the schools. 'I can send them comfort; perhaps pig, nicely roasted and basted with all sorts of mouth-watering sauces. Some capon and chicken, soft and white; freshly baked bread and a large barrel of the finest ale. Indeed, I shall send it tomorrow, early in the morning.' Thibault turned, slightly gesturing at his master. 'A gift from His Grace.'

'I will do what I can,' Athelstan replied slowly.

'Good. Very good.' Thibault clapped his hands like an excited child.

'The heads,' Athelstan demanded swiftly. 'Where are those heads, severed at the neck and soaked in brine for at least a month? Did you recognize them, Thibault?'

The Master of Secrets simply pulled a face and shrugged.

'Did any of you recognize them?' Athelstan gazed around. No one answered. 'In which case,' Athelstan persisted, 'may I see those heads, to inspect them?' Athelstan bit his tongue; he was tempted to ask about the mysterious prisoner but that might betray Sir John.

'Why?' Thibault asked. 'Those heads are not part of . . .'

'You asked us to investigate.' Cranston stirred himself. The coroner was becoming fidgety, his usual bonhomie fast draining away.

'I would like to inspect those heads when we want,' Athelstan insisted. The friar rose to his feet. 'And it's best if we begin now. Master Thibault,' Athelstan bowed towards Gaunt, 'Your Grace, is there anything,' Athelstan fought to keep the sarcasm out of his voice, 'that we should know? Master Oudernarde?' Athelstan turned towards the Fleming, 'I noticed poor Lettenhove seemed very agitated before the assault.'

'So he was,' Cornelius replied quickly. 'Brother Athelstan, you must have heard about the heinous attack on us as we journeyed to the Tower? We remained anxious, as did poor Lettenhove.'

'I understand that nothing has been disturbed and taken away from this chapel?'

'Nothing,' Thibault replied.

'In which case,' Athelstan bowed, 'I would like to begin. Your Grace, I need to examine this chapel.' Athelstan returned to his stool.

'You are quiet, Sir John,' he leaned over and whispered.

'Limoges, I shall explain,' Cranston murmured.

Gaunt rose to his feet. He nodded at Cranston and Athelstan then gestured at Thibault and the Flemings to follow him as he swept out of the chapel. Lascelles covered their retreat; the archers followed until only Rosselyn remained close to the doorway. Cranston glanced at Athelstan sitting so composedly on his stool; the friar just grinned and made a swift, soothing movement with his hand, a sign to wait. They both sat listening to Gaunt and his party clattering down the spiral staircase; only then did Athelstan move his stool closer to Cranston.

'Limoges, Sir John?'

'I shall tell you later,' the coroner hissed. 'But remember this, my little friar, Sir John is not frightened. He is tired, weary after drinking claret but not frightened.' The coroner tapped his boots against the floor. 'Oh, no, I am not frightened, but I am as wary as I would be if there was a rabid wolf in the room.' He rose to his feet. 'Let us begin.'

Athelstan did likewise. He slowly looked around that gorgeously decorated chapel. '*Primo*,' he pointed to the braziers, now full of grey scented ash. 'There were the explosions. As you said, Sir John, easy to fashion. Cannon powder or saltpetre in thick leather pouches, thrust into the hot coals – eventually they would break in the heat. The consequent explosion caused consternation; people would be looking at the braziers, nowhere else. *Secundo*.' Athelstan stifled a yawn, ignoring the wave of weariness. God knows he'd love . to be stretched out on his cot bed with Bonaventure sprawled at his feet. '*Secondo*,' he repeated, moving a stool, 'Lettenhove's marked and struck a mortal wound; he falls to the ground. *Tertio*, Master Oudernarde is attacked next, but only wounded. I suspect the barb was loosed a little off the mark.'

'And the severed heads?' Cranston asked.

'Good, Sir John. *Quatro*. Before our assassin flees, he somehow leaves those two severed heads by the rood screen and that, Sir John, is where the mystery begins. Look at this chapel. Remember this afternoon, how busy it was, thronged with Gaunt and his guests, servants, musicians, men-at-arms and archers. So I ask you. How could our assassin prime a small crossbow, take aim, loose and repeat the same action, then open a sack,' Athelstan walked across and tapped the rood screen, 'and place a severed head here.' He walked past Hell's mouth to the other side, 'And another one here, yet not be noticed?'

'Did he use Hell's mouth?' Cranston pointed to the great dragon's head tightly wedged in the doorway of the rood screen. 'Look at those gaping jaws, Athelstan. Our assassin could have crawled in with his crossbow . . .' Athelstan and Cranston pulled back the curtain at one end of the rood screen and walked into the sanctuary. Athelstan stared around, peering through the poor light.

'Dark,' he observed. 'See, Sir John,' he pointed to the heavy curtains hanging either end of the rood screen, 'these block out the light from the window of the transepts. There's the sanctuary lamp, but,' Athelstan sniffed at the candles on their five-branched spigot, 'once these are extinguished, murder could easily wrap its dark cloak around this holy place. Now Hell's mouth.' Athelstan swiftly scrutinized the back of the dragon's head, at least two-and-a-half yards high. He marvelled at the artifice for it was simply fastened to a high-legged table; each leg had a wooden castor while a black canvas cloth clasped to the back of the dragon's head covered the table entirely. In the gloomy light this did look like the rippling skin of a dragon. 'Very clever, Sir John. The dragon's head is simply a large mask with those splendid jaws fixed and wedged into the door of the rood screen. The rest of its body is quite simply a table and a canvas cloth. Now,' Athelstan pushed the canvas back and, going on his hands and knees, crawled beneath the table, the top of which was well above the gaping jaws. Athelstan peered through this; it provided a good view of the chapel nave as well as the stool marking the spot where Lettenhove had fallen. The elder Oudernarde, however, would have been much more difficult, if not impossible, to mark down. The assassin would have to move sharply to the right but, even then, his target would be blocked. Oudernarde had been standing that little bit closer to Hell's mouth. Moreover, there was the question of the two severed heads. Athelstan had wildly considered that both had been dropped through Hell's mouth, but surely that would have been noticed? They would have rolled, yet he'd seen them placed like ornaments either side of the dragon's head. Of course, Hell's mouth might have been moved? Was that possible? Athelstan scrambled out from beneath the table.

'Well, little friar,' Cranston grinned down at him, 'and what have you discovered?'

Athelstan dusted down his robe, got up and told him what he had concluded, before moving back into the chapel to examine the front of Hell's mouth. He pushed hard but the scenery was wedged between the edges of the screen and held tight by clasps. Cranston did the same from the other side. Hell's mouth was like a stopper in a wine skin. Athelstan reasoned it could be shoved loose but this would damage the clasps, the thick leather strips on either side, and there was no sign that this had happened.

'The Straw Men must have made sure Hell's mouth was secure,' Athelstan sighed. 'And yet, if it could be moved, the assassin might be able to place the heads, then push or pull it back in again. Of course,' he rubbed his face, 'that would have been seen or even heard; the clasps would have been broken, very obvious to detect. So, Sir John, the severed heads must have been put down in another way. Then there's the vexed question of the assassin having a clear view of Oudernarde. The assassin would only gain this by moving Hell's mouth, yet there's not a shred of evidence to suggest that happened.' Athelstan stood, arms crossed, staring down at the floor.

'I'm back in the schools, Sir John.' Athelstan scratched at a piece of wax on his wrist. 'You can only get a logical conclusion, a truthful conclusion from a logical, truthful beginning, yet that escapes me. Look, Sir John.' He nodded towards the now-empty doorway, 'Of your kindness, please ask Lascelles and Rosselyn to join us. Plead with them to bring two hand-held arbalests like the ones our assassin certainly used, as well as a quiver of bolts on a war belt.' He paused. 'Oh, yes, and a small inflated pig's bladder, the type children use as a ball.' Cranston looked surprised but shrugged and strode away, shouting for the archer on guard.

Athelstan stayed for a while.

'One assassin here,' he murmured, 'or could it have been two? And Barak? Murder, suicide or a simple accident?'

Athelstan left the chapel and went down the spiral staircase into the cavernous murky crypt. For a while he stumbled about with a cresset torch he'd taken from the stairwell. Eventually he lit every sconce, candle and lantern box in that dark, gloomy chamber. Athelstan walked up and down. 'This is a strange place,' he murmured. 'Most crypts are beneath ground level but this is the first floor of the White Tower.' He held the torch up. The crypt reminded him of a tithing barn: its paved stone floor was scrubbed clean with no matting, while the whitewashed walls lacked any ornamentation – even a cross. Apparently used for storing furniture, the crypt was bleak and soulless. He noticed how all the windows were shuttered and barred before moving down to where the shutters on the furthest window had been thrown back. According to all the evidence, Barak had tried to escape through this but had, due to some mishap, fallen to his death. Athelstan stood listening to the different sounds from both the stairwell and elsewhere in the Tower. Again, he heard the roaring from the menagerie and promised himself a visit to examine both the lions as well as to see for himself that great snow bear swimming in the moat. 'But that will have to wait,' he whispered. 'Barak's ghost is more important.'

Athelstan crouched down to examine the thick, oiled hempen rope with its tarred, twisted strands, which Barak had used in his abortive escape. The rope was secured tightly to a great iron ring driven into the wall. The rope had been pulled back after Barak's fatal use and simply tossed on to the floor. Athelstan picked it up, scrutinizing the heavy knots placed every twelve inches. He could detect nothing out of the ordinary. Such ropes were common in both the Tower and other castles in case of fire or if the stairway to St John's Chapel somehow became blocked. He sifted the rope through his hands and tugged hard, but the rope was sound in itself and firmly secured. He opened the shutters and flinched at the strong gust of icy wind; nevertheless, he persisted. He took the rope and threaded it out; it was long enough to allow someone to safely descend then jump to the ground below, the well-placed heavy knots providing some sort of hold for foot and hand. Athelstan leaned over the sill and peered down.

'What did happen to you, Barak?' he whispered to the darkness. 'Did you slip from the rope? Were you nervous? Why take the arbalest with you? Were you on the rope when someone pushed you?' Athelstan recalled the horrid wound to the right side of the dead man's face, the broken neck, the way the body had crumpled. 'I don't think you slipped.' Athelstan again peered over the window ledge: it was a dizzying drop to the cobbles beneath. 'Do you know what I think, Barak, God rest your soul? You didn't fall from the rope, you fell from here. Or, even more logical – and this would explain your savage wounds – you were thrown from here.'

Athelstan pulled the rope back and clasped the heavy shutters close. He leaned his hands on them and tried to make sense of his own thoughts. Such an escape could be depicted as probable. Barak the assassin could have easily checked both rope and shutters earlier in the day. According to the evidence, Barak carried out those attacks, left the severed heads and, when everybody else was fleeing the chapel, he joined them. That would be feasible. The rest would only be too eager to escape the White Tower but Barak slipped into the crypt. He certainly reached this window. Such an escape, Athelstan reasoned, from the fastness of this Tower would not be the first. Years ago Athelstan, while studying at Blackfriars, had used the top of the White Tower with its four unique turrets as an observatory to study the stars. Athelstan smiled at the memories. He'd also learnt a great deal about the Tower's history. How a number of prisoners, including a Welsh prince, Ranulf Flambard, Bishop of Durham, and Roger Mortimer of Wigmore had all escaped by rope from this great Norman keep. Indeed, hadn't one of them, the Welsh prince, fallen to his death? And yet . . . Athelstan felt a deepening disquiet about the accepted story of Barak's death. The evidence didn't appear correct; there was a lack of logic to it. 'Not only the details,' Athelstan murmured to the darkness, 'but the motivation. According to his comrades, there was no change in Barak in the hours or days before he committed these dreadful crimes.' Athelstan rubbed his face. Would, he wondered, the Upright Men have entrusted those severed heads to Barak? Yet there was no evidence, apart from what was found on his corpse, of any link between him and the Upright Men. According to Thibault nothing incriminating was found among Barak's personal belongings. Athelstan stood with his back to now-closed shutters. He peered through the gloom then walked across to the recess built into the far wall. The paving stones here were the same light colour as those of the chapel while, despite the dust and cobwebs, the walls had been recently whitewashed, probably as late as the previous spring. Athelstan took another cresset from its holder and went into the recess. He crouched down. Using the pools of light from both torches, he scrupulously examined both floor and wall inch by inch.

'May the Lord be thanked,' Athelstan prayed, 'I have found it.' He stretched out and touched the wall, certain those dark stains were small splashes of fresh blood on the plaster of the enclave. Athelstan put one of the torches down and sat with his back to the wall, rubbing the plaster with the back of his head. He turned so he was on his hands and knees. Barak, if he remembered correctly, was slightly taller than he. Athelstan scrutinized the wall and murmured a prayer of thanks. The small bloodstains were just above where the friar had rested the back of his head.

'Athelstan, Athelstan! Brother Athelstan!' The friar returned to the chapel, where Cranston, Lascelles and Rosselyn were waiting. The two soldiers were deeply intrigued by what Athelstan asked for but quickly agreed to help. First Rosselyn and then Lascelles acted as a would-be assassin.

'I want you to go beneath the table, behind Hell's mouth and,' Athelstan pointed to the two stools each marking the place where Lettenhove and Oudernarde had fallen, 'pretend to loose a bolt at the Fleming's henchman and then at Master Oudernarde. However, you are to do it twice. The first time you must pretend to have one arbalest, the next that you have two and the second is already primed. Now,' Athelstan insisted, 'you must use the gaping jaws of Hell's mouth as your vantage point. I suspect that, like me, you will find Lettenhove an easy target to mark; Oudernarde not so. Once you are ready, shout out. Sir John here will start counting.' After some confusion and a few false starts, Lascelles declared he was ready. Cranston had almost reached twenty when Lascelles declared he had used the same arbalest twice, and twelve when he used a second one already primed. Rosselyn was not so swift on either occasion, declaring how the war bow was his weapon, but Athelstan was satisfied. He now had a clearer idea of how long an assassin would take if he had used Hell's mouth as his screen, while both had confessed that aiming at Oudernarde was difficult. The friar also noticed how the two soldiers, being right-handed, wore the box-like quiver of bolts on the left side of their war belt.

'So you found the first mark easy enough?' asked Athelstan.

'Oh, yes,' Lascelles replied, nodding in agreement, 'but Oudernarde was very difficult.'

'To present the best target,' Rosselyn declared, 'Hell's mouth would either have to be dragged back a little or Oudernarde stand further from it.'

'I agree,' Lascelles murmured.

'Shall we move the scenery?' Athelstan asked. All four men pressed against the gaping jaws. Eventually the dragon's jaws snapped free of the rood screen to roll back on its castors. Athelstan carefully examined the thick leather straps which acted as both a cushion and a clasp to protect the edges of the rood screen. Athelstan patted the jaws. He would love to bring this to his church. He realized that the doors to most rood screens were about the same measurement. 'Very clever. They must calculate the gap in the rood screen, then adjust the leather straps accordingly, folding them into a wedge. Now,' Athelstan eased himself past the dragon's head, inviting the others to join him in the sanctuary beyond. Once they were, Athelstan and Cranston positioned Hell's mouth correctly and pushed it back so it wedged easily in the rood screen door, although not as snugly as before with two of the leather straps now damaged. Athelstan shook his head in disbelief. 'So it couldn't have been moved.' He spoke to himself. 'Well, well, well.'

'Brother, I have brought you the pig's bladder,' Rosselyn, hidden in the shadows, called out.

'Oh, thank you, bring it here. Please, all of you, go back into the chapel and stare at Hell's mouth.' Athelstan, lost in thought, stood staring at the black canvas sheeting as Rosselyn brought across the pig's bladder. Athelstan waited until he'd left, crouched beneath the table and pushed the ball through the gaping jaws. Cranston confirmed it rolled away from the rood screen. Athelstan just shook his head. How, how, how, he thought to himself, had those two severed heads been placed so carefully? If they had been despatched through Hell's mouth, although not as light or round as a pig's bladder, they would have certainly rolled and so been seen, even heard. Yet they had been positioned like two ornaments on a sill. Calling out to the rest, Athelstan left the chapel and walked down into the hollow, empty crypt, the torches still flaring fitfully casting shafts of light which made the shadows dance and shiver. They reached the window Barak had apparently used for his escape. Rosselyn opened the shutters, stared down and confirmed that Barak's corpse had been found just beneath.

'Did you or anyone see or hear the fall?'

'Brother, this is a January day. Darkness had fallen. A sentry by sheer chance stumbled over the corpse just lying there, the arbalest a short distance away. As I said, it was mere luck; the corpse might not have been discovered until daybreak.'

'And were the window shutters open or closed?'

'I don't truly know – perhaps almost closed. I sent one of my archers up to light the lantern box. I can't remember distinctly. Perhaps the assassin, once he was through, paused to pull them across – I mean, to hide any light.' Rosselyn stamped his feet, rubbing his hands. 'In brief, we found the corpse. We believed the assassin had been escaping through that window in the crypt when he slipped. An archer went up to light the lantern as a signal and,' he shrugged, 'that's all I know.'

'The shutters were probably closed,' Athelstan agreed. 'If they'd been open on a winter's day that would certainly attract attention. Anyway, gentlemen,' Athelstan stepped back, 'pretend you are the assassin. You are preparing to leave as Barak did – remember you are carrying a crossbow.' Athelstan watched as both men did the same, fastening the small crossbow to a clasp on their war belt before pulling their cloaks around them.

'I have it,' Athelstan murmured. 'Gentlemen,' he sketched a blessing in the air, 'I thank you.'

'What have you learnt, Brother?' Rosselyn seemed anxious, and Athelstan wondered why. Had he to report back to Thibault, or did he have personal reasons? Lascelles, on the other hand, remained cold and impassive, as he had throughout. Athelstan wondered if Lascelles, as Thibault's henchman, had reflected on this bizarre mystery and was speculating that the accepted story might not be true.

'Brother,' Rosselyn came out of the shadows, 'I asked you a question?'

'I'm sorry,' Athelstan apologized. 'The truth is I have learnt very little.' He paused as the bell of St Peter ad Vincula began to answer those tolling from the city, announcing the hour of Compline.

'We have lodgings here?' Cranston demanded. 'I'm becoming hungry, cold and, if the truth be known, exhausted.'

'Sir John,' Rosselyn reassured him, 'you and Brother Athelstan will share a chamber in the Garden Tower near the Watergate. The kitchens will serve you.'

'Before you leave,' Athelstan gestured around, 'I want this left as it is.'

Rosselyn promised he would do what he could, and both men left. Athelstan watched them go.

'Brother, you don't want to share your thoughts?'

'Well, not with those two, Sir John. One of them might be the killer.'

'But Barak?'

'Aye, poor Barak,' Athelstan echoed. 'We will let the dead sleep in peace for a while. Come, Sir John, your belly is rumbling like a drum.'

Outside the baileys and yards of the Tower were freezing cold. A thick river mist had descended to create a land of ghosts, broken only by the shouts of sentries, the neighing of horses and that deep, throaty roaring from the royal menagerie. Pinpricks of lights glowed from battlements and tower windows. Torches flared in their desperate fight against the chilly night breeze. Cranston and Athelstan were pleased to reach the Garden Tower; the smell from around the Watergate was offensive but the chamber on the ground floor of that squat, sinister-looking tower had been well prepared. A circular, comfortable room, the windows were not only shuttered but covered with heavy leather drapes embroidered with heraldic devices. The fire in the small hearth roared up the flue, the pine logs cracking and snapping. The lime-washed walls gleamed cleanly and displayed a crucifix with small statues of the Virgin and saints placed in niches. The servant waiting for them loudly assured Sir John that the cot beds were comfortable, while he would place more rope matting on the floor to curb the chill. The servant then offered to bring food. Cranston, bellowing how hungry he was, began to take off his cloak. Athelstan kept thinking about that desolate chapel. He walked towards the door.

'Sir John, wait here.'

'No, I will not,' Cranston barked. 'You are off again on your travels, little friar? Well, if you are, I will stay with you in this benighted place.' Athelstan told the surprised servant not to serve the food and, pulling up his cowl, walked back into the icy blackness. Cranston followed, cursing quietly. Athelstan stopped an archer who kindly led them down the steps into the gloomy dungeons of the White Tower.

'Oh Lord, save us, Brother,' Cranston moaned. 'What in Heaven's name are we doing?'

'The archer told me Barak's corpse is here, I want to see it. Come on, Sir John.'

The dungeons proved to be a stygian underworld of shadow-filled, stinking tunnels and enclaves. Torches glowed in their rusty holdings. Vermin, like little black demons, scurried across the pools of light. The reeking odour of decay caught their noses and mouths. A figure jangling keys lurched out of the murk. The burly-faced janitor immediately recognized Cranston, though the coroner could only shake his head when the man introduced himself as William Ockle, former assistant hangman at Smithfield. He asked their business. Athelstan replied and the janitor led them to a dungeon door, opened it and ushered them in.

'The Fleming has been taken to the death house on the other side of Saint Peter's,' Ockle explained between noisy mouthfuls of ale from a blackjack. He gestured at Barak's corpse thrown on to a dirty, sodden palliasse. 'God knows what His Grace will do with him. Perhaps,' he smacked his lips, 'his head will be lopped off, his limbs quartered and the bloody, tarred chunks will festoon London Bridge.' Athelstan crouched down, murmuring a prayer. He asked both the janitor and Cranston to hold the torches close as he re-examined the corpse. He turned Barak over to examine the back of his head, feeling the deep wound which he traced with his fingers. Moving the corpse back, Athelstan studied the entire right side of the face, pulped to a hideous, soggy mess.

'Do you want me to strip the corpse?' Ockle offered. 'I will have to sooner or later.' His voice became peevish. 'I lay claim to all his clothing, boots and possessions. I hope he is wearing an undershirt. My woman can wash it, then I'll sell it to the Fripperers in East Cheap.'

Cranston glared up at him. Ockle pulled a face. 'I was only asking . . .'

Athelstan searched the corpse. He could tell from the neck and other injuries that the entire right side had been badly bruised and crushed as Barak smashed into the cobbles. He examined the war belt with the quiver box hanging on the right side before moving to the hands. He sniffed at these, noting the mud stains though the nails were neatly pared and clean, the skin soft and smooth as any clerk's. Barak's wrists were also sleek, unmarked and bereft of any jewellery or covering. Athelstan recited the requiem, blessed the corpse and got to his feet. He gave Ockle a coin for his pains, left the dungeons and, ignoring Cranston's protests, climbed the spiral staircase leading back into St John's Chapel. He nodded at the archer on guard and stood in the centre of the nave, staring at the rood screen.

'Remember this, Sir John,' Athelstan pointed to the braziers, one to his right, the other to his left, 'the explosions occurred in each. Nearby stood Lettenhove and, across the chapel, Oudernarde. Along the transepts, the tapestries had been pulled up to reveal the food tables, servants were milling about. Now look at the rood screen: Hell's mouth seals its entrance, on either end of it hangs an arras of heavy damask.' He sighed. 'Remember that as I surely will.' The friar refused to say any more; he left the chapel with Cranston hurrying behind.

'Brother . . .?'

Athelstan waited till they had left the keep. Once out in the blistering cold, he paused and stared up.

'The sky blossoms are hidden, Sir John. We'll have snow tonight and it will lie thick.'

'Is Barak the murderer?'

'He was no assassin,' Athelstan whispered. 'God have mercy on him. He did not slip from that rope, he was hurled from that window, or that is what I suspect.'

'Why?'

'Gloves and wrist guards, Sir John, or the lack of them, but now I am famished.'

# PART THREE

## 'Ursus Marinus: Sea Bear'

T hey returned to their chamber, the snow falling in heavy flakes. Athelstan recalled the legend of souls tumbling from Heaven seeking a dwelling in human flesh.

'It will lie swift and rich,' Cranston declared, stomping up the steps. He was startled by a figure stepping out of a shadow in the stairwell inside. 'In God's name!'

'Aye, Sir John, in God's name surely.' The black-haired harpist pushed back his hood, the corner of his harp peeping out between the folds of his threadbare cloak. 'Sir John, good evening. Like you, I'm trapped here. I cannot leave till the morrow, and even then I will need a maintainer. You will vouch for me?'

'Of course.' Cranston grasped the harpist by the shoulder and pulled him into the pool of shifting torchlight. 'Brother Athelstan, let me introduce the Troubadour, former cleric, former soldier, a teller of tales and quite a few lies.' Athelstan, staring at the hollow eyes and pinched, sallow features beneath an untidy mop of hair, could well believe Sir John's description. The Troubadour, or whatever his real name, looked crafty and devious – indeed, the ideal choice to play Renard the Fox in any mystery play.

'Yet a most skilled harpist.' Cranston took out a silver coin and handed it over. 'He plucks the strings and they pluck at your heart. But, my friend, it's your eyes I need now. What have you seen?'

The Troubadour bit on the coin and slid it beneath his robe. 'I have wandered the Tower, when I can. Thibault has taken it over. There's great secrecy over the prisoner kept in Beauchamp. I tried to draw as close as I could. I even spent some money but to no avail. Those archers are Thibault's men in peace and war, body and soul. No one will speak about the prisoner – well, not openly.'

'And yet you have discovered something?'

The harpist grinned; his teeth were remarkably white and even.

'Definitely a woman, Sir John – she still has trouble with her monthly courses according to a servant who empties the slop jars. Another says she spends her days embroidering and requires needle, thread and thimble.'

'And?'

'She is definitely Flemish. She finds London food not to her taste, though she is partial to eel pies and lightly grilled fish cakes. However, she is no damsel in distress; she's not fair of face or lovely of form.'

'How do you know that?'

'Again, servants have glimpsed her with her veil pulled back. Sir John, they say she reminds them of someone, but they cannot actually place her.'

'Someone? Someone who?'

'This was an old servant who has worked here for many a year; she glimpsed the prisoner's face, it sparked a memory, but she cannot say which.' The Troubadour spread his hands. 'More than that I cannot say.'

'And the severed heads?' Athelstan asked.

The Troubadour's strange eyes blinked. 'Again, Brother, very little. I heard a whisper, just a rumour, that the heads really belonged to Master Thibault and were taken from his care when the Upright Men attacked him on his journey to the Tower. They also say that Thibault was looking for something, perhaps the severed heads, when he laid siege to the Roundhoop.'

'And the attack in the chapel?'

'Again, very little, Brother except, immediately after the second attack, the Flemings' secretary, the Mousehead?'

'Cornelius?'

'Yes, he and Thibault's bully boy, Rosselyn, abruptly left the chapel as if they were pursuing somebody. Remember I was with the minstrelling in the recess. They went down the stairs then Cornelius hurried back.

'Why, where did they go?'

'I don't know, Sir John. I suspect that they went out to ensure Beauchamp Tower was still kept secure.'

'Ah, of course!' Athelstan declared. 'They wondered if the attack could be linked to an attempt to free this mysterious woman.'

'Perhaps. I tell you this, the squires of the shadows . . .'

'Thibault's spies?'

'Yes, Sir John. They've been very busy throughout the city, as if they were searching for something, or listening to rumour.'

'They could be looking,' Athelstan answered, 'for what was plundered when the Flemings were attacked on their journey to the Tower – the severed heads. They would also be very interested in discovering if the news that Gaunt holds a special prisoner here has become common knowledge.'

'And so we, too, must get very busy,' Cranston murmured. 'Look, my friend, tomorrow you will be allowed to leave – I shall vouch for you. Thibault will see no danger in you. Now, once you have gone, seek out Muckworm. Tell him Sir John, sometime soon, desires to meet the leader of the tribes at the Tower of Babel.'

'Sir John, you wish to go there?'

'I have to. Now, my friend,' Cranston opened the door and Athelstan peered out; the snow was still falling. The troubadour slipped through and they adjourned to their chamber, all shuttered and closed, the braziers a mound of glowing bright coal, the fire in the hearth built up and roaring. A short while later, the servant who'd been waiting brought bowls of steaming hot chicken broth, slices of cold beef and pots of heavily spiced vegetables. Athelstan blessed the food and watched as Sir John cleared the platters and swiftly downed his wine. Afterwards the coroner, kicking off boots and loosening belts, clasps and buttons, stretched out on one of the cot beds. 'Well, little friar, what have you learnt?'

'A little, Sir John, but first, Limoges?'

Cranston raised his head off the bolster; abruptly realizing he was still wearing his beaver hat, he tore this off and tossed in on to the floor. He lay half propped, listening to the bell clanging from the top of Bell Tower above the constant growling from the animal pens. 'I must take you there, Brother, see the cages . . .'

'Limoges, Sir John!'

'Ten years ago, or just over, I was with Gaunt and his brother the Black Prince at the siege of Limoges.'

'Ah,' Athelstan interrupted, 'I remember this. De Cos the bishop?'

'Yes,' Cranston sighed, 'he refused to surrender the city. When it was taken, the Black Prince nearly had him killed – his flock certainly were. You may have heard the stories?'

'Garbled, tangled,' Athelstan replied, 'difficult to believe.'

'Then believe me, Brother, whatever you heard, never mind how dreadful it is, the truth is more heinous. I was there. I turned my horse at the Porte de Saint Marcel and rode back to camp. A nightmare, awful to see, horrible to hear! Unarmed men, women and children, brutally butchered, the streets bubbled ankle-deep in blood. Gaunt was there along with his black-armoured brother; they are both as guilty as each other. I mentioned the King's lions in their cages; Gaunt was like a ravenous, raging lion.' Cranston pulled himself up, wagging a finger at Athelstan. 'Now you know why I remained silent. You don't poke a lion, especially one that is both mad and bad. Oh,' Cranston's voice turned sweet in mimicry, 'Gaunt can be the perfect gentle knight, the gallant warrior, the courteous courtier, the righteous ruler,' Cranston's voice turned hard, 'as long as you do exactly what he's asked. Oppose him, especially in public, then prepare to experience the furies of Hell. Remember that – never forget it. The Upright Men and Gaunt richly deserve each other. Now,' Cranston continued, rubbing his hands, 'what have you discovered?'

'Two stories.' Athelstan made himself comfortable at the table. 'According to the accepted one, Barak is the assassin. Why, we don't really know. He may not have liked the rich and the powerful, in which case he was only one among a multitude. Anyway, according to the accepted story, Barak wedged that cannon powder in those two braziers,' Athelstan shrugged, 'an easy enough task. Travelling players use such powder to create their illusions. Barak could have done that and not been noticed. Sometime after the play, Barak crawled into the back of Hell's mouth and used the gaping jaws to mark down Oudernarde senior and Lettenhove. The former he wounded, the latter he killed.'

'Why do you still insist he used Hell's mouth?'

'Sir John, where else could the assassin hide to prime an arbalest then loose, not once but twice, and never be noticed? I mean, if we believe the accepted story?'

'Agreed, and?'

'Barak must have somehow moved Hell's mouth to strike as well as position those two severed heads. God knows where he got them from.' Athelstan laughed grimly. 'And God only knows to whom those heads belong? Who were those unfortunates? Why were they killed? Why are their heads here? God bless me, it is beyond answer. I suspect Master Thibault, who was so keen to seize those grim relics, knows the truth but will not share that with us. Nor,' Athelstan added, 'will he reveal the truth about his mysterious prisoner. Are those severed heads part of the mystery surrounding her, whoever she may be? Why are Gaunt and Thibault so concerned about a middle-aged woman, a Fleming who, according to the fickle memory of a servant, may have been in the Tower before?' Athelstan paused. He realized how silent it had become, as if the snow was enveloping this grim fortress in a thick white shroud. He recalled the stories of the ghosts who allegedly haunted the soaring, deep-dungeoned towers, the wraiths said to stalk its lonely courtyards and baileys.

'Your story, Brother?'

'Apparently, after he had done all this, Barak tried to flee – that's understandable. Using all the tumult and upset, Barak left the chapel for the crypt. He reached that window and, still clutching the arbalest, attempted to use the fire rope to escape. Again, according to the evidence, he slipped and fell to his death.'

'And,' Cranston asked sleepily, 'you challenge this?'

'Well,' Athelstan paused at a knock at the door; he opened it to see the servant, covered in snow, his face pale with cold, stood in the icy stairwell.

'Brother Athelstan, Master Thibault asks you to celebrate the Jesus Mass tomorrow after dawn.' The fellow hopped from foot to foot, scratching his grey beard and pulling at his cloak, doing a little jig to keep warm by stamping his feet.

'What is your name?' Athelstan smiled, fishing into his purse.

'Wolkind.'

'Well, Wolkind, there's a coin for your pains. Tell Master Thibault I will celebrate Mass. Now get you warm.' Athelstan sketched a blessing and closed the door.

'You were saying, Brother?'

'So I was.' Athelstan stood over a brazier warming his hands and smiling at Cranston who lay sprawled red-faced and content without a care in the world. 'I said there were two stories. The first is faulted so many times, I wonder if it's a complete lie.' Athelstan used his fingers to emphasize his points. '*Primo*. For Barak to use Hell's mouth as a cover he would have to detach it from the rood screen so that he could clearly strike Oudernarde as well as Lettenhove. He would also have to move it backwards and forwards to position those two severed heads, but we now accept that's nonsense. Hell's mouth was firmly wedged in the door of the rood screen. It had to be. Don't forget, Sir John, we watched the masque. Herod was pushed through those jaws. I saw no movement.'

'It could have been done afterwards and then repositioned?'

'I don't think so. Marks would have been left. The noise alone would have alerted people. Think, Sir John, the scenery would have to have been moved forward and back. Trust me, Sir John, it was not moved until we did it.'

'So how did Barak loose two bolts without being detected?'

'Sir John, that's the mystery, and it deepens. Barak, given the speed of his attack, must have used two arbalests already primed. So where is the second? Why should Barak only take one of them? Why hold it on a dangling, swinging rope while attempting such a dangerous escape? Why not place it on a hook on his war belt as Rosselyn and Lascelles did? Why was the quiver box on the wrong side? Barak was right-handed; the quiver should have been on his left not his right.' Athelstan pulled a face. '*Concedo* – I concede,' he continued, 'Barak may have simply made a mistake, but there is more. He wore no wrist guard as any archer should and, above all, no gloves.'

'You mentioned that before.'

'Sir John, Barak was going down a rope, hard and coarse.'

'True, true,' Cranston breathed.

'He would have burnt his hands. He'd have worn gauntlets – heavy ones – yet his hands were soft and unscarred. Then there are the injuries,' Athelstan continued, 'the right side of his face and body were smashed to pulp against the cobbles. Moreover, there is a deep wound to the back of his head, while I detected flecks of blood against the wall of that recess in the crypt.'

'You think he was struck at the back of the head and his body rested against the crypt wall before being hurled with great force, the arbalest pushed into his hands, from that window?'

'Yes, Sir John, I suspect that's the truth. Barak was no assassin but the victim of murder. Of course, my conclusion prompts other problems when we return to what happened in Saint John's Chapel. We do not know who was doing what, where and when. Indeed,' he laughed sharply, 'the only person who does is the assassin.' He turned at a loud snore. 'Sir John, are you leaving us?'

'Brother, I have to. I'm exhausted.'

Athelstan continued to stare into the red-hot coals which invoked memories of paintings of Hell he'd glimpsed in frescoes and illuminated psalters. He shifted his gaze and recalled the events of the day. The explosions in the braziers, that gaping gargoyle, the dragon's head. The crossbow bolts whipping across that beautiful chapel. Lettenhove and Oudernarde collapsing. Barak's twisted, battered corpse. And the reason for all this? Athelstan crossed himself then moved to check the draught cloths pinned to the bottom of the chamber door. He returned to the brazier. Where did this all begin? That furious affray at the Roundhoop? Athelstan recalled the young man hesitating with his sword before being struck himself, those words mumbled as he died about 'gleaning'. How some woman was to continue to glean. How he tried to raise himself as if looking for something. Was that just a man lost in the fever of his death throes? And before the attack at the Roundhoop, that savage assault on Thibault's party near Aldgate? It wasn't just an attack on Gaunt; the Upright Men had been searching for something – that enigmatic woman prisoner? Why was she so closely guarded? Why was she so important to Gaunt to be kept under such strict watch at the heart of his power? Undoubtedly there was treachery afoot, the one link between all these events. The attack at Aldgate, the murders in the White Tower. Somebody, pretending to be Gaunt's friend and ally, was really a vigorous Judas.

'Sir John?'

'Yes, Brother?' came the sleepy reply.

'The ambush near Aldgate – surely, for it was so well prepared, the Upright Men must have a spy close to Gaunt and Master Thibault?'

Cranston groaned and rolled over, one eye squinting up at Athelstan. 'Brother, for the love of God, go to sleep. The Upright

Men watch Gaunt as closely as he watches them. They could have easily learnt about the arrival of the Flemings at Dover and the intended route to London. The Upright Men have countless watchmen and spies.'

'But so carefully plotted and prepared?'

'Brother,' Cranston rolled back, 'good night and . . .'

He abruptly pushed back the blankets as the tocsin on the top of Bell Tower began to toll, a discordant, harsh clattering rousing the garrison. Athelstan unbolted the door and hurried out. The falling snow had created a sea of brilliant white against the black fortifications of the Tower. Athelstan glanced across. A glow of fire pierced the darkness brightening the night sky. Other doors were opening, men hurrying out, slipping and slithering across the snow in a clatter of mail and drawn weapons. Cranston, wrapped in blankets, joined Athelstan on the top step, spluttering as the snowflakes settled on his face. A shout echoed, followed by two strident blasts of a horn. Rosselyn strode out of the darkness.

'Brother, Sir John,' he gasped apologies, 'only an accident, a fire in the stables. I've directed men there; we will soon douse the flames.'

*'Ite missa est* – go, our Mass has ended.' Athelstan smiled at the small crowd of worshippers huddled within the rood screen of the rather severe sanctuary of St Peter's. Like Athelstan, they had struggled through the snow, at least a foot deep, as the sacring bell announced a very grey dawn. The Straw Men were there, as were Master Thibault, Lascelles and Oudernarde. Master Cornelius, Athelstan suspected, would be celebrating his own Mass much later in more comfortable lodgings. Cranston, who'd served as Athelstan's altar boy, rose from the sanctuary steps, stamping booted feet, rubbing his hands and noisily smacking his lips. He helped Athelstan divest. Thibault and his party promptly left but not before Lascelles curtly informed Cranston and Athelstan that his master would like to see them before they exited the Tower. Cranston grunted he'd break his fast first, then turned away to help Athelstan clear the sacred vessels from the altar. Once they'd finished and were about to leave by the narrow corpse door, the Straw Men, led by Samuel, came back under

the rood screen. Rachael had pulled up her hood to hide her gorgeous red hair in deference to being in church. She rested on Judith's arm; they and their companions, rubbing their hands for warmth, stopped before Cranston and Athelstan, shuffling their feet. Samuel went to speak but thought otherwise. He closed his mouth, fingering his lips.

'Well?' Cranston barked. 'What do . . .'

Athelstan touched him on the arm. 'You have come to ask about Barak?'

'Yes, we have, Brother.' Judith stepped forward, her impish face set in a stubborn twist. 'We are all here, except Eli, but he's a lazy slug-a-bed.'

'And?' Athelstan asked.

'Do you think . . .?' Rachael blurted out. 'Well, we don't. We have been discussing this. Barak cannot be the murderer. He just cannot be, I mean . . .'

Athelstan grasped the young woman's mittened fingers; her green, cat-like eyes crinkled in amusement.

'Look,' Athelstan smiled at her then round at the rest. 'Gaunt regards you as his mummers, his players, yes? He favours you. He patronizes you.'

'Yes,' Samuel conceded, 'he pays us well.'

'I'm sure he does.' Athelstan released Rachael's hands even as he glimpsed a swift, startled look in Samuel's eyes. Athelstan immediately wondered if there were other reasons why Gaunt and Thibault favoured these strolling players.

'So . . .' The friar took Judith by the elbow, guiding her and the rest out of the church by the narrow side door.

'So what?' Judith asked.

Athelstan scratched his head. 'I don't think Barak was responsible; I don't believe his corpse should be abused. I need to see Thibault. Sir John and I entertain serious doubts about the accepted story but that can wait. Let's break our fast in the guest house refectory.'

They went out into the crisp morning air. The darkness was thinning. Torches moved. Cries and shouts rang out as the Tower community were roused. Women trudged through the snow with buckets for the well. A few children, swathed in motley cloths, played in the snow. High on the Tower parapet walks, torches and braziers glowed. Horses neighed greedily from the stables to be answered by roars and growls from the royal menagerie. Dogs gingerly nosed the snow and barked furiously as they floundered in a drift. Athelstan watched an old greyhound, brindle coloured, desperately trying to get back to its mistress, who was offering a titbit to eat. Smells and odours wafted from latrines, kitchens, lay stalls and wash chambers. The snow had ceased falling but everything was shrouded in white. The great magonels, trebuchets, catapults, sheds and other siege weapons rose like monsters frozen in the snow. Sills and ledges, roofs and cornices – even the great three-branched gallows, each arm displaying a frozen hard cadaver, were encrusted in frosty ice. Cranston led them along the side of the pebble-dashed church. Athelstan knew there would be no stopping him. The coroner was famished, already savouring the cooking smells billowing from the kitchens. Cranston moved as fast and as keen as a strong lurcher. Athelstan walked behind listening to Judith's chatter – how she hoped they could visit St Erconwald's – when he heard the whirr, like the wings of a bird, and a crossbow bolt smacked and splintered against the wall of the church. He abruptly stopped. Cranston turned. 'Get down Athelstan!' he screamed. He dragged the friar by the arm, pulling both him and Judith down just as another bolt whirled over their heads. Crouching in the snow, Athelstan felt the ice seep up the sleeves of his gown. Cranston drew his dagger. The rest raced back to the corpse door as another barb shattered noisily against the church wall.

'Harrow! Harrow!' Cranston bellowed at the top of his voice, raising the alarm. Doors were opened. Archers, men-at-arms and servants came spilling out as Cranston continued to shout. Athelstan, still crouching in the snow, glanced at where the spent barbs lay, then across at the looming mass of the White Tower. He scrutinized the log piles, the engines of war, the wooden staircase and its supporting scaffolding, the unhitched carts and hand barrows.

'There'll be no more,' he murmured, getting to his feet and pointing across.

'Look, Sir John, a company of archers could lurk behind any of those barriers and then disappear.' He brushed the snow from his gown, calling out to the rest gathered just within the corpse door that it was safe. Rosselyn, cowled and cloaked, war bow strung, hurried up. Athelstan briefly explained what had happened, gesturing across at the impedimenta close to the White Tower.

'Whoever it was,' he declared, 'hid there but now he has gone. I hope he hasn't taken my appetite with him.' He showed Rossleyn, the captain's hardened face all pinched and severe, where the crossbow bolts had hit before trudging on through the snow into the welcoming warmth of the refectory. At the buttery hatch servants were ladling out bowls of boiling hot oatmeal spiced with nutmeg and thick dark treacle. Athelstan collected his and went over to a stool close to the fireplace. He took out his horn spoon, murmured a blessing and began to eat, allowing both the heat of the food and the glow from the fierce fire to calm him. Athelstan, as always after Death's dark wings had brushed him, mentally recited both the 'Confiteor', an act of sorrow, followed by the *'Deo Gratias'*, a prayer of thanksgiving. He ate and calmed himself staring up at the roughly carved woodwose in the centre of the mantle, a hell-born face with popping eyes, wild hair, pig's snout and gaping, moustached mouth. The others joined him. Cranston bustled over.

'You are correct, Brother, the devil's bowman must have stood close to the White Tower, cloaked in white. God knows there is enough there to hide behind.'

'Not very accurate, was he?' Athelstan lifted a spoonful and carefully sipped at the oatmeal. 'More of a warning than anything else.' He stared around. 'Who's missing?'

'Eli.' Rachael began to tap her feet nervously. Athelstan gazed towards the half-open door; a raven perched there, a huge bird, black, fat and sleek, its yellow curved beak jabbing at the snow. A visitor from Hell, Athelstan wondered, watching it strut like a devil, unafraid of the human bustle around it.

'Eli never sleeps this late.' Samuel rose from his stool, putting the earthenware bowl on the ground. Athelstan, sensing a growing unease, also got up.

'Where does Eli lodge?'

'The Salt Tower.'

'The rest of you stay.' Athelstan pointed to Samuel. 'But you come with me.'

'And where you go,' Cranston gobbled the remains of his oatmeal, 'I shall certainly follow.'

They left the guest house, booted feet crunching on the snow. The ravens had gathered. A dense flock of black glossy feathers, sharp beaks and empty eyes, hungry for any titbits or scraps of refuse. The garrison was also stirring. The hot smells from the stables mingled with the fetid odour from the animal cages. Day had broken and the real business could begin. A butcher and his two apprentices were slaughtering pigs in a small compound near the kitchens. The chilling squeals of the animals grew strident on the freezing morning air as blood from the slaughter seeped in dark red rivulets under the wicker fence. Another apprentice stood close by with a club driving away dogs maddened by the smell. Athelstan glanced away. They moved carefully, side stepping the burly washerwomen with their huge round tubs as well as soldiers, surly and freezing with cold after their duty along the ice-bound parapets. Children played snow-balls, shouting and yelling as they were hit or fell. The pounding of hammers and the scrape of metal echoed from the smithies. Deep in his heart Athelstan wished to be away from here. The Tower was a strange and narrow place, its atmosphere unsettling. Above all this activity brooded the great soaring donjons, walls and towers. Athelstan recalled how his parishioners believed these dark stones housed demons and other malevolent spirits. He had also heard the stories about its miserable dank dungeons, the secret torture chambers; of corpses being burnt in the dead of night, their ashes being tipped into the river. The Tower was a secret maze of passageways and tunnels, a place where people were taken and never seen again, alive or dead. A house of blood, Athelstan brooded, and he wished to be rid of it.

They reached the entrance to the Salt Tower. Cranston gestured at Samuel, who led them up the freezing spiral staircase. Athelstan gripped the guide rope fastened to the wall. Torches flared and danced in the brisk draughts which came whipping through the narrow windows and murder slits. They reached the first storey. Another set of worn steps led up to an iron-studded door, black with age, its great iron ring flaked with rust. Samuel knocked then kicked with his booted foot, shouting Eli's name. There was no reply. Again, knocking and kicking brought no response. Samuel scrabbled at the broad eye slit, yet even his dagger was unable to pull back the wooden slat.

'Stuck with the dirt of ages,' Samuel muttered, stepping back. Cranston tried but could gain no response. Others were gathering in the entrance below. Rossleyn came up the stairs, shaking the snow from his cloak. The door was examined.

Rossleyn peered through the keyhole before banging with the pommel of his dagger at the top and bottom of the door. 'Locked and bolted,' he announced. 'The key's there. I'm sure the bolts are in their clasps.'

The stairwell was becoming thronged. Athelstan went and looked in a narrow recess close by; there was nothing but dust. He whispered to Cranston then pushed himself by the others, going down out into the mist-hung morning. He walked around the Tower, trying to ignore the rank odours from a nearby midden heap. He paused and stared up at the window to Eli's chamber, its heavy wooden shutters sealing what must be a simple box-shaped opening.

'Probably shuttered both inside and out,' Athelstan muttered. He studied the sheer face of the Tower wall. 'And that would be very difficult,' he whispered, 'to scale, especially during a snow storm at the dead of night.'

'Are you praying, Brother?' Cranston, his face almost hidden by the low-pulled beaver hat and the high muffler on his cloak, stood grinning at him.

'No, Sir John, just preparing to meet another child of Cain. That door is locked and bolted from the inside. If Eli is in there, he must be either dead or senseless – probably the former. A young man, the victim of a knife or club rather than any falling sickness. I hope for the best but plan for the worst. You have delivered my instruction . . .?'

'The door will be forced but no one will enter before we do,' Cranston agreed. 'Rosselyn is acting all officious but this tower falls within my jurisdiction . . .' Cranston broke off, grabbing Athelstan by the arm and leading him back as the sound of shouts and a dull thudding trailed from the Tower. Someone had piled rubbish into a makeshift brazier. Cranston and Athelstan stood with the gathering crowd warming their hands. The friar let his mind drift back to the very start of all this – that attack near Aldgate, or was it something before that? Athelstan suspected it did. The malignant root to all this still laid hidden, murky and tangled, richly nourished by treachery. Who was the traitor in Gaunt's entourage who had informed the Upright Men about that cavalcade, the Flemings and their mysterious prisoner? In turn, who was the Judas among the Upright Men, the one who revealed to Thibault that fateful meeting at the Roundhoop? Were the Warde family really spies sent into the parish of St Erconwald's to ferret out such mischief? A shout followed by a crack from the Tower startled Athelstan from his meditation. Rosselyn appeared in the doorway.

'Sir John, Brother Athelstan, the door is forced. You'd best come . . .'

Athelstan and Cranston squeezed by the broken door into the Tower chamber. The room was poorly lit. All torches and rush lights had long burnt out, while the braziers were simply mounds of dead grey ash. Athelstan walked carefully across the squelching rushes. Eli's corpse lay almost in the centre of the chamber; the gore from the hideous wound to his face had congealed into a fearsome, dark red mask. Athelstan crouched, his stomach heaving. Eli's face had been shattered by the crossbow bolt embedded deep between his eyes. The barb had ploughed a furiously bloody furrow; the face had almost collapsed, the bolt thrust so deep the small, stiffened feathers of its flight had merged with the ruptured skin. Eli was fully dressed, his dagger still in its belt scabbard, boots on his feet. A wine cup lay nearby where it had apparently rolled from his fingers. Athelstan picked this up and sniffed it but caught only the slightly bitter smell of dried claret. He murmured a prayer, blessed the corpse and stared round that bleak chamber. Others tried to come in but, at Athelstan's hushed request, Cranston ordered them to stay outside in the stairwell. Both coroner and friar rigorously scrutinized that shabby room – its flaking walls, the mush of reeds on the floor, the untidy cot bed with its grey linen bolster. Eli's saddlebag and purse contained paltry items: a paternoster ring, some coins, a Santiago medal and a greasy, tattered manuscript, its pages bound by twine containing extracts of some mystery play clumsily copied from an original. Athelstan picked up the small wine jug and platter; he sniffed at these but detected nothing untoward. Athelstan then joined Cranston by the door, now leaning against the wall to the left of the entrance. Ancient and sturdy, the door was at least five inches thick; its stiffened leather hinges had cracked, as had the bolts at both top and bottom. The lock, too, was wrenched, the heavy key, still inserted, twisted by the pounding when the door was forced.

'*Jesu Miserere*,' Athelstan whispered. 'How could this happen?' He studied the eyelet; the slit was about six inches wide and the same length. The moveable slat itself had a heavy stud screwed into one end so the person inside could pull it backwards and forwards. Athelstan grasped this. He pulled with all his might but he couldn't move it; nor could Cranston.

'Stiffened with age,' Rossleyn stepped into the chamber, 'the wood's become wedged tight, a common problem in the Tower.' He tapped the door. 'The cold, the damp.' His voice trailed off.

Athelstan, shaking his head, walked back and crouched by Eli's corpse. From the stairwell he heard the moans and cries of Eli's companions as the news of the murder spread. The shouting drew closer. The Straw Men gathered in the doorway. Rossleyn ordered them to stay back but Samuel and the rest spilled into the chamber. Rachael, her red hair all loose, knelt beside Athelstan, sharply rocking backwards and forwards. Judith staggered towards the bed and simply lay down, thumb to her mouth, staring at the corpse. Samuel took one look at the shattered face and turned away, one hand over his mouth as he stumbled to the jake's pot to be sick. Samson and Gideon crouched by Rachael, comforting her, whispering that Judith needed her. Athelstan swiftly intoned the *De Profundis* and the requiem. He blessed the corpse and got up. 'Sir John,' he declared, 'we are finished here.' He helped Rachael to her feet, beckoning at the others to gather around.

'Eli, last night did any of you visit him?'

'No,' they chorused.

'And nothing strange,' Cranston insisted, 'nothing untoward occurred?'

'Nothing, Sir John.' Samuel wiped his mouth on the back of his hand. 'Eli retired. He left the refectory just as the bells were tolling for Compline.' He shook his head, 'I do not know, I cannot explain . . .'

Athelstan let them go and called over Rosselyn. The captain of archers sauntered across.

'Brother?'

'The fire last night?'

'From what I know, a simple accident. A candle fell out of a lantern box on to some dry straw. The fire was fierce but soon doused. Why?' Rosselyn indicated with his head. 'Do you think this was somehow connected?'

'I don't know.'

'Anything else, Brother?'

'No, no thank you.' Athelstan paused and watched him walk away. 'Pardon my lies, Sir John, but I think it was,' Athelstan whispered, 'and I'm not too sure how. As for Eli's murder, I wonder. Was he slain because he saw something when hiding under that table? He was the nearest to the rood screen and Hell's mouth.'

'Possible,' Cranston conceded.

'And the greater mystery,' Athelstan declared. 'How was a young man in a locked, secured chamber, its door firmly sealed, the windows,' he pointed, 'shuttered within and without – how could such a young man be murdered by a crossbow bolt?'

Athelstan repeated the same question sometime later in Thibault's chancery chamber, a comfortable, elegant room draped in heavy ornate tapestries with the richest Turkey cloths across the floor. Oaken furniture gleamed in the light of pink-coloured candles and the glare of flames roaring in the stone hearth. The Master of Secrets, half man, half shadow, Athelstan thought, sat enthroned behind a polished walnut table. He was swathed in a fur-lined cloak. On either side sat Oudernarde and Cornelius. Behind him stood Lascelles with Rosselyn guarding the door. Athelstan repeated the question about Eli's death. Cranston slurped noisily from his goblet of hot posset, drawing a look of distaste from the prim-faced Cornelius. Thibault threw down his quill pen and leaned over the table, his soft face lit by the flaring candles. Despite the opulence, the heavily scented warm air, the crackling fire and the hot posset warming his belly, the Dominican sensed the ice-cold harshness of Thibault's soul.

'Brother Athelstan, you argue that Barak is not the assassin but a victim?'

'He may be the assassin, but he was definitely the victim of murder. How and why?' Athelstan shrugged. 'I have expressed my doubts. I shared the same last night with Sir John. I assure you of this. The passing hours, a good night's sleep and celebrating the Eucharist have not changed my mind. The attack on us this morning confirms my doubts. An assassin still lurks here in the Tower. I suggest Barak did not murder Lettenhove, or,' he bowed imperceptibly at the Fleming, 'wounded your august father. True, Barak may have been used by the assassin but . . .'

'Yes, yes,' Thibault interrupted testily, 'you have aired your doubts but you have no explanation as to the truth behind any of these murders, be it Lettenhove, Barak or Eli?'

'You are correct, or why I was attacked this morning.'

'I'm sorry that happened,' Thibault retorted. 'Rosselyn informed me about it.'

'Is there anything certain?' Cornelius jibed.

'You have studied logic, Master Cornelius?'

'Of course.'

'Then you know that in this life nothing is certain, except the fact that there are uncertainties.'

'You play with words,' Oudernarde grated, eyes glittering with anger. 'My henchman lies murdered, my father sorely wounded.'

'I am truly sorry for that, Magister.'

'We expected better of you.' Oudernarde jabbed a finger. 'My Lord of Gaunt and Master Thibault talk highly of your work, Brother Athelstan, and that of your companion, the Coroner of London . . .'

'For the time being.' Thibault's threat was almost hissed. Cranston, sitting with his eyes half closed and wishing the pain in his belly would fade, simply opened his wallet and drew out his seals of office. Athelstan grasped his friend's arm. Thibault smiled and spread his hands.

'I mean,' the Master of Secrets fought to curb his temper, 'you could be promoted to higher favour.'

Cranston snorted noisily and put the seals away.

Athelstan tapped the table edge. 'You want certainty, Magister? I will give you certainties. First, a killer haunts the Tower. Who he is, how and why he slays is, for the moment, a mystery. Secondly, the Upright Men have a hand in this. Thirdly, you have a spy among the Upright Men; they certainly have one in your company. Fourthly,' Athelstan brushed aside Thibault's attempt to protest, 'the two severed heads which suddenly appeared in the chapel of St John disappeared equally swiftly during the attack on your company near Aldgate. Fifthly, Master Oudernarde, you brought those severed heads from Flanders. Sixthly, the attackers took these but their real prize was your hooded prisoner, probably the woman who now lives in splendid but closely guarded isolation in Beauchamp Tower. Seventhly, Barak was not the assassin but was murdered to appear so. Eighthly, Eli's death is a complete mystery. How can a young man, locked and bolted in a most secure chamber, be killed by crossbow bolt loosed to his face, yet no such weapon be found in that chamber?' Athelstan took a deep breath. 'So, yes, masters, good sirs all of you: certainties, however uncertain they may appear, have been established.' Athelstan picked at the three knots on his waist cord symbolizing his vows of poverty, chastity and obedience. 'I would like to inspect those severed heads,' he continued, 'and I would dearly love to meet your mysterious prisoner, or at least be told why she is so mysterious.'

Cranston coughed noisily to hide his grin, clearing his throat as he stared up at the vaulted chamber roof. Thibault picked up his pen, smoothed the quill plume feathers then used it to beckon Lascelles. The henchman leaned over the chair to hear his master's whisper and slipped like some black wraith from the chamber.

'For the time being,' Thibault almost lisped, 'our prisoner is not your concern, Brother Athelstan.'

'Ninthly,' Athelstan almost shouted, 'Sir John and I need to be busy. We need to reflect, to discuss, possibly even search. Master Thibault, in a word, we need to be gone. I have one favour to ask. My parishioners will have undoubtedly appreciated My Lord of Gaunt's gifts, and they would rejoice if the Straw Men, albeit in mourning for two of their members, could visit Saint Erconwald's. My parishioners would love to see their performance, while it would give me the opportunity to question the troupe further.' Athelstan paused as Lascelles slipped back into the room carrying a leather sack. Athelstan suspected what it contained.

'The Straw Men can wait but you have our permission to leave.' Thibault smacked his lips. 'As for the heads . . .' He snatched the sack from Lascelles and placed it on the table. 'Take them, Brother Athelstan. You have our authority, and that of the King's Coroner in London, to hand them over to Master Robert Burdon, Custos of the Gatehouse of London Bridge and

Keeper of the Heads, to add to his collection above the gatehouse.'

'And their crime?' Cranston demanded, leaning across to pluck up the sack.

'For the moment that must remain secret, Sir John.' Thibault waggled his fingers. 'Suffice to know, they were traitors who deserved their fate.'

'We all deserve our fate; only God's mercy saves us from it.' Athelstan pushed back the narrow chair and rose to his feet. He bowed, and with Cranston carrying the sack, walked to the door.

'Brother Athelstan?'

'Yes, Master Thibault?'

'You say we have a spy in our company. I find that difficult . . .'

'It always is,' Athelstan retorted. 'A Judas hides behind his kiss which,' he gestured around, 'is why I must return to question people here, and that includes you, Master Thibault.' Athelstan nodded at Rosselyn to open the door and they left. Once outside Athelstan winked at Cranston. 'Let us divert ourselves, Lord Coroner. The royal menagerie? Perhaps we'll visit that, but I must see this great snow bear.'

Cranston needed no further encouragement. He led Athelstan across baileys and courtyards, skirting frozen white gardens, herb plots and snow-covered outbuildings, past their own lodgings and through Hall Tower along Red Gulley to St Thomas' Tower which fronted the wide deep moat. Even before they entered the great cavernous cell on the ground floor, Athelstan smelt the thick, rancid odour of rotting fish and putrid meat, so dense and cloying it made him gag. The bear keeper, who rejoiced in the name of Artorius, a bulbous-eyed, bald-headed fellow, round as a tub, his unshaven face glistening and reddened from the coarse wine he was enjoying, was at first hostile and surly. However, he was only too willing to take Cranston's coin and show them what he called his 'pride and joy'. He raced up the steps on the side of St Thomas', gave them each a pomander and unlocked the iron-barred door. He beckoned them into the reeking darkness, took a cresset from its holder and began to light a long line of other torches fixed into the wall.

Athelstan could only stare in disbelief. The entire ground floor of St Thomas' was a huge cavern with a pointed vaulted ceiling.

Most of it was taken up by a huge cage: the bars, placed very closely together, were driven into the ground and rose to meet similar poles of the finest steel driven horizontally into the far wall. The flaring flames of the sconce torches shimmered in these. Athelstan noticed how there was a gate built into the cage where the vertical bars had been cut to form a square filled by a thick oaken door so as to allow the keeper to put in food or, if he wanted, enter the cage itself. Athelstan stood, transfixed. Despite the coarse but powerful-smelling pomander drenched in lavender and pinewood, the reek was intense. Athelstan coughed and spluttered. He held the pomander close as he walked carefully forward. The ground was greasy under foot. Athelstan slipped and slithered as he made his way down the aisle past the cage. He grasped a pole of the cage and his heart skipped a beat as a great dark shape lurched out of the shadows. He stepped back and stared in disbelief as the light from the cresset torches above him grew stronger. The bear approached the bars on all fours. Abruptly aroused from its sleep, it reared up on its hind legs. Its black-edged snout sniffed the air, huge jaws opened in a roar, massive paws flailed in the air. The friar was taken by the bear's sheer ferocity, but also by its heart-throbbing magnificence.

'A gift from the King of Norway,' Artorius sang out. The bear was at least three yards high and, despite a few stains from lying in its cage, the animal's hide was a brilliant thick, white fur. Athelstan had seen many a mangy-coated travelling bear much smaller and black furred; usually broken and infirm, fed on ale slops and discarded food, these hobbled along, muzzled and chained like beaten dogs. This was different. The snow bear was certainly chained: a massive leather collar circled its thick neck with a finely wrought, very long silver-like chain secured to one of the cage poles; this allowed the animal considerable freedom of movement.

'Behold Maximus,' Artorius declared, 'truly the king of all beasts!' Athelstan could only agree. He had never seen such a splendid creature. Maximus, startled from his sleep, lurched forward and crashed against the poles, his black, red-rimmed eyes with their hard, unblinking stare conveyed his sheer ferocity, his large, massive jaws open to display teeth as long, white and sharp as ivory daggers. Maximus again crashed into the cage

poles before lumbering on all fours to a broad, iron-plated door
built into the far end of the Tower.

'The finest steel of Milan,' Artorius declared, tapping one of
the bars. 'A gift from the Sforzas, as is the chain.'

Athelstan stood back, viewing the cage in the strengthening
light of all the torches which were now lit. Maximus appeared
to dislike the glare and the heat; he stood with his back to them,
pushing at that gate with his head.

'The best steel,' Cranston breathed. 'It would have to be.'

'True, Sir John,' Artorius replied. 'Maximus can take a man's
head off, and has, with one bite or sweep of his paw.'

'Is he so savage?' the coroner asked.

'On a full stomach Maximus can be as content as a pig; he
will even play with you,' Artorius nodded. 'And I mean that,
though even then you have to be very careful, yet he is mild
enough. However, once he's hungry or if he smells blood or
worse, both, I do not like being in here, finest steel or not.'
Athelstan studied the cage again; the snow bear was a marvel
and so was this. Cunningly devised, the close-set poles stretched
from wall to wall, cordoning off most of this cavernous chamber.
Maximus kept pressing his head against the gate in the wall
leading on to the wharf.

'He is hungry and wants to go swimming; he hopes to catch
fish. Come, I'll show you.'

Athelstan and Cranston followed. The friar noticed how the
aisle was broad enough but he followed the keeper's advice and
kept as far away from the bars of the cage as possible.

'It has been known,' Artorius sang out, 'for Maximus to suddenly
make a lunge. One thing about him which always surprises our
visitors, despite his bulk, is that he can be as swift as a
greyhound.'

'Like someone else I know,' Athelstan whispered. He winked
as Cranston turned and glared at him. Artorius opened the door
at the end of the aisle and led them out on to the broad, snow-
swept wharf which ran alongside the moat. Despite being
constantly fed by the river, the water here had begun to freeze:
sheets of ice bobbed on the surface, the cold was bitter and a
thick river mist twisted above the quayside. Artorius walked to
the outside entrance to the cage. Maximus was now banging

noisily. The keeper pulled back the heavy bolts and lifted the huge bars. Artorius leaned these against the gate and hurriedly withdrew back through the door, beckoning at Cranston and Athelstan to follow. Once inside Artorius lowered the small door hatch so his visitors could have a good view. Athelstan glanced to his left; Maximus was now shoving the gate open. It creaked noisily and the bars on the other side fell away.

'Deliberately so,' Artorius whispered. 'The gate is heavy. The bars delay Maximus so I have enough time to get back in here.'

'And how do you get him back and seal the gate?' Athelstan asked.

'A juicy piece of meat placed at the far end of the cage oozing blood. Maximus loves that. He knows his routine, which is as fixed as any monk's horarium. Maximus becomes busy with his food. I close over the gate with a hooked pole, pull the bolts across and place the bars back down.' He paused. 'Now, watch this.' Maximus had pushed open the gate. Athelstan glanced through the door hatch, fascinated by the bear's speed. Maximus, the long chain rattling out, raced across the wharf and plunged into the icy moat, revelling in the splashing water.

'It's safe now,' Artorius declared. He opened the door and led them out.

'Is it safe?' Athelstan asked anxiously.

'Maximus loves to swim and fish,' the keeper reassured him. 'He'll be there for hours.'

'Fish?' Athelstan asked.

'Oh, yes,' Artorius replied, 'once he caught a porpoise swept in by the river. Maximus will eat anything and everything.' Athelstan just stood and watched. Maximus was swift and confidently plunging up and down, swimming expertly – sometimes only his massive head protruded above the surface. The silver chain, fine and delicate in appearance, was very strong. Maximus had the freedom to swim although not to reach the far side of the moat.

'God be praised!' Athlestan whispered, crossing himself. 'For such splendour! Sir John, I think we should go.'

They thanked Artorius and left St Thomas' Tower, going out through the Lion gate, the roars and snarls from the menagerie ringing in their ears. Athelstan refused Cranston's offer to see

the other beasts; instead he plucked Sir John by the sleeve and
led the unresisting coroner into the sweet onion-smelling tap
room of the Hook of Heaven, an ancient tavern which overlooked
the Thames. They cleaned their hands in the bronze basin hanging
by a chain from the rafters in full obedience to the warning
carved around the rim: 'Wash with water your hands so clean
that, on the towel, no spot be seen.' Once done, Athelstan ordered
blackjacks of ale and bowls of thickened chicken stew. Cranston
had remained ominously silent during their visit to the snow bear.
Athelstan suspected Sir John was reflecting deeply on Thibault's
hidden threats and the menaces which swirled around them. He
wanted Cranston to lighten his mood.

'We will do our duty, My Lord Coroner,' Athelstan whispered
as he polished his horn spoon and took a generous mouthful.
'Let us reflect, Sir John, warm our bellies and,' he gestured at
the sack, 'fathom these mysteries further. Now listen. You must
return to your chambers in the Guildhall. Yes? Lady Maude will
also be hungry for your embraces. However, make careful scrutiny
of this. Search among the Spicers of Cheapside, discover everything you can about Humphrey Warde. Sir John, you remain
silent. You have been so . . .'

'The tribes.' Cranston finished his soup. 'Brother Athelstan,
my little friar, my friend: Barak is dead, Lettenhove slain, Eli
mysteriously murdered, but these are only bubbles on the surface
of this morass. Brother,' Cranston put his spoon down and grasped
the friar's hand, 'believe me, the tempest has been sown. God
help us,' he murmured, 'we are going to reap the corpse-makers'
storm.' The coroner, still distracted, gathered his thoughts. 'I have
business, little friar, so have you, and the hour candle burns.'

They left the tavern. Cranston, lost in his own thoughts, turned
off up an alleyway leading to the city. Athelstan, grasping the
bag with its grisly contents, moved towards the bridge. The
Angelus bells began to peal. Traders, merchants, hucksters and
apprentices were all preparing to cease trading in order to break
their morning fast. Most of these were swathed in cloaks and
hoods against the biting cold. The air was riven with shouts and
cries. People pushed and shoved towards the cook shops,
alehouses and taverns. Beggars, blue with cold, whined for alms
and shook their clacking dishes or tapped their canes. The

'stealthy night shapes' as Cranston called them, were also busy
– the sneak thieves, the shadow stalkers hungry for prey. Bailiffs
and beadles, determined on their food, hurried a line of miscreants to the great stocks next to the bridge. A sheriff's man pushed
a moveable, three-branched gallows with the cadavers of house
breakers stripped naked, their dead flesh a pasty white, along the
thoroughfare. A herald went before them, declaring the gallows
proclaimed the dire consequences of breaking the King's peace.
How their wolfish souls, guilt-steeped and sin-scorched, had
received their just desserts from both God and man. A relic-seller
in a snoop cap followed, hoping to trade among the gathering
crowd, loudly declaring he had holy fragments of the Seven
Sleepers of Ephesus for sale. Behind him a singing cleric
bargained with a funeral party escorting a corpse, stitched in its
deer-skinned shroud, to chant the death psalms.

Athelstan, head covered, pushed through this throng on to the
bridge. He ignored the fishy, oozing stench from the river as he
did the sweet flavour from the public ovens where the morning
waffles, cakes and pastries had been baked. He did not look to
the left or the right, ignoring the thunder of the Thames as it
broke against the starlings of the bridge, the clacking of water
mills and the constant noise of the traders crammed into the
narrow causeway which ran between the houses and shops either
side. He passed Becket's chapel. On its steps a wandering
preacher, standing next to a bonfire of burning rubbish, its
creeping flames spluttering in the wet mist, screamed with
scorched throat his dire prophecies. How the souls of London's
citizens were polluted by carnal lust. How Christ would soon
come again, a brilliant flaming figure appearing like a gorgeous
rainbow in the storm-swept skies above London.

Athelstan walked on, knocking away the apprentices plucking
at his sleeves and the fleshy-mouthed whores who sidled up
whispering what delights they could offer. Athelstan ignored
such harrowers of the dark. Nevertheless, the world and all its
business still pressed in. A group of Newgate bailiffs pulled
two river pirates to the balustrade overlooking the river. Ignoring
their screams, the officials tied nooses around the prisoners'
necks and toppled them over. Athelstan glimpsed a prostitute
on her knees before a costermonger, feverishly loosening the

points of his hose as both sheltered in a narrow runnel between
two soaring houses. Athelstan looked away but his eye was
caught by other scenes. A beggar, one leg crushed by a cart,
lay dying beneath a stall, attended by a Carmelite. Two courte-
sans from The House of Imminent Pleasure just beyond the
bridge sauntered by swathed in cheap finery and even cheaper
perfume. A group of armed knights, gorgeous pennants
proclaiming John of Gaunt's arms, forced their destriers through
the crowd. Curses and insults were thrown. The leading knight,
visor down, lowered his lance and the crowd swiftly parted. A
gust of river wind, heavy with the smell of rotting fish, buffeted
Athelstan. The friar felt dizzy, disconcerted, as if he could feel
the pent-up anger and lusts of the people around him. He took
a deep breath and moved on, reaching the end of the bridge
and the steps either side leading to the upper stories of the
yawning bridge gate.

Athelstan climbed these, knocked on the iron-studded door
and was ushered into what the mannekin Robert Burdon called
his 'workshop'. Custos of the Bridge and Keeper of the Heads,
Burdon was scarcely five feet tall, a small, pot-bellied man who
loved to dress in blood-red taffeta, the colour of what he jokingly
called his 'fraternity of the shearing knife'.

In the chambers above Athelstan could hear the screams and
shouts of Burdon's brood of children.

'Brother Athelstan! Brother Athelstan, come deeper in.' The
friar walked up the macabre chamber, long and narrow, lit only
by arrow-slit windows, its wooden floor scrubbed clean, as was
the long table which ran down the centre of the room. On shelves
along the wall ranged rows of freshly severed heads; these had
been washed in brine and recently tarred at the neck, glassy eyes
above gaping, bloody mouths gazing sightlessly at him from
under half-open lids. Athelstan refused Burdon's offer of refreshment. He explained why he had come and placed the sack on
the table. Burdon, calling blessings down on Sir John, undid the
twine and brought out both heads. Clicking his tongue noisily
as he critically examined them, the mannekin picked each up,
sniffed at them in turn, wetted his fingers and stroked the grey,
wizened skin of the two severed heads. He then examined the
cut necks. Athelstan had to turn away when Burdon prised open

the mouths, poking around with his fingers. Once finished he placed both heads in a space along the shelves.

'Do you know, Brother,' Burdon smiled, 'at night, when darkness falls like a sheet of blackness and the river mists billow in, they come for their heads. Oh, yes! Heart-stricken, bloated and dangerous, the ghosts, the terrormongers, rise from the dismal woods of Hell. They gather here, ushered in by the night hags, a synod of wraiths.' Athelstan stared at him in disbelief.

'True, true,' Burdon lifted his hands towards the shelves, 'the ghosts of all my guests. I hear them pattering up the steps. Sometimes I glimpse them, smaller than me, hell-borne goblins. They bang on the walls. They gabble like Abraham men then they whisper, a sound like roasted fish hissing on a skillet. But,' Burdon rose to his feet, 'not these two. You see, their ghosts cannot cross the sea though their heads did, mind you. I detect salt water on their skins, while I'm sure both were severed not by an English axe but a two-handed broad sword, the execution weapon of Brabant?' Burdon raised his eyebrows. 'Flanders? Both heads are dry. The skin withering, the carrion birds will soon peck them to the bone. One head belongs to an old woman, the other to a fairly youngish man. Both have had their tongues plucked out.'

'So,' Athelstan sketched a blessing in the direction of the heads, 'two heads brought from Flanders by Gaunt's agents. They were undoubtedly the victims of judicial decapitation, probably carried out in secret. Before execution, their tongues were plucked out, the usual statutory punishment for those guilty of grievous calumny and slander. Both heads were to be shown to My Lord of Gaunt.' Athelstan paused. 'I suspect the heads were taken by the Upright Men during their assault near Aldgate and searched for when Thibault's men stormed the Roundhoop.'

'I heard about both incidents, Brother. I took custody of a number of heads . . .'

'Well, Robert,' Athelstan clasped him on the shoulder, 'you have two more.' He bowed and walked towards the door, reluctant to say any more. After all, Master Burdon might be Thibault's spy. The friar whispered goodbye and walked into the freezing cold.

# PART FOUR

## *'Vermis: The Serpent'*

The light was dying. People, wrapped in cloaks, mantles and hoods, hurried home. The Southwark gallows rose fearsome and sombre through the murk, the corpses hanging there already freezing hard. The stocks nearby were full of miscreants, locked by neck, wrist or ankle. The moans of the prisoners were so pitiful Athelstan begged the bailiffs, for the love of God and the honour of Sir John, to free them. A couple of coins provided the necessary encouragement. Athelstan walked up the main thoroughfare into the tangle of alleyways leading towards his church. The friar paused, still lost in thought. 'The heads were severed in Ghent,' he murmured, 'their tongues plucked out beforehand. They must have uttered some terrible slander against My Lord of Gaunt, but what? Something connected with that mysterious prisoner?'

'Brother, are you well?' Athelstan blinked and stared at the sharp features of Ranulf the rat catcher peering out at him from the shelter of his tarred, pointed hood. Ranulf lifted his cage carrying his ferocious ferrets, Ferox and Audax. 'All quiet at the church, Brother. Master Thibault's gifts disappeared in the twinkling of an eye. Slices of roast pork and stoups of ale. Well,' Ranulf shook his cage, 'Moleskin the boatmen's shed is plagued by rats. The cold has driven the enemy out into the open,' and, muttering to himself, Ranulf wandered off, swaying slightly on his feet.

Athelstan continued up the alleyway on to the open enclosure before St Erconwald's. The old church rose eerily in the murky light under its carpet of frozen snow, a white wilderness which only emphasized the dull, black mass of the sombre church. A beacon light, lit by Mauger the bell clerk, glowed from the steeple. Candlelight flared behind the shutters of the death house where Godbless and his goat sheltered. Athelstan stared around at the sheer bleakness. He wondered what visions lurked here beyond the veil? He walked to the cemetery lychgate. Did the Soul-harrier, Satan's apostate angel, hide among the gravestones? Did the shadow spirits, the wandering wraiths and shade-souls, hover to plot dark designs against the living? Athelstan closed his eyes. Was Godbless right? Did the dead swarm here like larvae, squalid ghosts, eyes the colour of boxwood in faces of waxen yellow? The beggar claimed he had heard their night shrieks. Athelstan rubbed his eyes. 'And you, Friar,' he quietly accused himself, 'are becoming tired and your brain fanciful.' He took a deep breath, tried to clear his mind and went in search of where Benedicta had hidden the house key. Once he found it, he ensured Philomel was comfortable, unlocked the door and walked into the stone-flagged kitchen, clean-swept, tidy but very cold. Athelstan took a taper to the hour candle. He lit the spigots and lantern horns before firing the braziers and the kindling in the hearth. Benedicta had left a lamp with perfumed oil of the anointment of roses to sweeten the air. A scratching at the door disturbed the friar's enjoyment of the fragrance. He allowed Bonaventure in and the cat immediately joined the friar at the hearth. Athelstan pulled across the two rods; from each hung a small cauldron on a chain, one containing oatmeal, the other a soup, thickened and seasoned with herbs and onions. The room slowly thawed, the savoury smells from the pots curling out. Once the food was ready Athelstan prepared two bowls for himself and a pot of oatmeal for Bonaventure. The friar sat at the table, blessed both himself and the cat and ate slowly, staring into the flames.

'Where do I begin, Bonaventure?' he murmured. The cat scarcely lifted its head. 'Just like Sir John, absorbed in your food. Well, let me explain. There are two camps. My Lord of Gaunt's and that of the Upright Men, who definitely have a cell here in Saint Erconwald's. Each party has a spy deep in the other's household, and so it begins.' Athelstan gulped a spoonful. 'Gaunt brings his agents the Oudernardes from Ghent. They escort a mysterious prisoner, probably a woman, along with those two severed heads: one belongs to a young man, the other to an older woman. Both must have spoken some hideous slander against Gaunt, hence the removal of their tongues before their heads were severed. The gruesome remains were probably brought to

London as trophies as well as proof of a task well done, of clacking tongues being silenced forever.' Athelstan supped another mouthful. 'The Upright Men stole the heads during that attack but failed to capture the mysterious prisoner. I wonder, Bonaventure, who gave them such excellent intelligence of where Gaunt's party would be at a certain time on a certain day in the depth of winter?' Athelstan waved his spoon at Bonaventure. 'At the Roundhoop Thibault struck like a hawk. Who among the Upright Men told him about such a meeting?' Bonaventure, who'd licked his bowl clean, cast an envious eye on those of this strange little friar. Athelstan pushed the oatmeal towards his dining companion. 'Not the best of banquets, Bonaventure, but at least it's hot. Now, what did really happen at the Roundhoop? Something definitely did but I can't place it. What did that young man mean when he said the woman should continue gleaning? And what was he looking for? Some people might say he was all feverish due to the shock of death but I don't think so.'

Athelstan paused, listening to the faint sounds from outside. Darkness would be falling, and the freezing cold would keep most of his parishioners indoors. 'I wonder,' Athelstan put down his spoon and stroked Bonaventure, 'has Gaunt, my learned cat, truly placed a spy here in my parish?' He stared at the crucifix fastened above the hearth. 'None of my parishioners were present in Saint John's Chapel, thank God.' Athelstan swiftly crossed himself. 'But Bonaventure, a clever assassin certainly was.' Athelstan rose to put a log on the fire; when he turned back Bonaventure was finishing his soup. 'Wretched cat!' Athelstan whispered. 'But who was that Judas man in the chapel? How did he kill? At first I suspected he used Hell's mouth to shield and hide himself but, to do that, he would have to detach it from the rood screen, and that never happened.' He breathed out noisily. 'Yet how could that assassin loose two bolts and not be seen, leave those severed heads and not be detected? And how did the assassin trap Barak in that crypt, strike him at the back of the head, strap on the war belt, thrust a crossbow into his hand then hurl him from that window?' Athelstan shook his head. 'All a great mystery, even more so Eli's death. Imagine a chamber like this, Bonaventure. No secret entrances, the window shuttered both within and outside, the door locked and barred. So how was

Eli killed by a crossbow bolt? The eyelet was sealed and stuck?' Athelstan moved to the door. 'Even if it wasn't, if I open the eyelet here and slide the shutter back, I'd see a weapon thrust against the gap. I'd already be vigilant – that's why we use an eyelet – even more so if I glimpsed a crossbow.' Athelstan went and stood before the hearth. 'And that mysterious fire? I am sure it was a diversion so Eli's killer could slip through the darkness. Why Eli? A simple player? To spread terror or,' Athelstan wagged a finger, 'did he see something untoward in that chapel? Or was he simply murdered because he might have done? Yes,' Athlestan rubbed his hands, 'that's a start. After Oudernarde was struck, everyone, including myself, was at the far end of that nave, except Eli. Why was he slain? And, above all,' Athelstan went back to his chair, 'how was it done?' He stared into the fire. As he stroked Bonaventure, his eyes grew heavy so he put his head down on his arms and slept. A loud knocking on the door eventually aroused him. Athelstan glanced at the hour candle – an entire ring had burned. He hurried to the door.

'Brother Athelstan, it's me, Flaxwith, and two of my bailiffs.' Athelstan drew the bolts and let them in. All three were draped in cloaks and mantles, mufflers and hoods pulled close. Flaxwith's mastiff stayed obediently outside; he and Bonaventure had met before and both nourished a lasting hatred for each other.

'Sir John sent you this.' Flaxwith handed over a small cream-coloured scroll tied with a green ribbon. Athelstan undid this, offering his visitors blackjacks of ale. They refused but gratefully ladled out some of the hot soup while Athelstan read the item-ized list of information about Humphrey Warde and his family. The details were succinct and clear. According to Sir John, Warde was a very successful spicer who'd mysteriously left his shop in Cheapside. Rumour had it that he'd fallen on hard times. However, Sir John had learnt on good authority from whisperers in the Guildhall that Warde still enjoyed a lucrative trade with the spicery department of Gaunt's wardrobe as well as those of the royal household.

'Spices be damned!' Athelstan whispered, rolling up the scrap of parchment.

'You sound exactly like Sir John.' Flaxwith put down the bowl, smacking his lips.

'Master Flaxwith, come with me. Leave one of your men to guard my house. He may eat and drink whatever, within reason. Bonaventure will tell me if he doesn't.' Athelstan grabbed his cloak, put on his stout walking boots and, followed by a surprised Flaxwith and one of his bailiffs, swept from the house. It was a black night, freezing hard, the ground under foot glitteringly treacherous, a trap for the unwary. The friar recalled the attack on him outside St Peter's. Was that against him or someone else? To kill or to frighten? Athelstan hurried past his church, his mind teeming with problems and questions. God bless both him and them but what if Pike and the others were correct? Humphrey Warde could well be a spy, a cockle planted deep in Athelstan's wheat field, a collector of intelligence for his sinister masters at the Savoy palace. Athelstan walked on. The snaking lanes and paths were deserted. Chinks of light gleamed at windows and doors. Snow slid from roofs peppered with icicles. A rat scrabbled across the frost. A black shadow pursued; in the corner of a runnel the hunted gave an eerie screech as it was caught. From somewhere a voice chanted a common song and then faded. Athelstan reached Rickett Lane. Down under the leaning, cramped, crooked little houses, much decayed and held up by crutches, Athelstan found Warde's narrow, two-storey tenement. The front was boarded up but the door hung slightly open, unlatched and unlocked. A cold and unreasoning dread seized Athelstan as he pushed back the door. Inside the stone-flagged passageway was lit by greasy tallow candles in their niches. Somewhere a child whimpered. Athelstan paused. The house was cold but the air fragrant from the smells of crushed spices stored in the small shop immediately to his left. Athelstan was about to walk on when he glimpsed the shadow slumped between the two tables where the spices were prepared and weighed. He grabbed the box lantern off its hook just within the doorway and walked in. Humphrey Warde lay sprawled on his back, the crossbow bolt almost buried in his chest. The blood from the wound had clotted in an icy puddle. Athelstan murmured a prayer and moved on. Katherine Warde lay face down in the small kitchen, killed by a crossbow bolt to the back of her head. In a small cot beside her, baby Odo murmured fretfully.

'Raise the hue and cry!' Athelstan whispered to a shocked

Flaxwith who had followed him in. 'Shout "Harrow" and rouse the parish!' He tapped the small cot. 'Baby Odo needs attention.' In the small comfortable solar above, Humphrey's two children, Laurence and Margaret, had been struck down. Laurence almost blocked the threshold; the barb had sliced his throat, the blood splashing out to stain both lintel and floor. Margaret had been thrown back in the comfortable window seat, the embroidery she had been working on slipping through her fingers as the bolt smashed into her chest, a direct hit to the heart. Her eyes stared in glassy horror, her slack mouth encrusted with blood.

'These are nightmares,' Athelstan whispered. 'The blackest sins have been committed here. The demons gather. God have mercy on us all.' Flaxwith touched him on the shoulder and pointed to a parchment scrap nailed to a wooded settle nearby. Athelstan plucked it down and read the scrawl.

'When Adam delved and Eve span
Who was then the gentleman?
Now the world is ours and ours alone
To cut the Lords to heart and bone.'


Sir John Cranston gazed down at the four bloody corpses stretched out on a canvas sheet in the spice chamber. Athelstan had swiftly finished the rite for the dead and informed the coroner of what he had found. The lane outside was packed with people. The wardsmen had been alerted by the ringing cries of 'Harrow! Harrow!' Bladdersniff, the local beadle and constable, despite his topeish ways, had roused Athelstan's parishioners. Baby Odo was being looked after by a family. Now the rest of the neighbourhood, armed with staves, clubs, cudgels, daggers and maces, gathered in the freezing cold.

'Father, we are here.'

'So you are.' Athelstan beckoned Watkin and Pike into the small chamber. 'Just one question.' Athelstan's face was drawn in anger, eyes hard, no smile or understanding look. 'One question.' Athelstan repeated. 'On God's eternal judgement on your souls, the truth!' he hissed. 'Are you responsible for this?'

Watkin and Pike gaped in horror at the blood-drenched corpses.

'Under the ban!' Watkin exclaimed. 'They must have all been placed under the ban! Father, I swear, if they were, the order was not known or carried out by us.' Watkin scratched his face. 'The Wardes were a nuisance; they actually learnt very little, nothing more than most of the parish know. Well,' he shuffled mud-caked boots, 'until that attack on the Roundhoop.'

'*Juravisti iuramentum magnum et non poenitebet vos*,' Athelstan replied, quoting the solemn legal phrase. 'You have sworn a great oath and you cannot repent of it, yes? You and yours,' Athelstan pointed at both of them, 'had nothing to do with this. If you did, I shall, with bell, book and candle, solemnly excommunicate you from the steps of the sanctuary of our church. Damned Watkin! Damned to the fires of Hell for all eternity! Cursed in your waking. Cursed in your sleeping. Cursed in your eating. Cursed in your drinking. Bereft of the sacraments. No Eucharist, no shriving, no anointing, no baptizing.' Athelstan's words rolled like the peal of doom, echoing out along the passageway and into the street beyond. Watkin and Pike stretched out their hands, the solemn gesture when taking an oath.

'Father, on our souls,' Watkin couldn't take his eyes off those corpses, 'we swear on our souls.'

'If you were involved,' Cranston barked, 'once Holy Mother Church finished with you, the hangman will begin.'

'Father?' Huddle the painter, accompanied by Benedicta, pushed his way by Watkin and Pike to stare aghast at the carnage.

'How?' Benedicta whispered.

'Never mind.' Athelstan softened. He picked up a leather sack and thrust this at her with the keys to both church and house. 'Benedicta, these are Humphrey Warde's papers: some ledgers and a psalter. Put them in the parish chest, make sure they are safely secure. Please look after everything. I have to accompany Sir John.'

'King's business,' the coroner lugubriously intervened. 'Despite the late hour, I need Brother Athelstan and, when we are finished, I'm afraid it's back to the Tower.'

'Ensure all is safe,' Athelstan urged Benedicta. 'Go to Father Walter at Saint Ethelburga's, ask him as a favour to send his curate to celebrate the Jesus Mass for you tomorrow. Huddle?' The painter stepped out of the shadows, his stained fingers clutching the skin of his face now whiter than the driven snow, his eyes two large pools of terror. He could not stop staring at the corpses.

'Huddle,' Athelstan gently shook the painter's shoulder, 'Huddle, what is it?'

'So gruesome, Father, so savage, so much blood. I was . . . I was only talking to them, I . . .' Huddle turned and fled into the street to retch and vomit noisily.

'Take care of him,' Athelstan urged Benedicta. 'Tell him to look after our anchorite; they must continue with their paintings. Now,' Athelstan forced a smile and sketched a blessing, 'all of you must leave. Benedicta, do look in on baby Odo, take care of everything.'

Once the chamber was cleared and the shop door closed, Athelstan sat on a high stool and stared owl-eyed at Sir John. 'So, I am to accompany you?'

'I'm afraid so,' the coroner replied evasively. 'Yea, even into the Valley of the Death.' Cranston eased himself into the chamber's only chair. 'The centre doesn't hold,' Cranston murmured as if to himself. 'All things are falling apart. A violent storm is coming.' He pointed at the corpses, 'Do you believe they were spies?'

'God forgive Gaunt,' Athelstan whispered. 'But yes! Warde depicted himself as a spicer who had fallen on hard times, forced to leave his house and shop in Cheapside. Nonsense! That was a sham, a play, a little masque. Your enquiry, Sir John, proved that. The truth is that Warde supplied precious spices to the Royal households. He was Gaunt's man and cheerfully indulged in this pretence – he came and took root here. A man needed by the community, everyone wants to do business with a spicer, especially in the depth of winter when our meat is old and heavily salted. Nutmeg, mace, cloves and cinnamon are in great demand. Warde and his children would have good custom, at least in theory. They would visit houses, get to know families. Katherine would mingle with other women. All the chatter and gossip of the community would flow around them. They would collect, sift this and pass it on. Precious information, be it who was close to the Upright Men, or even the time and date of meetings like that at the Roundhoop.' Cranston made to object.

'Clever and cunning, an entire family acting as a subtle shield for a spy. Sir John, I can guess your objections. According to Thibault's plan, the Wardes should have settled in Saint

Erconwald's as comfortable as Bonaventure in my kitchen, yet they didn't. From the very start they were marked down – distrusted, suspected. So, how did the likes of Watkin and Pike who, most of the time, do not know what day of the week it is, realize this was all a subterfuge?'

'And the answer?'

'You know it, Sir John. The Upright Men were informed about the Wardes by their spy in Gaunt's retinue. And yet there is a further problem. If Warde was discovered so swiftly, distrusted so deeply, what real danger did he pose? How could this poor spicer find out about a secret meeting at the Roundhoop? If they were so blatantly Gaunt's spies, why not just drive them out? Why this?'

'Punishment? The ban?'

'Oh, come, Sir John, you and I both know people are buying and selling information on all sides, all the time. What puzzles me,' Athelstan rose to his feet, 'is the devastatingly harsh punishment. The Wardes were spies but, and this is the paradox, they also seem to have been protected while they were here. Why? By whom? Well, at least until now.' Athelstan surveyed the herb and spice jars along the shelves. The spicer was an orderly man: everything was in its place and clearly tagged, except one jar just on the edge of the shelf, pushed the wrong way round while the cork stopper on the top was not fully secured. Athelstan took this down and turned it. 'Dust of poppy seed,' he read the tag. 'An opiate. Why is it out of place, put back wrongly, hurriedly? Did the killer help himself? Was Warde preparing something for him when the assassin struck? Did the murderer ask for an opiate as a pretence? Did he need it? This is where I found Warde. Was our spicer enticed into his shop and silently slain?' Athelstan held up the jar. 'As you know, I have been through the house. Apart from this jar, Sir John, there is no real disturbance, no sign of resistance or a struggle.'

Athelstan blessed the corpses again.

'You imply that some other person or group, apart from Thibault, were protecting the Wardes?'

'Yes, Sir John, I mean here in Southwark. Warde was distrusted so he was isolated; he never posed a real danger because he remained on the outside. Why didn't Thibault just withdraw him?

Why didn't Warde recognize the truth and leave? More importantly, why didn't the Upright Men, or their cell here at Saint
Erconwald's, just drive him out? Why did such apparent tolerance
abruptly end in a savage massacre?' Athelstan shook his head.
'Yet Watkin, and I believe him, maintains this is not their work.
Are the Upright Men innocent of this? Thibault, surely, would
not turn on his own spy – so is there a third party, another group
with their own grievances – but who? Those in the Tower are
forbidden to leave. Ah, well.' Athelstan sighed. 'Where to now,
my friend? This Valley of the Shadow of Death?'

Cranston jabbed a finger at the door. 'Brother, we have a
meeting at the Tower of Babel in the Cloisters of Hell, Whitefriars,
to be precise. I am – we are – going to do business with Duke
Ezra of Caesarea, leader of the rifflers, ruffians and roaring boys.
I want to question him and one of his henchmen, the Herald of
Hades, about what they know.' Cranston squeezed himself out
of the chair. 'Gaunt and the Upright Men both pride themselves
on their knowledge. Believe me,' Cranston ran a finger across
the spice counter, 'they know nothing compared to Duke Ezra.
All my spies, such as the Troubadour or Muckworm, report only
what they have learnt from Duke Ezra and his coven, who speed
throughout this city like a colony of rats. They sneak along
runnels into the dingy dens, mumpers' castles and dark dungeons
of the counterfeits, the cozeners, the coney-catchers and the Jacob
men. You'll find them in taverns and alehouses, cook shops and
bakeries. They thrive in the mansions of the mean as well as
those of the wealthy. Palaces, friaries, priories, abbeys and monasteries are not free of them either.' Cranston donned his beaver
hat. 'And now we go to the very source. Let's leave all this horror
to Bladdersmith and his wardsmen.'

Within the hour, having collected his writing satchel and other
items for his continued stay at the Tower, Athelstan joined
Cranston in the royal barge, specially summoned for the journey
across the Thames from the Bishop of Winchester's steps to those
of the Temple. A perilous, freezing, choppy journey. The night
was black as ink. The heavy wherry, despite its careful manning
by royal bargemen, shook and shivered as it breasted the swells
and turbulent tide pools of the Thames. A sea mist was gathering
to block out the north bank so only the beacon lights in church

steeples and the flaming bonfires of rubbish heaps lit along the
different quaysides pierced the murk. Athelstan sat clutching his
writing satchel. Around him huddled Cranston and his bailiffs.
The mastiff whined against the cold; Flaxwith, tender as a mother
with child, tried to soothe it. The bargemen, hooded and masked
against the biting breeze, bent over their oars, pulling in unison
to the soft chant of the prowman. The air reeked of salt, fish and
sweat. Other barges and wherries swept by, the lanterns on their
sterns glowing fiercely. Athelstan wondered about the Fisher of
Men, that enigmatic recluse who, from his Chapel of the Dead,
harvested the Thames of corpses, assisted by his henchman,
Icthus, and other grotesques. Would they be busy on a night like
this? The prowman called out an order and the barge turned a
little to port, juddering as the river caught it. A bell sounded
hollow and sombre in the dark. A barge laden with produce broke
from the mist and cut across the bows of their craft. Athelstan
tensed, Cranston cursed. The wherry swerved a little. The danger
passed and they aimed like an arrow towards the host of torches
flaring along Temple steps. They swiftly disembarked. Flaxwith
and his companions ringed them, swords and daggers drawn, as
they moved into the hideous underworld of the city. They entered
a maze of narrow, crooked lanes, alleyways and runnels which
snaked around the decaying, crumbling houses. Some of these
were beginning to pitch forward, turning the paths beneath into
hollow, dark tunnels, the sky blocked out by the leaning storeys
and jutting gables. Dungeon-like doors, barred and studded,
remained sealed shut, though Athelstan glimpsed light through
the eyelets. Above them shutters abruptly opened only to slam
shut just as swiftly. Box lanterns glowed on the end of their
chains. Now and again a shout would ring out a warning.
'Cranston,' a voice called. 'Cranston and his minions.'

A hunting horn brayed. 'Let them pass.'

Another voice bellowed, 'Allow those who come to pay service
to our Duke safe passage.' Shadows floated across their path.
Ghostly shapes emerged out of doorways and alley mouths. Naked
steel would glitter then disappear. Athelstan watched his step but
the ground under foot was surprisingly firm and clear.

'Saltpetre,' Cranston whispered, 'they have their own dung
carts to clear the muck and spread that. Duke Ezra always looks

after his own.' They left the lanes and crossed a square where a mixture of smells wafted to greet them: the stench of dirty clothes on unclean bodies mingled with odours from the tallow chambers, melting rooms and tanners' yards which thronged the area. Beggars raced across the square to meet them – 'ill-looking vermin' as Cranston described them with their long, dirty beards, their heads covered in old stocking tops. The hunting horn brayed twice again and these promptly scuttled away. They went down a further street, turned a corner and entered another square. On the far side of this rose an ancient gateway illuminated by a veritable forest of torches fastened to clasps above the yawning entrance and along its crenellated wall top; from these broad, silver-edged black banners swirled in the night breeze.

'The Castle of the Fleet and Newgate Dogs. The Tower of Babel. Believe me, Brother, there are more bodies buried in its cellars and streets than in your graveyard. If you cross Duke Ezra, you are not punished, you simply disappear. Be on your guard. This is the place of jabbing daggers and slashing blades. Prepare to enter Satan's dark pavilions, the tents of Hades, the bowels of Hell; false of heart and sick of soul are its citizens.' Cranston turned to Flaxwith and the bailiffs. 'They have given me their word, but remain careful. Do not draw your weapons unless I tell you. Do not wander off even for some glimmering mort or pretty doxy. So sheath your swords and follow Sir John into the Valley of Gehenna.' Cranston led them across the square. Trumpets bellowed and the great gates swung open, allowing them into the notorious sanctuary of Whitefriars. This was the home of all the greasy, grimed rogues: the cogging naves, the courtesy men, the nighthawks, the nugging maids, the cheaters, shifters, cross-biters, the naps and the foists, the knights of the dusk and the squires of the sewers, the rifflers and the rutters.

Despite its reputation, Athelstan was surprised at how clean the lanes were. The smell of mulled sack hung heavy in the air, wafted out of the brightly lit taverns and ale shops. The houses were mean and shabby but, despite the cold, doors and windows remained open, the streets lighted and warmed by roaring bonfires and crackling braziers. At first glance this beggar's town was not a hive of dark dens but a busy ward with markets still doing business selling goods – stolen, of course, from elsewhere. The ladies of the night

strolled in their tawdry finery under the supervision of their two
guardians: the venerable Mother of the Kind Matrons – Athelstan
did not dare ask Cranston to explain this – and the Mistress of the
Wicked Wenches. Lazarus men, as the coroner described them,
kept order in the streets with club and cudgel. They passed a large,
shabby house. Flaxwith agreed with Sir John that it was the infamous
Cutpurse Manor, where pickpockets were tutored. They passed an
ancient chapel, the Church of the Condemned, served by a defrocked
priest called the 'Vicar of Hell'. The crowds in the narrow lane
parted before them. Curses were shouted at Cranston but he ignored
them. The coroner plucked at Athelstan's sleeve and pointed to
where two old ladies stood in the door light of the aptly named
Devil's Tongue tavern. Athelstan peered at them as he passed; their
faces were caked in paint, pursed lips brightly carmined.

'Nightshade and Belladonna,' Cranston murmured. 'Two old
ladies who visit to nurse and give their victims poison – eternal
comfort, a quiet way to go into the dark. One day, Athelstan, I'll
catch them in the act and hang them out of hand.'

They moved on. Athelstan noted that they had a discreet escort,
'Tyburn Sprigs', as Flaxwith described them, hooded and visored
with the insignia of a red, three-branched scaffold sewn on to
their cloaks. The lane twisted and turned and they entered a
square. In the centre rose a huge Pity, a life-size cross bearing
a carving of the crucified Christ; a little beyond this a fountain
still gurgled despite the freezing cold. Athelstan exclaimed in
surprise. The cobbles had been cleared of all slushy dirt so they
gleamed in the light of the great flambeaux lashed to heavy poles
driven into the ground. Three sides of the square were bounded
by outhouses, storerooms, stables, smithies and workshops all
closed up for the night. Directly opposite them rose a majestic
mansion of Cotswold stone with a sloping tiled roof, smoking
chimney stacks and mullioned glass windows lit by glowing
lamps, their wooden sills painted a smart blood red. The mansion's
majestic entrance door of shimmering black oak stood at the top
of wide, earth-coloured steps lit by merrily burning braziers under
a row of cresset torches. Cranston and his party moved across.

'No further!' a voice called. Men emerged out of the shadows;
mailed and helmeted, they wore surcotes boasting the green and
gold cedars of Lebanon.

'No further!' the voice repeated. 'Sir John, Brother Athelstan, you may go on. Master Flaxwith, you and your men must stay. They will be entertained. Come, come,' one of the guards beckoned.

'Go,' Cranston murmured. 'But act prudently.'

Cranston and Athelstan were led up the steps. The great door swung open; shadowy figures welcomed them along the gleaming, oak-panelled gallery, past chambers locked and secured. Pure white candles glowed in their wall clasps. Alabaster oil jars exuded both light and a delicious perfume, the fragrance mingling with the most mouth-watering smells of cooked food. Guards stood discreetly in the shadows. Now and again the gleam of their steel was caught by the light. They reached the end of the passageway and were welcomed into a sumptuous chamber hung with cloth of gold; thick Turkey rugs stretched across a layer of coarse rope matting, carpeting the floor. Tapers glowed by the dozen while lowered Catherine wheels, their rims crammed with perfumed candles, provided more light. A fire leapt vigorously in the black stone hearth to the right of the dining tables. Brilliant white samite cloths covered these tables while their every plate, jug and trancher were of the richest metal, studded with jewels.

'Welcome, Sir John, Brother Athelstan!' The towering, bald-headed, bushy bearded man in the throne-like chair at the centre of the high table gestured to the empty seats on his left. 'Sit, eat and drink.'

Cranston and Athelstan sat down. The goblets before them brimmed with red and white wine and herb-tinged water. Athelstan crossed himself as a servant appeared out of the shadows to serve portions of veal and a ladle of savoury vege-tables and herbs. Duke Ezra of Caesarea toasted his guests and then turned back to whisper to his companions. Cranston sat and ate, as comfortable as if he were in the Holy Lamb of God. Athelstan simply pretended. He glanced swiftly around; there were about a dozen other men present, lean, pinched faces staring out of pointed hoods. Gang leaders, Athelstan concluded, men summoned to render their account at this robber's exchequer. Eventually the hushed conversation ended. Duke Ezra rose from his seat and walked around the tables arranged in a square, going behind the seats, praising his disciples. He reminded them of their oaths of loyalty. Abruptly he paused behind one of his captains. Athelstan stiffened as he glimpsed the battle mace Ezra clutched. The duke's burly face had turned puce red; spittle bubbled at his lips.

'No Judas sits at my board,' he roared, 'drinks my wine, eats my food and clasps my hand.' Then the mace came whirling down. His victim half turned; he was struck a second blow which sent blood and brains splattering on to the sheer samite cloth. A third blow and the man's head cracked like a shell as he collapsed sideways.

'You came here to pay your tithes,' Ezra raised the brain-splattered mace, 'not to withhold what is Caesar's. You must render to your ruler what is your ruler's. Now my beloveds, you may go. Take this dog's carcass and bury it beyond the sight and memory of man.' The rest of the company, stony-faced, chilled by the sudden violence, pushed back their chairs and rose. They lifted the corpse of their comrade, bowed to their host and left. Duke Ezra watched them go and leaned his elbows on the table, fingers laced together, smiling benevolently at what he now termed his 'special guests'.

'No murder, Sir John.' He pointed at the door. 'Edmund Rastner, also known as "Brillard", also known as "Rummage", also known as "Deverel",' Ezra waved a hand, 'wanted in Bedfordshire, Lincolnshire, Norwich and Bristol.' Again the airy wave. 'I killed a wolfshead according to statute law. But,' he smiled in a show of strong, gleaming white teeth, 'we are not here to discuss that. You would like some blancmange?' He suppressed a grin, 'Blood red and laced with nutmeg, no?' He pointed to the wine jugs carved in the shape of water horses. 'Do help yourselves. Oh, by the way,' he gestured around the chamber, 'it may look as if we are alone but of course, Sir John, we are not. You recognize that?'

'Naturally.' Cranston smiled back. 'The only time you will be really alone with me, Duke Ezra, is when I take your head on Tower Hill.'

The self-styled Duke threw his head back and roared with laughter.

'*Tempus fugit*,' Athelstan murmured.

'Time flies indeed, Brother.' Ezra stopped laughing. He dabbed his eyes with a napkin and drank deeply from his goblet. 'And thus comes the hour of darkness.' Ezra turned sideways on his throne, peering at Athelstan out of the corner of his eye. 'I know you full well, Brother.'

'I wish to God I did.'

Ezra smiled and shook his head. 'Your world, Brother, is divided into good and bad.'

'And yours?'

'Bad and those bad men trying to be good. You and Sir John belong to the latter. I truly believe that. You're trying to make sense of our world. I gave that up years ago, Brother. I simply exploit it. Now,' he turned to face them squarely, 'let's make sense of it. Gaunt's party was betrayed. The attack at Aldgate? They wanted to humiliate our noble Regent, seize those severed heads and, above all, capture that mysterious prisoner, yes?' Ezra didn't even wait for an answer. 'Magister Thibault, that weasel in human flesh, now believes that a traitor lurks close to his master. He has you to thank for that knowledge. Thibault certainly has a traitor-spy in your parish, Brother, though I understand that has now been taken care of.

'Murdered,' Athelstan intervened. 'The Wardes were slain in cold blood.'

'Master Humphrey was certainly Gaunt's spy,' Ezra agreed, 'a clever ploy. Warde was betrayed by the Upright Men's spy in Gaunt's retinue – you've probably reached that conclusion yourself. As far as the assault at the Roundhoop is concerned, that was Master Thibault's revenge.' Ezra slurped noisily from his goblet. 'Reflect very carefully,' he sniffed. 'As for the deaths in the Tower, Gaunt must be furious. The Upright Men are openly claiming that Gaunt and his coven are not safe even at the very heart of their power.' Duke Ezra grinned. 'A true mystery, a public mockery! Gaunt's guests attacked in full view of the leading citizens of London. What a shame! As for the assassin, young Barak?' Ezra shook his head, 'I do not believe he is the guilty one. The murder of Lettenhove and Eli proves that no one is safe. The assassin is like a fox in a chicken run, he is killing whom he wishes. Gaunt looks weak and helpless, that is what is sweeping the city. Guests killed, severed heads left, a member of his favourite acting group slaughtered mysteriously.'

'Do you know anything fresh?' Cranston jibed, 'or are we here to marvel at your wisdom and knowledge? You have power, Duke Ezra, but so do I.'

'Something else is being planned,' the gang leader retorted quickly, stung by Cranston's jibe. 'What, Sir John, I do not know. There is chatter about a gathering at the Tower, or around it.' Duke Ezra sipped from his goblet. 'Tell Gaunt to leave there,' he continued. 'The Upright Men will play him hard and fast, make it appear as if he is besieged, driven from his power, frightened of even being in his palace of the Savoy. Also tell him,' Ezra paused, 'that despite all his precautions, the secret prisoner, or so the gossip runs, poses a direct threat to him.'

Athelstan leaned forward. 'What do you mean?'

'Nothing, for the moment.'

The friar stared at this notorious wolfshead. For a few heartbeats he caught fear in Ezra's face and voice, as if this self-proclaimed Duke knew how far he could go. Gaunt's mysterious prisoner seemed to mark the limit. So who was she? Athelstan wondered. If Gaunt thought Ezra would meddle with his prisoner he'd send troops into Whitefriars and hang this outlaw leader from his gatehouse.

'I will give His Grace the Regent your kind advice.' Cranston toasted Ezra with his goblet. 'But you know why we are here. I want to meet the Herald of Hades. If there is mischief afoot, he'll have snouted it out as swiftly as a hungry hog with a truffle.'

Duke Ezra stared at the blood brimming on the samite cloth.

'Sir John,' he did not lift his eyes, 'the Herald of Hades – you want to speak to him?' He raised a be-ringed hand, the precious finger stones dazzling in the light. 'So you shall. But not now.' Ezra grinned. 'He has been very busy on my behalf across the Narrow Seas in Ghent. You may meet him the day after tomorrow, on one condition.' He drew a small scroll from the cuff of his velvet-laced jerkin and held it up. A figure stepped out of the darkness and took this round to Cranston. The coroner unrolled it. Athelstan glanced quickly at the list of names under the heading of 'Newgate'.

'My beloveds, Sir John, all intended for the Elms gibbet at Smithfield. I know you have pardons prepared. I want my beloveds back.'

Cranston, fingers to his lips, studied the names. 'Not these two.' He tapped the parchment. 'Crail and Layburn ravished an innocent maid and throttled her; they must hang.'

'Really, Sir John?'

'They will hang,' Cranston declared defiantly, pushing back his chair. 'I viewed her corpse. Barely twelve summers old, she was. I have seen a cat treat a rat with more respect. God wants them for judgement.'

'No mercy?'

'None!' Cranston shouted. 'But these three others, the Plungers . . .'

'Plungers?' Athelstan queried.

'Professional cozeners,' Cranston whispered. 'One pretends to fall in the Thames, the second pretends to rescue him, and the third organizes a collection for both the so-called victim and his saviour.' He tapped the parchment. 'These three,' he raised his voice, 'have allegedly dipped into every stream, river and brook in and around London. I know this unholy trinity; they've had the gristle in their ears pierced and an "F" branded on their shoulders, yet they still keep plunging.'

'Old comrades,' Duke Ezra declared mournfully, 'Sir John, they truly are my beloveds.'

'All three will be pardoned.' Cranston rose to his feet. 'On one condition: I never see their ugly faces this side of the Thames again.'

'Then go in peace.' Duke Ezra also rose. 'The Lord be with you, Brother Athelstan, Sir John.'

'And with your spirit too,' Athelstan quipped back.

'You will arrange it personally, Sir John, the morning after tomorrow as the execution cart leaves Newgate?'

'I'll be there. And the Herald of Hades?'

'Sir John, he will await you . . .'


In the ruined nave of the derelict church of St Dismas, which stood in a thick clump of trees to the north of the old city wall, Simon Grindcobbe and the other leaders of the Upright Men had gathered their cell drawn from Massingham, Maldon, and other villages of south Essex. This was a safe, deserted place. Once a prosperous village, the great pestilence had swept through with its scythe and reduced both church and village to a haunt of ghosts. Outside the wooden crosses and stone memorials in God's Acre had crumbled and fallen. Only the towering memorial stone on the top of the great burial pit bore witness to the church's former history as well as the horror that had silenced it forever. Grindcobbe, Tyler and Straw now sat cross-legged behind the preacher John Ball as he knelt before the crumbling altar and intoned their chant.

'Nations in their greatness, he struck.'

'For his love endures forever.' The voices of the fifty fighters rolled back like a crashing wave.

'Kings in their splendour he slew.'

'For his love endures forever.'

'Sihon, King of the Amorites.'

'For his love endures forever.' The response grew even stronger.

'On the earthworms their land he bestowed.'

'For his love endures forever.'

'Kings in their splendour he slew.'

'For his love endures forever.'

'Og, the King of Bashan.'

'For his love endures forever.'

'On the earthworms their land he bestowed.'

'For his love endures forever.'

'Kings in their splendour he slew.'

'For his love endures forever.'

'Edward, tyrant of England.'

'For his love endures forever.'

'Gaunt the usurper.'

'For his love endures forever.'

Grindcobbe turned. The fighters, heads and shoulders cowled and mantled in tarred leather, faces hidden behind black mesh masks, were now in a trance, chanting the responses to John Ball's hymn of destruction. Grindcobbe rose and walked up the crumbling sanctuary steps into the darkened sacristy. 'Are you there, Basilisk?' he called out.

'I am.'

Grindcobbe peered through the murk; the far outside door, hanging off its latch, swayed in the breeze. 'You have met our spy in Gaunt's household? You must be surprised?'

'No surprise, Master Grindcobbe. This entire city seems up for sale.'

Grindcobbe laughed softly. 'When you decide,' he added, 'deal with him. He has served his purpose. He only feeds us morsels, what he wants to. One day Gaunt will catch him out. The torturers will tug him apart to discover what he knows. More importantly, to protect himself, he might kill you. Anyway,' he continued, 'tomorrow, just after the Angelus bell, let all chaos break out. Have the postern gate loosened. You have wreaked great damage. More must be done.'

'Who is that prisoner?' The basilisk's voice was scarcely above a whisper.

'Rumour abounds,' Grindcobbe replied evasively. 'Once we seize her, we shall have the truth about Gaunt's shame. We will topple him off his high throne. We will make the people wonder. We will present him as a spectacle, a prince who can't even rule the Tower. Remember, once the Angelus bell has tolled.'

'I shall remember,' came the whisper. The sacristy door swung open and the basilisk slipped like a ghost into the night.

'There is an assassin on the loose who swept through my parish like some winged demon. This murderer annihilated an entire family.' Athelstan gripped the lectern in the chapel of St Peter ad Vincula. The friar had returned to his lodgings in the Garden Tower late the previous day; he'd immediately demanded an audience with Magister Thibault, where Cranston had passed on Duke Ezra's warnings. Thibault had heard them out, tapping fingers against the arm of his chair before informing them that he would reflect on all this and meet them on the morrow.

'The Straw Men must also be present,' Athelstan demanded.

Thibault had nodded and said he would reflect on that as well. Now Gaunt's Master of Secrets, together with his henchmen and the bland-faced Cornelius, sat on a cushioned bench before Athelstan; on the other side ranged the Straw Men. Judith was openly agitated, her eyes screwed up in fear. She stared at Athelstan, who once again sensed the tension between Judith and her male companions, whose attempts to sit close were brusquely refused. Rachael leaned forward, red hair straggling down, green eyes wide in shock. Master Samuel sat combing his beard with chewed fingers. The burly Samson had the look of a pole-axed ox while the effete Gideon twirled a lock of hair between his fingers. Next to these, leaning against the pillar stood Rosselyn, hood pulled back, his grim face twisted in a look of disbelief.

'I mourn for you, Brother,' the captain of archers spoke up, 'but I swear, nobody here left the Tower yesterday. Ask my men. I was here all day; I can vouch for everyone else. My Lord of Gaunt's instructions, reinforced by Master Thibault, are most clear. None of us are to leave. None of us did.'

'Who was murdered?' Rachael asked, shifting the hair from her face.

'Nobody you know.' Athelstan sighed. 'A spicer and his family,' he glanced swiftly at Thibault, 'though I believe they were known to you.'

The Master of Secrets just shrugged as if that was a matter of little concern. 'We cannot leave here,' Samson protested. 'Brother Athelstan, I thought we were to visit your parish to perform a passage from a mystery play?'

'Not now,' Thibault snapped. 'Not till these mysteries are solved. Nobody leaves.'

'I will.' Athelstan voice thrilled with defiance. 'I shall. I need to. I must revisit the Roundhoop.'

'Why?'

'To refresh my memory.'

'About what?'

'I shall know that, Master Thibault, when I remember it.'

'And I am the King's own officer.' Cranston, sitting in the sanctuary chair next to the lectern, spoke up. 'I shall go where I want. I have business in the city tomorrow. King's business.'

'Which is?'

'If you were King, Master Thibault, I'd tell you.' Cranston got to his feet. 'But you are not, so I shall not. We are finished here, Brother. We've been told that no one left the Tower yesterday.'

Athelstan murmured his agreement. He felt weary. He'd slept late, risen and celebrated his Mass, now this. The friar stared down the church at a faded wall painting depicting St Peter's confrontation with the arch-magician, Simon Magus. Magus had tried to fly, only to be brought crashing back to earth by the prayer of St Peter. Athelstan smiled to himself. He felt that he was also stumbling around despite going hither and thither in pursuit of this or that. Power games were being played. Pieces were being shifted on the board. Forces gathered – Gaunt on one side, the Upright Men on the other. In between was himself, Cranston and St Erconwald's. Nevertheless, there was something else, something that constantly dogged Athelstan's secret thoughts. He was exasperated because he felt weary, because he was failing to resolve these problems. To confront a mystery, to enter it as he would a maze, to thread his way through to the centre and so prove there was no mystery was Athelstan's great passion. He felt physically and mentally depleted if he was not involved in that, or if he started but failed to make headway. In truth, he loved entering that maze perhaps even more than being a Dominican priest, a friend of Cranston, or the spiritual leader of his flock. An absorbing . . .

'Brother Athelstan,' Thibault mocked, 'are you praying?'

'I wish to God I was,' Athelstan retorted. 'Believe me,' Athelstan breathed in deeply, 'I need to visit the Roundhoop, then we shall return.' He smiled at Judith, Rachael and the other Straw Men. 'Perhaps we shall then stage our own play?'

'Meaning what?' Cornelius demanded.

'Oh, we shall go back to Saint John's Chapel. I want to recreate where everybody stood, to establish how that skilful assassin could wreak such damage.' Athelstan blessed the air as a sign that he had finished. He collected his cloak and chancery bag from the corner of the sanctuary and left the chapel by the corpse door. Once outside he finished dressing against the cold, thanking God for the thick serge leggings under his robe. Cranston was similarly attired. The morning was freezing cold; a thick mist had wrapped itself about everything, a moving shroud which made the eyes wince and the lips curl as it nipped exposed flesh. No fresh snow had fallen but the ground under foot was like polished glass. Athelstan and Cranston gratefully accepted the walking canes Rosselyn offered. The captain of archers accompanied them down to a postern gate and allowed them through. The ward outside, Petty Wales, was busy, though this was one of the wastelands of the city. The slippery lanes, derelict houses ranging either side, were cold and filthy hovels where illness and ignorance ruled like lords. Hunger-haunted faces stared out at them. Frozen fingers picked at chestnuts roasting in a dirty pan above a rubbish heap which had been doused in filthy oil and set alight. Nearby stale bread, hard and black, was on sale with sausages and dripping from dead dog preparations. The beggars clustered so close together it looked like a mass of rags covered one huge body with many pinched faces. Cheap tapers glowed from tawdry box lanterns, spots of yellow which pierced the thickening whiteness.

They reached the Roundhoop and went up the steps into the musty, circular tap room. The place was dark and the shutters were closed – only candlelight broke the gloom. Athelstan stared around as Cranston ordered two blackjacks of ale. Minehost was new. Athelstan could recognize no one from that previous dramatic and bloody visit. Goodmayes, the tavern master at the time, had been killed along with his servants. Athelstan took his blackjack and joined Cranston in the shabby window seat close to the meagre glow of the hearth fire.

'Brother, your thoughts?' Athelstan glanced round; the only customers were chapmen and tinkers sheltering from the cold.

'The killings at the Tower,' Athelstan began, 'were very mysterious. Clever and subtle, they caused deep confusion, heaping great shame on Gaunt. Look at how he is now depicted. Don't forget, Sir John, Gaunt has assumed the power of Regent. He may call himself that but I understand that it has never been approved by parliament. He is not as secure as he thinks and this bloody business at the Tower weakens him further. Gaunt is being depicted not as a great prince but a jackanapes, a fool, a weakling who cannot even protect his own in the Crown's greatest fortresses. My friend, I have no idea of how these murders occurred – none whatsoever. We have deduced a few truths about those severed heads but who they were remains a mystery. The murders of Eli and Barak are buried beneath layers of deceit and lies, not to mention clever trickery. The Wardes were murdered, bloody, gruesome deaths yet, at the same time, so swift, so silent with no evidence of any alarm or resistance. The assassin appears to have moved from chamber to chamber like a welcome guest who, at the same time, proved to be a bloody-handed slayer.'

'And here?' Cranston gulped from his blackjack. In truth the coroner was deeply uneasy and out of his depth. He resented being locked up in the fastness of the Tower with the treachery and deceit of Gaunt and his party swirling about him. He was the King's law officer; he dealt with murder and dispatched its perpetrators to the gallows. He glanced wistfully at Athelstan; surely this little friar with his probing eyes and sharp wits would find a path out?

'And here?' Cranston repeated. Athelstan rose and walked to the centre of the tap room. He recalled that bloody affray. He was standing here when it occurred; he had turned, desperate to reach the door. The Upright Man had confronted him. He'd been looking beyond Athelstan – at what? Then the arrows had flown. The Upright Man had collapsed. Athelstan had knelt beside him. The friar chewed the corner of his lip. The dying man still had that questioning look in his eyes even as he babbled about some woman gleaning. Athelstan felt a tingle of excitement. He was sure that young man's swift, brutal death was linked to these mysteries. He could offer no logical reasoning or evidence to justify such a conclusion, just a suspicion which nagged at his brain as a dog would a bone.

'Tomorrow,' Cranston called out, 'we must be at Newgate.'

'And today, Sir John, we must take care of the present evil. I need to go through Humphrey Warde's papers. Sir John, if you are leaving the Tower, I would be most grateful if you could collect them from the parish chest in Saint Erconwald's.'

Cranston finished his blackjack and stood up. 'I certainly want to be free of the Tower. I promise to give Benedicta a kiss from you. I also want to make my own enquiries. I will collect those papers and rejoin you soon enough.'

# PART FIVE

## *'Jocus: Dramatic Scene'*

Athelstan sat in his chamber in the Garden Tower and stared at the wall. He felt slightly sleepy, but a growing chorus of shouts and yells kept distracting him. Athelstan rose, straining his ears, then horns brayed and bells clanged. He hurried to the door and went out on to the steps. He stopped in surprise: men, women and children, accompanied by barking dogs, were running for their lives out of Red Gulley which snaked past Bell Tower. They kept pointing back, shouting about some horror as they slipped and slithered in the snow. Athelstan did not know what to do. He heard the words 'St Thomas' mentioned but no one stopped to explain, fleeing across to any open door to fling themselves in. After the crowd came the royal beastmaster dressed in the livery of the King's household, accompanied by his minions. They were dragging nets and the beastmaster was trying to organize others to hold long poles with flaming cresset torches lashed on the end, into a line. Behind these rose the howling of the Tower mastiffs, echoed by a more fearsome roar. Athelstan watched the entrance to Red Gulley and gaped in disbelief. He thought his eyes were deceiving him. The mastiffs came streaming through the gateway leading from the gulley, then turned as a pack to confront Maximus the great snow bear. Maximus, his snout and paws covered in blood, stood up on his hind legs. The animal still wore his collar, the long, silver-like chain attached to it swung backwards and forwards and proved no real obstacle to the bear's movements. Maximus, massive head forward, jaws gaping, roared his defiance at the mastiffs. Two of these, their blood lust roused, streaked in, racing across the packed snow, bellies low, crushing jaws open for the bite. Trained to hunt as a pair, the mastiffs aimed to seize each of the hind legs and hamstring their opponent. Maximus, however, was too swift. He abruptly dropped to all fours. Shifting slightly to one side, he swiped the nearest dog a killing blow which smashed the mastiff's head to pulp. Maximus then moved just as swiftly as the second mastiff turned to flee, only to flounder in the snow. The great bear pounced, trapping the dog's haunches between his paws, pulling it back in a flurry of bloody snow for the death bite to the nape of its neck. The rest of the hunting pack hurtled in. Maximus, pounding the corpse of the dead dog, reared up, paws threshing the air. The royal beastmaster screamed at a company of archers who had moved forward notching their bows not to loose. Maximus, who seemed to sense the danger, now turned from the dogs and lumbered back towards Red Gulley. The dogs followed. Maximus turned again. The dogs retreated but the beastmaster seized his opportunity. The cresset torches soaked in pitch and tar were now burning fiercely.

Athelstan stood, fascinated. He could tell from the way the royal beastmaster worked that animals escaping from the menagerie were not a rare event in the Tower. The mastiffs were called off and the moving wall of fire proved too much for Maximus. He roared one final defiance and allowed himself to be driven out of the inner bailey down Red Gulley towards his cage in St Thomas' Tower. Athelstan was sure the bear would be safe. A king's animal, not even Gaunt could order its destruction. Athelstan recalled that magnificent beast rearing up, the chain swinging about. How had he broken free? Athelstan felt his stomach pitch. He had seen that cage. Artorius had been very careful. Athelstan was sure this was no accident or mere chance. He was tempted to go down and see but realized the royal beastmaster would have the area tightly guarded while Athelstan could offer very little practical help. The friar walked back into the Garden Tower and re-entered his chamber, leaving the door off the latch. He closed his eyes and recalled Maximus' cage. The sinuous chain tied to a pole, the gate to the moat tightly secured, the door he and Cranston had used to view the bear. Athelstan opened his eyes. He was sure Maximus' escape was deliberate and he doubted very much whether Artorius was still alive. He paused at fresh cries and shouts echoing from outside. Had the bear escaped again or forced his captors back? The cries and shouts grew stronger. Athelstan felt his stomach tense. Had Maximus been released just to cause confusion and chaos? Was it the precursor for something else? Athelstan rose to his feet; he just wished Cranston was here.

'Brother Athelstan! Brother Athelstan!' The friar hurried to the door and flung it open. Rachael, red hair streaming, stumbled in a flurry of snow. Now and again she'd stop to help Judith: Samuel, Gideon and Samson followed, hastening towards the Garden Tower, gazing fearfully behind them. The Straw Men reached the friar, gasping and breathless.

'Is it the bear?' Athelstan asked.

'No, no.' Rachael pointed back. Athelstan followed her direction. He could now hear the crash and slither of steel, the cries of men locked in deadly combat. The tocsin on top of Bell Tower boomed out as the beacon fire beside it flared into life. Athelstan urged the Straw Men into his chamber.

'Get your breath back,' he advised and went out on to the steps. Other bells were tolling. Fires flamed against the dark sky. Men-at-arms and archers hurried across out of Red Gulley where they had been busy helping the beastmaster. The roar of the lions only deepened the death-bringing din now clear on the freezing air. Officers of the garrison hurried about dressed in half armour, clutching an assortment of weapons. Athelstan went back into the Tower, closing the door behind him. He told the Straw Men to remain where they were but, chattering with fear, they begged him to stay with them. Judith particularly was beside herself with fear, crouching beside Rachael, who put a protective arm around her companion's shoulder and drew her close.

'She's terrified of bears!' Samuel explained. 'That's why she ran away from her father. Brother, what is happening? What should we do?'

'I need to find out what is wrong.' Athelstan pointed to the ceiling. 'It's too dangerous to leave.' He crossed to the door and turned. 'What did you see?'

'Some hostile force,' Samuel declared. 'They appeared as if from nowhere.'

'I'd best go up.' Athelstan opened the door. 'I . . .' He broke off as three archers, war bows slung across their backs, cresset torches in their hands, burst into the stairwell. They pushed Athelstan aside with shouts that the fortress was under attack and that the alarm beacon on top of the Garden Tower had to be fired. They clattered up the winding steps, Athelstan and the Straw Men hurrying behind, and reached the top. The archers flung open the door which swung in the freezing, pummelling breeze. The Tower top was sanded for better grip, the pitch-smeared beacon already primed and soon lit, the leaping flames providing a welcome burst of heat. Athelstan hurried to the fighting platform beneath the crenellations and peered over. The tower baileys were now caught up in confusion. He could glimpse the royal beastmaster trying to seal off all entrances to St Thomas' Tower. To the north, however, around the Wardrobe Tower, hastily gathered members of the garrison were being driven back by a well-organized phalanx or schiltrom of men armed with shields and swords, a screed of archers around them. The fighting looked intense, the enemy bowmen loosing at any who approached while their main battle group steadily advanced.

'They are fighting to reach Beauchamp!' Athelstan cried out.

'The prisoner,' one of the archers muttered. 'It's the Upright Men; they are after Gaunt's prisoner. God save us.' He added bitterly, 'Whoever she may be, she will be the death of many a good man today.' Athelstan grabbed him by the arm; the archer turned. Athelstan could tell by the look in the man's face that he had said too much.

'Don't worry.' Athelstan smiled. 'I will not report you. The prisoner? You have seen her?'

'Brother, I trust you. I was in the escort which brought her from Dover. God save us!' The man leaned closer. 'Don't you realize, Brother, those attackers are our brothers, peasants like me.' He shook his head. 'I have said too much.'

'You have told the truth,' Athelstan whispered. 'God knows, my friend, we seem to live a life where right and wrong merge.'

'They are breaking through!' another archer yelled. Athelstan stared down. The attackers, tightly packed together, were pushing the defenders back. The danger had been recognized. Men-at-arms, hobelars and archers were gathering before Beauchamp to block its entrance. A futile move as the enemy was moving too fast, while the Tower archers dare not loose lest they hit their own, still closely engaged with the enemy.

'What can we do?' Rachael wailed.

'What should we do?' Athelstan retorted. 'This is not our fight.'

A hunting horn brayed, followed by a trumpet blast. Athelstan hurried across to the other side of the tower. Loud cries of 'Harrow! Harrow! *Dieu Nous Aide! Dieu Nous Aide!* Saint George! Saint George!' rang out. Men-at-arms, armoured knights, hobelars and archers were now pouring into the inner bailey around Bell Tower. Crown standards and pennants blazed in a riot of blue, red and gold, the royal leopards clear to see. The unexpected reinforcements paused to arrange themselves into battle formation. Archers to the front and flanks, men-at-arms and knights to the centre, they moved forward, a mass of bristling steel. A trumpet blared. They paused. The archers raced forward, war bows strung. Up they swung and a rain of black shafts rose against the grey sky to fall like sharpened hail on the attackers. The Tower garrison, who'd first engaged the enemy, realized what was happening and swiftly retreated, leaving the enemy exposed to another hissing attack. Again and again the arrows rained down. The defenders of Beauchamp also moved forward. More trumpets shrilled. The mass of mailed men gathered just beyond Bell Tower surged forward. Athelstan breathed a prayer, a plea for the souls being so cruelly loosed from flesh and bone. The massacre had begun.

An hour later, summoned by Thibault, Athelstan sat on a stool in St Peter ad Vincula. A Court of Oyer and Terminer had been set up. A great table bearing a copy of the Gospels, a royal standard and an unsheathed sword lay next to Thibault's commission 'to listen and terminate' Crown matters. The Master of Secrets was the principal judge, Lascelles his associate, Cornelius his scribe. Athelstan realized it was all a pretence. Indeed, according to statute, the rule of law had been suspended. Thibault had been very quick to point out the underlying legal principle, enshrined in the Statute of Treason proclaimed by the present King's grandfather Edward III. Once the royal banner had been unfurled and displayed, all those caught in arms against it were adjudged rank traitors; sentencing was just a formality, gruesome death a certainty. Only a dozen prisoners had been taken. The dying wounded had been roughly tortured, interrogated and then dispatched with a throat-cut from a misericorde dagger. All the prisoners refused to speak, to confess, to accept any pardon or any commutation in return for betraying the Upright Men. Sentence had been swiftly delivered: all faced summary execution. Thibault had asked Athelstan to shrive any who asked for the sacrament. Athelstan's earlier fears were also realized. The release of Maximus had been deliberate, to cause as much chaos as possible before the attack.

'Some accomplice in the Tower,' Thibault had hissed at Athelstan, 'killed the keeper, released the chain on the bear and opened the gates.'

'And Artorius?' Athelstan asked. 'How . . .?'

'Slain by a bolt through the forehead; indeed, that's all that remains of him.' Thibault smiled slightly, as if he found it amusing. 'Just imagine, Athelstan, a savaged head with a crossbow bolt in it. He was killed, the chain released and the doors left open.'

Athelstan closed his eyes and murmured a prayer. The assassin had been very cunning. At first Maximus would have moved slowly, giving the killer an opportunity to escape. Only then would the formidable bear begin to wander, attracted by the smell of blood from his now-dead keeper.

'Where was Artorius killed?'

'In the aisle beside the cage. The place is awash with blood.'

'How did the assassin get in?' Athelstan asked. 'Artorius was careful.'

'What does it matter now?' Thibault had declared. 'Their plans certainly failed.' During the swift trial Athelstan had learnt how Thibault, alerted by Duke Ezra's warnings and perhaps his own spy, had secretly prepared two war cogs, 'The Glory of Lancaster' and 'The Blanche of Castille'. They had slipped through the morning mist and used that as a cover to drop anchor off the Tower quayside. Once the tocsin had sounded and the beacons lit, both cogs had disgorged their fighting men to trap and kill the Upright Men. Now the doom. Thibault summoned each of the survivors before him and stripped off their hoods, masks and weapons. Peasants, young and old, striplings as well as veterans, they all proved to be obdurate. They refused to recognize the court, to give their names or say anything about their families or their villages. All ignored Thibault's offer of clemency so all were condemned to '*Mort Sans Phrase*'

– immediate execution. Once sentence was passed the prisoners were hustled out. Athelstan accompanied each of the condemned. They were forced to kneel on the frozen, snow-covered grass. Athelstan crouched beside each, listening to their litany of sins, trying to provide what comfort he could. He'd whisper the absolution, bless the condemned, rise and step back. The headsman's assistants forced their victim to lie face down on a great log, twisting his head sideways. The executioner, feet apart to steady himself, brought up his great two-edged axe and severed the neck with one savage cut. Athelstan just continued to stare at the ground, whispering the *De Profundis*, moving aside as the blood shimmered across in sparkling red rivulets to soak and warm the ground. The gore-gushing trunk was pushed away, the head doused in boiling water and tossed into a basket to be displayed along the Tower wharf. Athelstan stayed to the bitter end, determined to pray for each soul.

They all died bravely. They betrayed no bitterness towards him but cursed the judge who condemned them. They did whisper a few words about themselves: how in the main they were from Massingham and Maldon in Essex, parishioners of St Oswald's, their priest Father Edmund Arrowsmith. Athelstan kept such information to himself. When the executions were finished, he left that blood-drenched place, pushing through the crowd, ignoring the questions of Samuel and the other Straw Men. Back in his chamber, Athelstan warmed himself over one of the braziers. He gulped some watered wine then lay on his bed, staring up into the darkness. Some time later the latch rattled. Cranston swept into the chamber, doffing hat and cloak and placing a leather sack beside Athelstan's bed.

'I know what happened. Rosselyn told me. It's like a flesher's yard out there. At least thirty heads. Those killed or executed already decorate poles along the Thames. Thibault is beside himself with glee.' Cranston took a sip from his miraculous wine skin. 'Stupid bastard! Tensions are rising among the garrison – you know why?'

'I feel the same,' the friar answered, dragging himself up on the bed. 'I am a yeoman's son, Sir John, a tiller of the soil, an earthworm. So are many of the archers and hobelars who kill their own kind to protect cruel lords.' Athelstan put his face in his hands.

'You are down in spirit, Brother.' Cranston clapped him on the shoulder. 'You deserve better. God knows I've been given that. Today I kissed the Lady Maude and cuddled my two poppets. After that the world didn't seem so terrible.'

'No, Sir John, it's a beautiful world, just turned and twisted by our sins. Look,' Athelstan paused as the bell of St Peter ad Vincula clanged marking the hour. 'I don't want to go out there,' he whispered. 'Not now.'

'You were saying?'

'Gaunt has enough wealth in his palace of the Savoy to ensure no one in London starves. There are enough empty comfortable chambers in this city to house all our vagrants. Enough food to feed the starving. Enough cloth to dress the naked. Sufficient religious houses to shelter the sick and witless but we human beings don't think like that. We put the self first, second and third, an unholy trinity against anyone who happens to be our neighbour.' Athelstan sighed. 'Thus endeth of my homily, Sir John. Let us return to what we are good at. We hunt murderers, trap them, confront them and despatch them to judgement. So, let us begin.' Athelstan got off the bed, picked up the sack and moved across to the chancery table. 'As I said, I do not wish to leave. I have looked on enough blood. Sir John, I'd be grateful if you would visit the chapel in the White Tower. Summon whoever you can. Try to recreate what happened. I hope to join you there. Perhaps we might also visit the death chamber where Eli died.'

Cranston took another gulp from his wine skin, gathered his cloak and left. The coroner was pleased that his little friend wished to be by himself. That enigmatic friar, like any good lurcher, was casting about for a scent. The hunt had begun!

After Cranston had left, Athelstan emptied the contents of the sack on to the table, the manuscripts from Humphrey Warde's house, ledgers, bills, memoranda and the beautiful calfskin-bound psalter. Athelstan opened this and was immediately intrigued. Warde had been a spicer, and had apparently commissioned this especially for himself. The author and illuminator of the psalter had described the history of spices, especially the mystical qualities of certain herbs and plants as well as the role spices played in Man's constant war against the demons. The miniature bejewelled pictures depicted devils bubbling in a huge cauldron containing, according to the inscription written beneath, oil, resin, garlic, myrrh, cloves and cinnamon. In one picture a flying serpent-devil with scaly wings was being pierced by shafts of henbane and hemlock. Next to this a miniature displayed Satan's eye, huge as a fist, open and luminous, flaring with malevolent life, being assailed by thick clouds of frankincense from a golden thurible. Another picture showed a demon in a shape of a huge slug tortured by the holy oil poured over him while a fellow demon was being showered with sacred chrism. Athelstan read on, fascinated, turning the stiffened leaves as he half listened to the sounds of the garrison and the eerie noises of the Tower. At one point he rose and pulled across the wheeled brazier for greater warmth. He glanced around. The juddering candlelight made the shadows shift and rise as if another world, a secret one, thrived here in this bleak stone chamber. Athelstan rubbed his fingers over the spluttering coals. 'Yet there is another reality,' he whispered to his own shadow. 'This straight and narrow place shelters an assassin, a soul throbbing with hatred, who exults in dealing out sudden and mysterious death.'

The attacks on the Flemings he understood, the murder of Warde was brutal yet logical, but why the Straw Men? Athelstan returned to the psalter, leafing through the pages till his eye was caught by an exquisitely illuminated full page picture of Lucifer falling from Paradise. Athelstan stared, shivering at the chill which abruptly seized him. '*Jesu Miserere.*' He prayed softly. 'Jesus, have mercy on us. Is it possible?' Athelstan put the psalter aside and pulled across the bills and memoranda. He sifted through these, searching for items bought and sold while listing Master Warde's customers. Athelstan revised what he had written, looking for a pattern, and eventually found it. He threw the quill pen down, staring at what he had written. 'Warde was a spy,' he murmured. 'He was sent into my parish to listen, collect and report, but he was not the hand which wielded the dagger – he was only the glove.' Athelstan beat his breast. '*Mea Culpa! Mea Culpa! Mea Culpa!* My fault entirely, I was too quick to judge those two rogues, God bless them. Watkin and Pike were correct. A Judas man did, and is, sitting at the heart of our community.' Athelstan rose and carefully collected his papers, now determined to join Sir John in the White Tower. 'I will not tell him my suspicions,' he murmured, 'not here in this

murky, treacherous place where the walls listen and deceit flour-
ishes thick and rich as any tangle of weed.'

Athelstan took his cloak and braved the freezing weather.
Night was edging in. Daylight was swiftly fading. The Tower
garrison was preparing for sleep. Figures and shapes slid through
the ever-present mist. Athelstan glanced towards Beauchamp
where torches flared above the doorway, gleaming on the
armoured mail of the guards. 'I wonder who you really are?'
Athelstan whispered to himself. He made his way across the icy
ground into the White Tower, up the stairs and into St John's
Chapel. Cranston, Lascelles, Cornelius, Rosselyn and the Straw
Men were gathered there. Athelstan smiled to himself. The
coroner had exercised his authority. The chapel itself hadn't
changed much since the day of the killing. The heavy tapestry
curtains still hung between the pillars on either side, screening
off the aisles or transepts where the food tables had stood. The
bloodstained turkey carpet and matting had been removed but
Hell's mouth still stood wedged into the entrance of the rood
screen. On either side of this hung the heavy arras concealing
the left and right aisles flanking the sanctuary. Athelstan stared
around and, ignoring the hubbub of conversation, walked out of
the chapel, down the steps and into the cold darkness of the
crypt. He took a cresset from its holder and went along to the
far window. He stared at this then crossed to the small recess
where Barak's body must have lain. Athelstan was convinced
Barak was no assassin. He'd either been killed or felled uncon-
scious here, then swiftly dragged up, the arbalest and war belt
used to depict him as such. Those shutters had been opened and
Barak's body violently hurled out. He heard raised voices so he
walked back up the steps to join the rest in St John's Chapel.

Cranston had persuaded Rachael to act as Oudernarde, Samuel
as Lettenhove. The rest of the Straw Men were arguing about
where they were on that day. The others were just as vague about
their whereabouts, especially Rosselyn and Cornelius, who never
mentioned anything about their swift departure from the chapel to
check on Beauchamp Tower. Eventually Cranston imposed order.
He reached a consensus that Oudernarde and Lettenhove had been
standing on opposite sides of the chapel.

'As were the two braziers when the small explosions occurred,'

Cranston declared. 'They caused the first confusion, then Lettenhove was struck, followed by Oudernarde. Yes?' They all murmured in agreement. 'And the assassin,' Cranston pointed down the chapel towards the door, 'could not have stood or knelt there; he would have been glimpsed by the guards or the musicians, yes?' Again, everyone agreed.

'In the aisles either side,' Samuel offered but then shrugged as he realized the foolishness of what he had said.

'The killer,' Cranston answered, 'if he had stood in the aisles, would be in full view of all those pressing around the food tables. The assassin first loosed at Lettenhove then somehow moved across the chapel to release a second bolt at Meister Oudernarde. And that,' the coroner wagged a finger, 'is the mystery. How could this assassin carry, prime and loose not one crossbow bolt but two then hide his weapon, all without being seen?'

'Not to mention producing those two severed heads,' Athelstan intervened. He walked to the rood screen, gesturing with his hands to either side. 'Both are found halfway along either side of Hell's mouth. Of course,' Athelstan pulled at the arras on the right side of the rood screen, 'the assassin may have hidden behind this, loosed the bolt then moved swiftly across the sanctuary behind Hell's mouth to the other arras and done the same again, then pushed out those two heads. And yet for one person this would be difficult, very difficult.'

'And we were there,' Rachael spoke up. 'I'm sure we were, collecting costumes, masks and other items.'

'And I went behind to check all was well.' Rosselyn, crouching at the foot of a pillar, spoke up. 'I saw nothing untoward.' He rose clumsily to his feet. 'And remember the crossbow was never found.' Athelstan did not answer him; he was desperately trying to recall what had been happening when those crossbow bolts had been loosed. He pointed to one of the polished oblong tables on which the food had been served.

'Please, if you could bring one of those over here.'

Samuel and Rosselyn did, moving chairs and putting the table down in the centre of the chapel. Athelstan asked them to gather around.

'Look,' he smoothed the top of the table with his hand, 'the chapel of Saint John is a rectangle stretching west to east. On the eastern side here,' Athelstan pointed to the top of the table, 'stretches a line which includes the rood screen and the arras hanging either side. The entrance through that rood screen is blocked by Hell's mouth.'

'Are you sure,' Lascelles intervened, 'that the assassin did not hide there? You can survey the room from it, prime a crossbow then loose.' Lascelles shrugged. 'I know it can be done – we tried that. I appreciate your objections but it remains the only possibility.'

'I suspect the assassin wanted us to believe that,' Athelstan replied. 'But for the crossbow to be used correctly, Hell's mouth would have to be prised loose and pulled back. No evidence exists that took place. When we did pull it back, the tight fastenings were broken. If the murderer had done that, it would have been obvious; someone would have noticed.' The Straw Men loudly agreed, adding that they had all worked to place it there.

'Hell's mouth,' Samuel spoke out, 'is our pride and joy. In the main it can be wedged in the door of most rood screens. Rachael here always polishes and paints it. To move it as you describe, Brother, would have been nigh impossible. The paint work would have been scuffed, the fastenings would have been broken and the noise alone would have attracted attention.' Athelstan, nodding in agreement, gestured to the side of the table.

'These are the aisles or transepts. On that day they were busy, food and drink tables stood here, guests and servants moved about. The same is true here.' Athelstan grasped the end of the table. 'This is the entrance – guards stood there. Musicians were busy in the recess, people were coming and going.' He shook his head. 'So where did our assassin lurk and successfully and secretly loose two crossbow bolts?' His question was greeted with silence. The friar shrugged. 'Sir John, my apologies but my sermon may have proved too long. I am even sorrier that all it did was pose questions.'

The coroner grinned, picked up his cloak and bowed at the assembled company. 'Gentlemen, Mistress' Rachael and Judith, I thank you for your attention.' And the coroner, taking a sip from his wine skin, headed for the door. Athelstan swiftly sketched a blessing and hurried after him.

'Sir John?' Once they were outside Athelstan plucked at the coroner's sleeve. 'I apologize, but this mystery hounds me . . .'

'No need to apologize.' Cranston clutched Athelstan's hand and squeezed it. 'I am baffled, you are baffled, we are baffled. All that you said in there is what I was trying to express.' He let go of the friar's hand. 'Anyway, what brought you up? I thought you were busy with Warde's manuscripts. Did you find anything which might explain the massacre of him and his family?'

'No,' Athelstan replied evasively. 'Perhaps the Upright Men were involved? But come, Sir John, while we are braving the cold, let us visit Eli's chamber.' They trudged through the snow. The guard inside the Salt Tower allowed them up to the death chamber. Carpenters had been very busy. The door had been rehung on new freshly oiled leather hinges with gleaming bolts and a new lock. Cranston remarked on the speed and skill of the repairs as Athelstan began to search around. There was very little. Eli's possessions had been removed. The chamber was cold, empty and bleak. Athelstan returned to the door. He closed it over, drew the bolts and turned the well-greased lock. He then crossed the chamber to examine the window shutters but swiftly deduced that these had not been opened since late summer or early autumn: the bar was secure and covered in dust. Athelstan, puzzled, stood chewing his lip. This chamber has no secret entrance, so how had Eli been killed? He returned to the door and examined the eyelet. The slit looked unchanged, about six inches long and the same in breadth; the small wooden shutter had been replaced and now slid easily backwards and forwards. Athelstan pulled this open and stared into the darkened stairwell.

'An assassin with a small hand arbalest could loose a bolt quite easily through that slit,' Athelstan remarked. 'Except . . .'

'Except what, my dear friar?'

'Except when Eli was murdered that shutter was firmly stuck.' Athelstan stamped his feet against the gathering cold. 'And even if it hadn't been, Eli would have surely been cautious. I mean, that's the whole purpose of an eyelet, isn't it, to determine friend or foe? Eli was young, alert and vigorous; even if that shutter could slide back, problems remain. Let us analyse it,' Athelstan wagged a finger, '*causa disputandi* – for the sake of argument.

Let us suppose that the shutter could be moved. Now, logically the assassin standing outside would have knocked, perhaps even called out, yes?'

Cranston nodded.

'Eli must have asked who it was? Satisfied with the answer, Eli pulled back the shutter. He would certainly flinch at an arbalest being pushed up to the slit and move very swiftly out of danger. Yet in the end all this is fiction,' Athelstan closed the door, 'that couldn't have happened, as the shutter was held fast, stuck.' Athelstan laughed sharply. 'Even if it hadn't been, and Eli was satisfied with his visitor, why not just open the door? Why bother peering through the eyelet in the first place?'

'Brother, one question?'

'Yes, Sir John?'

'Can we resolve these mysteries?'

'At first sight, Sir John, no, though logic dictates, and God demands we do so.'

The mournful tolling of the Newgate bell was answered by that of the nearby church of St Sepulchre; the bells boomed out across the sleet-swept, blood-strewn concourse in front of the soaring iron-bound gates of London's greatest and grimmest prison. Despite the harsh winter's day, fleshers, butchers and their minions were busy hacking and hewing the carcasses of cattle, pigs and birds of every kind. Apprentice boys raced about with tubs and buckets crammed with steaming entrails, giblets and offal. The morning air was rich with the raw stench of slaughter, heavy with the tang of salt and brine. Scavengers, human, animal and bird, flocked to fight over globules of flesh and the occasional chunk of meat. Around these surged a crowd, leather boots, wooden sandals and, in some cases, bare feet squelching in the gory mess of blood, snow and filthy mud. Citizens hoped to buy a bargain though at the same time the great gates of Newgate were kept under close watch. When these abruptly swung open, people surged forward to greet the death carts which came rumbling out, escorted by men-at-arms wearing the city livery. Cranston and Athelstan, who'd been sheltering in the porch of the aptly named tavern The Roast Pig, stepped out and waited. Duke Ezra had insisted that the pardon for the three plungers be served here.

'So everyone can see his power,' Cranston whispered. 'A better mummer than any of the Straw Men, Ezra loves a spectacle. We have to do what he says – the Herald of Hades will be watching, hah!' Cranston pointed at the black-garbed executioner, his face concealed by a red mesh mask, sitting by the driver of the first cart. 'Your friend the anchorite, the Hangman of Rochester.' Cranston marched across. The line of carts now stood still as the undersheriffs in fur-lined cloaks organized their posse or *comitatus* to divide; three carts for the Elms of Smithfields, three for the gallows at the Forks by Tyburn stream. Cranston took off his beaver hat and pulled down his muffler so he would be recognized, then handed one of the undersheriffs the three pardons. Athelstan could only stand and pray for all he saw and heard was most pitiful. Some prisoners lolled half drunk in the carts, others protested and yelled their innocence, a few sobbed bitterly as family and friends gathered to make their final farewells. The reeking stench of unwashed bodies clothed in filthy rags all coated in Newgate slime was nauseous. Athelstan, whispering his Aves, moved to where the hangman sat.

'Good morning, Giles.' Athelstan deliberately used the anchorite's real name. 'God have mercy on you.'

'Soon done, soon finished,' came the hoarse reply. 'I'll visit Tyburn first then a city courier will escort me across to Smithfield.'

'You'll go back to your cell at Saint Erconwald's?'

'And to my painting, Brother.'

'You and Huddle?'

'Father,' the anchorite leaned down, eyes gleaming through his mask, 'we could transform your church. I mean . . .' He broke off as cheers and cries broke out. Athelstan glanced down the line of carts. The three plungers had been taken off the death tumbrils. Manacles and chains removed, they grasped their pardons and danced like fleas on a hotplate. Athelstan realized why Duke Ezra had insisted it be so – a public demonstration of his influence and protection for those he called 'his beloveds'. The three plungers were suddenly enveloped by a small mob who hurried them away lest any official might change his mind.

'You must go,' Athelstan grasped the hangman's black gauntleted hand, 'to make sure their deaths are swift and painless. God have mercy on them all.'

'In the twinkling of an eye,' the hangman replied, 'from this vale of tears to Heaven's gate before they realize.'

The mounted men-at-arms now imposed order, beating away the crowds and ordering the carts to go their appointed route. Cranston seized Athelstan's wrist and pulled him aside. They walked briskly. Cranston pushed his way through the crowds, stepping around puddles and pits of refuse, knocking away the grasping hands of apprentices and beggars who importuned for trade or alms.

'God knows,' Cranston growled, 'when the Herald will make his appearance, but it's the Holy Lamb for us, Friar, a tankard of ale and the juiciest, freshest mince beef pie.'

They reached the tavern and revelled in the sweet warmth of the tap room, the fragrance from herb-strewn pine logs mingling with the savoury tang of hams, cheeses and vegetables hanging in snow-white nets from the black beams. The ruddy-cheeked Minehost ushered them to Sir John's favourite window seat. They'd hardly sat down when Athelstan heard his name called and a lean, hatchet-faced man dressed in black robes like those of a Benedictine monk stepped out from the shadows of the inglenook. Athelstan stared at that sharp face, the foxlike eyes, the cropped auburn hair, the lips twisted ready to mock, talon-like fingers splayed as he stretched out a hand to clasp that of Athelstan.

'You forget so soon, Athelstan?'

The friar stared in disbelief. 'Eudo!' Athelstan clasped the newcomer's hand. 'Eudo Camois, or Brother Luke as I knew you in the novitiate. I heard . . .'

'You probably heard right, Brother. Luke the Dominican priest who became a forger and a counterfeiter, defrocked and rejected by the followers of Saint Dominic, yet greatly appreciated by the noble Duke Ezra.'

'You are the Herald of Hades?'

'And a little more,' came the sardonic reply.

Athelstan stared at this former Brother who had won a reputation as an astute scholar and a brilliant calligrapher even though this had proved to be his path to perdition. Luke had fallen from grace. Athelstan could well understand the temptation: forged licences, letters, charters and memoranda were a constant and very rich source of gold and silver. Cranston introduced himself then turned away to order. The herald went back into the shadowy inglenook to collect his small chancery pouch and rejoined them just as the scullion served their table.

'The business in hand?' Cranston demanded, making himself comfortable.

'Ah, yes. The business in hand.' The herald sipped from his tankard and stared around the tap room. 'I have to be careful.' He grinned. 'Gaunt or the other gang leaders would pay well for what I know. Anyway, Duke Ezra has told me all. Now,' he lowered his voice, 'the Oudernardes? They have been very busy in Ghent, the city of Gaunt's birth.' He sipped from his tankard. 'There have been great stirrings there . . . rumours.'

'About what?' Athelstan asked.

'As you know, the Flemings are Gaunt's allies; he needs them to threaten France's northern border. He also needs Fleming money but that's politics. The rumours are different. I heard about those severed heads; that of an old woman and young man, yes?'

Cranston agreed.

'Tongues plucked out?'

'So I believe,' the coroner replied.

'Decapitation is punishment enough. The removal of a prisoner's tongue beforehand signifies the victim has committed slander.'

'And?' Athelstan asked.

'They were mother and son.' The herald continued to whisper. 'She was a midwife, he a scrivener attached to the cathedral in Ghent, a letter writer, a drawer up of bills and memoranda. Now, according to rumour, she claimed that in the year of Our Lord 1340—'

'The year of Gaunt's birth?' Cranston demanded.

'Yes, remember Edward III and his wife Philippa of Hainault were in Ghent. Philippa's pregnancy was reaching its fullness. The accepted story is that she gave birth to the Prince who now calls himself Regent and uncle to the King. But there is another story,' the herald laughed sharply, 'repeated by the former owners of those two severed heads, that Queen Philippa did not give birth to Gaunt but to a female child. No, no, no,' the herald raised a hand to still their protests, 'that's what rumour dictates. The hush and push of a whisper which crept from the birthing room at the convent of Saint Bavin in Ghent where Philippa had settled some months before her confinement.'

'But why such a rumour?' Cranston demanded, intrigued by this royal scandal. 'King Edward already had three sons – why was it so important to have a fourth?'

The herald pulled a face. He was about to speak when the tavern door opened and two local beggars who plagued Cranston's life slid into the tap room. Before the one-legged Leif could hop over, accompanied by Rawbum who as usual was loudly complaining about the savage burns to his backside caused by sitting on a pan of boiling oil, the coroner twirled each of them a coin. Both beggars, praising Cranston in his public and private parts to the ceiling, ensconced themselves safely on the other side of the tap room.

'There was something wrong with the child, wasn't there?' Athelstan asked. 'It must be that. Edward III never lacked sons.'

'Brother, you can read my mind,' the herald agreed. 'Rumours, or so I learnt, claim the child was disfigured by a great purple birth mark here.' The herald traced the right side of his face from brow to chin. 'We all know,' the herald continued, 'how the Plantagenet brood prides themselves on their golden hair, fine figures and handsome faces. This disfigured child, according to whispers, was regarded as a cuckoo in the royal nest. Philippa, or so the story goes, panicked and changed her disfigured daughter for the lusty son of a peasant. This story is as old as Gaunt, some forty years. However,' he sipped from the tankard and stared round the tavern, 'the story was always kept confidential.' He tapped the side of his nose. 'Only those in the know but,' he drew a deep breath, 'the Upright Men have suborned leading men in both the city and at court.'

'The Upright Men learnt about this rumour?' Cranston asked.

'True, Sir John. The Upright Men sent their agents to Flanders hunting for a possible weakness, above all evidence, eager to sift among the debris of yesteryear.' He smiled. 'My master Duke Ezra thought he'd also join the others snouting around this trough of rich, royal pickings, which is why he sent me to Ghent. I'm not too sure if the Upright Men were successful but they certainly found out about the heads and Gaunt's mysterious prisoner. Can you imagine, Sir John, if this did become public knowledge and was trumpeted abroad. How Gaunt the great Lord, the enemy of the Commons, is no more than a mere peasant himself with no right to any power?'

'But this is all a lie.' Cranston shook his head. 'Scandal, gossip and rumour flourish as thick as weeds about royal births and deaths. Look at the fate of Edward II, supposedly murdered in Berkley Castle. Stories still circulate that he in fact escaped and became a hermit in a monastery in northern Italy.'

'Ah, yes, but here there is proof. Someone who may claim that she, not Gaunt, is the true child of Edward III – that she was born of a queen who abandoned her in a Flemish convent.' The herald hunched closer, his voice falling to a whisper, long, bony fingers jabbing the air. 'I confess,' he struck his breast in mock sorrow, 'that this is only hearsay, but remember, Sir John, the mysterious prisoner was hooded and masked. Why is that? Is it because she has more than a passing resemblance to either Edward III, Philippa or both?'

'True, true,' Cranston murmured. 'I knew Philippa very well; I once wore her colours at a tournament. I'd certainly recognize Philippa's daughter if I met her. Philippa was quite distinctive in her looks, small and dark.' Cranston's fingers flew to his lips, 'Oh Lord and all his angels!' he exclaimed.

'What is it, Sir John?'

Cranston tapped the side of his face. 'If I remember correctly,' he whispered, 'I heard a rumour that such a birth defect did appear in Philippa's family. I'm sure. John of Hainault, who joined our Queen Isabella in her invasion of England in autumn 1326, a redoubtable knight, a fierce warrior, also had that purple birth mark here on his right side going down on to his neck.'

'Be that as it may,' the herald continued, 'that old woman who lost her head, the midwife, was also living proof. She allegedly claimed to be living in the convent at the time as a handmaid to one of Philippa's ladies. She actually witnessed the exchange.' He shrugged. 'Whether that's true or not, I cannot say. God knows what she intended. However, she gave such information to her son the scrivener, who drew up one of those anonymous hand bills which, as you know, are usually nailed to a church door or a public cross. Was it to be blackmail, disruption for the sake of it or just to arouse public interest? However, the Oudernardes, through their own scrivener Cornelius, heard of this, and both mother and son were arrested and brutally tortured.'

'How do you know this?' Athelstan asked.

'How do you think, Brother? Duke Ezra has his allies in Ghent – they too have gangs. I spoke to no less a person than the torturer Cornelius used to question both mother and son. He's a mute.' The herald grinned. 'But unbeknown to his master, he is a former monk, a Carthusian, very skilled in the sign languages such monks use in their priories.'

'And you, my friend,' Athelstan smiled, 'are just as skilled, if I remember correctly. Anyway, what happened then?'

'Both confessed and provided the whereabouts of the woman whom they claimed to be the King's daughter. She was sheltering in the same house she was born in, Saint Bavin outside Ghent. Oudernarde sent urgent messages to Gaunt and, at the same time, seized and imprisoned the woman. She wasn't ill-treated but the mother and son were no longer needed. They were hustled out to a lonely wood, their tongues plucked out, their heads severed. Gaunt of course wanted to see their heads as proof. Above all, he wanted to meet that woman,' the herald spread his hands, 'so the Oudernardes journeyed to England. Of course, the Upright Men, like the hungry lurchers they are, keenly followed the scent. Gaunt's other agents were also busy, not just the Oudernardes but the Straw Men as well.'

'What?' Athelstan leaned across the table. 'What are you saying?'

'The obvious, Brother Athelstan. The Straw Men are Gaunt's agents. They are his spies, that's why he patronizes them. They are very good at it. Master Samuel is a collector, a sweeper up of rumour and gossip. They are suited to such work. They travel from hamlet to hamlet, to this village or that; they perform in chapels or churches, castles or manor houses, priories or monasteries. Samuel was once a member of Gaunt's household. He's now well placed to listen to the whispers in the shires around London: the power in strength and numbers of the Upright Men, the names of local leaders, what weapons are being collected and where they are stored.'

'Like the breeze,' Cranston murmured, 'you are right. The Straw Men come and go where they please.' The coroner shook his head. 'Do the Upright Men know this?'

'They may well suspect.'

'Which is why,' Athelstan spoke up, 'the Straw Men have suffered.'

'I have heard about the murders in the Tower.' The herald picked at the crumbs on Cranston's platter. 'Certainly punishment is being meted out to Gaunt and his minions, both Fleming and English, while his authority is publicly mocked.

'And that includes the Wardes being murdered, an entire family?'

'Strange.' The herald raised his hands in a gesture of peace. 'From the very little I know, the Upright Men were not responsible for those slayings.'

Athelstan nodded his agreement. He entertained his own suspicions about who was spying on whom. The herald drained his tankard and got up. He shook Cranston's hand. Athelstan rose and they exchanged the *osculum pacis* – the kiss of peace. The herald stepped back, tears in his eyes. 'You must think, Brother, that I lost my vocation. The truth is I simply found it. I tell you this, my friend: Gaunt, the Upright Men, the great lords of the soil, the poor earthworms – the revolt gathers pace.'

'I know,' Athelstan conceded, 'as I suspect you are going to warn me.'

'No, Brother, far from it.' For a brief second the herald's face grew soft, losing that sardonic twist. 'I always liked you, Athelstan. I won't give you warnings or advice, just a promise.' He stretched forward, pulled Athelstan closer and whispered in his ear. 'On the Day of the Great Slaughter,' the herald hissed, 'when the strongholds fall, I will protect you.' He stepped back, hands raised in peace. '*Pax et Bonum*, Brother.' Then he was gone.

Athelstan picked up his chancery bag.

'Brother Athelstan?'

'I am going back to Saint Erconwald's, Sir John, to confront a Judas.'

# PART SIX

## 'Deperditio: Destruction'

Athelstan pushed open the corpse door and walked into the musty darkness of his parish church. Bonaventure, sprawled in front of one of the braziers, languidly lifted his head then flopped back. Athelstan, followed by Cranston, entered the nave. The friar crouched to scratch behind the cat's ears. He knelt, comforting Bonaventure as he stared at the pool of torchlight in one of the transepts: the anchorite and Huddle were busy drawing the chalk outline of an angel guarding the gates of Eden with a flaming sword. Both painters stopped their hushed, heated discussion and came out to meet him.

'All went well at Smithfield and Tyburn?' Cranston asked.

'As soft as spring dew,' the anchorite replied, wiping his hand. 'But you haven't come here to enquire about the souls I have dispatched.'

'No,' Athelstan declared. 'I need a word with Huddle about parish business.'

'About what?' Huddle's long, pallid face wrinkled in concern.

'Oh, this and that.' Athelstan gently guided Huddle away from the transept and up under the rood screen. No braziers glowed here, nothing but the faint twinkle from the sanctuary lamp and the day's dying light piercing the narrow windows. It was cold. Huddle began to shiver, so Athelstan went across into the sacristy and brought back one of his robes.

'Here, Huddle, for a short while be a Dominican.' The painter swiftly donned it then sat on the sanctuary stool. Athelstan brought two more so he and Cranston could sit before the now very agitated painter.

'Father,' Huddle glanced fearfully at Cranston, 'what is this? Why is My Lord Coroner here?'

'You have nothing to fear,' Cranston replied, kindly hiding his own curiosity about what Athelstan really intended.

'Sir John is my witness.' Athelstan leaned forward. 'I will whisper, Huddle. I mean you well. I have come to save your life if not your soul.'

Huddle's terrified eyes spoke more eloquently than any words. 'Father, what do you mean?'

'You are the Judas man here in Saint Erconwald's,' Athelstan accused. 'You, Huddle, who cannot resist a game of hazard, the roll of dice or the spin of a coin. Deep in debt, aren't you, and just as deep in the counsels of the Upright Men? Your fellow parishioners thought Humphrey Warde the spicer was a spy. He was nothing more than a clever distraction, a catspaw; after all, who would really trust a newcomer, a former resident of Cheapside? My parishioners blamed him for betraying their cause to Gaunt but Warde was only a conduit, wasn't he? A man who was visited by the real spy, namely you, the parish painter who had to purchase certain mixtures for his frescoes, not to mention those small oyster shells which you use as your colour dish. Or, then again, you need certain spices which are used to preserve paints and brushes. You, Huddle, had every excuse to visit Warde and you certainly did. Much safer, more logical than meeting some stranger dispatched by master Thibault, who'd soon be noticed here in Southwark or, even worse, you, Huddle, being seen with him.' Athelstan paused. 'And even more dangerous, Huddle, having to cross London Bridge to be glimpsed in that tavern or this, entering or leaving the Tower or Gaunt's palace of the Savoy.' Athelstan grasped Huddle's paint-daubed hands. 'No, Huddle, you were the spy and you passed the information on. You visited Warde quite regularly to buy this or that, be it lime or resin or some other ingredient. He could take you into the back of his house where you could talk. You delivered your information which he then dispatched to his masters at the Savoy. God knows how he did that – in a package of spices, a small tun of fresh herbs, a pannier of condiments?'

Huddle simply licked dry lips.

'It was only a matter of time before suspicion was quickened – how there must be a traitor in the parish of Saint Erconwald's.'

'But Warde was never accepted into the community,' Cranston murmured.

'No, but he was a spicer; he lived here, he could listen to the gossip and chatter which flow like God's own rain along the crooked lanes and runnels of my parish. And you helped that, didn't you, Huddle? It diverted attention from the true traitor; you'd fan the fires of suspicion while acting all righteous. Who knows, you probably offered to place a special vigil or watch on Warde through your regular visits to him.' Athelstan squeezed Huddle's hands. 'You certainly did visit him. Warde's bills testify to that but . . .' Athelstan picked up his chancery bag and took out the psalter; Huddle quietly moaned and closed his eyes. Athelstan leafed swiftly through the pages and thrust the book towards the painter who opened his eyes and stared at the page which Athelstan tapped with his finger.

'A unique picture, Huddle: Lucifer falling from Paradise. Now most artists depict Satan as a grotesque with a monstrous head, scaly body and the wings of a giant bat, dragon or some other monster. But this is most original. Look, Lucifer is still God's light-bearer, a beautiful young man.' Athelstan pointed towards the transept where the anchorite was still busily working. 'You copied such a unique idea for the wall painting you and the anchorite have just completed. You did not visit Warde to watch but to talk; you became his friend though a traitor to your own kind. You provided precious information about the Upright Men and received your thirty pieces of silver, or whatever.' Athelstan fell silent. Huddle, despite the robe, shivered so much his teeth rattled. 'Warde became your friend,' Athelstan repeated, 'so much so he let you read his psalter.'

'If Watkin and Pike discover your treachery,' Cranston had now overcome his surprise, 'friend or not, they will hand you over to the Upright Men. They will take you to some desolate place. It might be days before you die.'

'I didn't kill Warde and his family,' Huddle blurted out. 'I had nothing to do with that but, there again,' Huddle swallowed hard, 'neither did the Upright Men. Watkin and Pike swore that the Wardes had not been placed under the ban.'

'Why not?' Athelstan asked. 'I am curious.'

'The Upright Men themselves were not sure about Warde, were they?' Cranston plucked at the front of Huddle's gown. 'They too began to wonder how a spicer, distrusted by the local community, could learn so much – not just parish chatter, gossip and rumour but important matters. How did Thibault learn that an ambush was being planned on a freezing, snowbound January morning near Aldgate? Or even worse, that meeting of the Upright Men in the Roundhoop.' The coroner let go of Huddle's robe; the artist put his face in his hands and quietly sobbed.

'It's true,' he whispered, taking his hands away. 'Father, I confess. I love the roll of the dice, the chance of hazard. At the beginning of Advent I visited the Crypt of Bones.'

'A cozener's paradise,' Cranston whispered.

'At first I won my wagers.'

'Of course you would,' Cranston jibed. 'They always let you win, at first, to lure the bait, to set the trap and so catch the coney.'

'I played against Lascelles, Thibault's man.'

'Lascelles!' Athelstan exclaimed. 'Oh, Huddle, they must have been hunting you.'

'Lascelles is well known,' Cranston declared, 'for carrying cogged dice. Despite his funereal looks, Lascelles is a roaring boy and a very, very dangerous one. He would have Minehost at the Crypt of Bones in the palm of his hands.' The coroner narrowed his eyes. 'I am sure you were given the best claret, fine foods, the attentions of some buxom wench.' Huddle just nodded mournfully in agreement. 'And so the stage is set,' Cranston declared. 'You have won! You are celebrating, you are fuddled, you play again and you are trapped.'

'I lost heavily,' Huddle agreed. 'Lascelles turned nasty.'

'So what did he offer?' Cranston asked.

'To cancel my debt and receive his winnings. I became desperate. He offered me a path out of all my difficulties. I agreed but pleaded that I would need some protection. I explained how the cell at Saint Erconwald's was fast and secure. Lascelles promised that I would be given help. He told me that Warde was Gaunt's man, body and soul. He had been promised great rewards, an indenture to have the monopoly of the sale of spices to the royal wardrobes at the King's palaces of Sheen, Woodstock and Westminster.'

Cranston whistled under his breath. 'A veritable fortune!'

'Warde said he had done this before. He came to Southwark to receive information as well as report on anything untoward.'

'Such as?'

'The massing of armed men, especially along the approaches to the bridge.'

'Naturally,' Cranston declared. 'When the revolt breaks out, the bridge will be the one stronghold vital to any successful enterprise.'

'Anything else?' Athelstan insisted.

'Oh, to discover where weapons might be stored.' Huddle glanced away. 'I informed Warde how our bows, clubs, swords and daggers were all buried with Watkins' father.'

Athelstan closed his eyes and shook his head.

'You see, Brother, the plan worked. Well, at least for a while. The others never suspected. I explained how I visited the spicer to buy my own materials and used that to keep him under close watch.'

'Instead you betrayed the Upright Men at Aldgate and the Roundhoop.'

'Yes, on both occasions, the Upright Men stayed here in Southwark the day before and then moved across the bridge in disguise.' Huddle shrugged. 'Master Thibault could make of that what he wanted.'

'And the most recent attack,' Cranston demanded. 'On the Tower?'

'After the Roundhoop,' Huddle confessed, 'the Upright Men became very suspicious and wary of the cell at Saint Erconwald's but it was too late for them. I culled rumours about fighters being brought in from Essex. Provisions had to be bought, hiding places secured before they crossed the bridge.' Huddle's voice faltered. 'I passed the information to Warde that the Upright Men were gathering for an attack. That's the last time I saw Warde alive.' The artist's voice broke. 'Humphrey was a good man. He had been promised so much by Gaunt. He didn't deserve to die . . .'

'Why,' Cranston demanded, 'didn't the Upright Men drive Warde out, visit him at the dead of night, terrify him into confessing? I mean,' Cranston gestured at the friar, 'my good friend here was perplexed about that – almost as if the Wardes were protected?'

'They were,' Huddle asserted himself, 'by me – let me explain. Lascelles informed me how Humphrey Warde's stay in the parish had not been successful. He'd discovered only what everyone knew. I mean, father, it's common knowledge about Pike, Watkin and Ranulf, isn't it?'

Athelstan quietly agreed.

'The Wardes were a laughing stock,' Huddle continued. 'I was to change this. At first I gave him mere morsels about where weapons were hidden. Lascelles eventually came back. He sent menacing messages through Humphrey that he needed meat, not just the gravy. I provided information about both the Roundhoop as well as the ambush planned near Aldgate. Now,' Huddle rubbed his hands vigorously as if he was trying to wash them, 'up until then I had always protected Warde. I informed the Upright Men how Warde was stupid and to let him run. Better him, I argued, than Thibault send in someone more dangerous. Of course, that all changed after the Roundhoop was stormed . . .'

'Oh, Huddle,' Athelstan whispered, 'can't you see what you have done? The ambush at Aldgate, the Roundhoop affray and the most recent attack on the Tower followed in very swift succession. The Upright Men must have now concluded that Warde was a very dangerous spy. Worse, they will be casting about further. How did Warde acquire such information? It's only a matter of time before they turn on you, the very man who assured them that Warde was a nonentity. Yes, yes,' Athelstan murmured, 'you are wrong, Huddle. I believe the Wardes were placed under the ban but, because the entire cell in Saint Erconwald's is now tainted, Watkin and Pike were not consulted or informed. I suspect, my friend, a similar judgement has been passed against you.'

Huddle put his face in his hands and began to sob. Athelstan stared hard at this painter whom he had come to love and care for. He had shriven Huddle at Lent and in Advent. He had listened to his secret sins, about his attraction to young men and the thoughts and desires this provoked, as well as his sense of deep shame and guilt. How he tried to lose himself in the world of hazard and chance. Athelstan always heard him out and insisted that Huddle express himself in those beautiful wall paintings which brought to life dramatic stories from the Bible.

'Father, what will you do? What can I do?'

'You cannot stay here, Huddle.' Athelstan smiled bleakly. 'You know that. You have committed the sin of Judas and, whatever their cause, betrayed those who truly trusted you.' Athelstan steeled himself against Huddle's heartrending sob. 'Trust me,' Athelstan continued, 'as God made little apples, the Upright Men's suspicions about you will now be hardening into a certainty. They will not entrust judgement to the likes of Watkins and Pike.'

Huddle closed his eyes and sighed deeply.

Athelstan rocked backwards and forwards. 'Indeed, I must tell you this, Huddle. The Upright Men have their own traitor in Thibault's household. It may be only a matter of time before he learns the truth and passes such information on, if he hasn't already.'

Huddle would have jumped to his feet but Athelstan pressed him on the shoulder. 'Or worse,' he hissed, 'do you think Lascelles will let you go? Do you think just because the Wardes are dead, Master Thibault doesn't want more information? I assure you, Huddle, whether you like it or not, before the week is out you will face judgement from both camps. You are in this, Huddle, to the death.' Athelstan leaned forward and cupped the artist's face in his hands. 'So, you are truly finished here. You cannot stay in Saint Erconwald's, yet I will not, I cannot, hand you over to a gruesome death.' The friar paused to collect his thoughts.

'Father, please!'

'Listen, Huddle. The Dominicans have a house on the outskirts of Durham near Ushaw Moor. You are to go there and hide. I shall write to the father guardian, a friend, a man I trust.' Athelstan took his hands away. 'You must become a lay brother for a while. Use your talents to decorate their church.'

'And Father, what will you do?'

'I shall tell my parish council how my order has been greatly impressed by Huddle's marvellous talent. How they needed one of their churches decorated with paintings before the great feast of Easter. How you were reluctant to leave, but I was insistent. Now,' Athelstan pointed to the corpse door, 'Go to the priest's house and wait for me there.'

Huddle left, closing the door quietly behind him. Athelstan made to rise when a thud and clatter at the door made him startle. He hurried down, opened the door and saw Huddle sprawled back, eyes staring, limbs thrashing, hands clutching at the yard-long feathered shaft embedded deep in his chest. Athelstan cried out even as another arrow shaft whipped by his face to clatter against the crumbling door jamb.

'In God's name!' Cranston, crouching low, dragged both Athelstan and the dying artist back into the church, slamming the door shut just before a third arrow shaft thudded into it. Athelstan sat down on the cold paving stones gazing helplessly as Huddle, eyes fluttering, lips bubbling a scarlet froth, legs and arms shaking, choked on his own blood.

'What is the matter?' The anchorite hurried across to stare in hushed desperation at his former colleague's death throes. He knelt down, clutching Huddle's hand, but the blood welling out of the chest wound as well as from his mouth and nose showed Huddle was in his last extremities. Athelstan remembered himself. Leaning down beside the dying man, he feverishly whispered the absolution, followed by the invocation to God's angels to go out and greet the departing soul. Sir John left him to it, abruptly opening the corpse door then slamming it shut just as swiftly before another shaft thudded into the wood.

'What shall we do?' the anchorite murmured. 'What is happening here?'

Athelstan leaned across, pressing a finger against the anchorite's bloodless lips.

'You are Giles of Sempringham, the Hangman of Rochester, the anchorite. You live here by my grace and favour. You will say nothing,' Athelstan insisted, 'and I mean nothing, about what you have seen or heard today. Do you understand? If you do break confidence, you and I, sir, are finished. Do I have your solemn word?'

The anchorite nodded, raising his right hand as if taking the solemn pledge.

'Now,' Athelstan breathed, 'what weapons do we have?'

'I have a crossbow,' the anchorite offered.

'Against an assassin!' Cranston grunted. 'Armed with a war bow he could kill us in the blink of an eye?'

Athelstan gazed down at Huddle. The painter now lay quiet, the death rattle faint in his throat, the great chest wound drenched in blood.

'Was it me?' Athelstan whispered. 'Did the assassin think he was loosing at me or you, Huddle, dressed in the robes of a Dominican?' Athelstan's stomach lurched at the way death had so casually brushed him. 'Brother?' He glanced across at Cranston. 'You know what I'm thinking, Sir John?'

'God knows,' the coroner replied.

'What if, what if, what if,' Athelstan broke free from his fear, 'what if doesn't matter. A killer lurks outside. He wants to end our lives as you would snuff a candle flame. Well,' the friar wiped sweaty hands on his robe, 'Huddle is now past all caring and gone to God, while we, sirs, do have a very powerful weapon.' Athelstan rose and went across into the dusty bell tower. He seized the oiled ropes and pulled vigorously, tolling the bell, ringing out the tocsin, time and again, until he heard the shouts of his parishioners as they hurried across the icy waste outside to discover what was wrong.

Athelstan stared round the chancery chamber, shuttered and warm, in the King's lodgings at the Tower. The smooth sheen of the oval table before him glinted in the dancing glow of candlelight. Outside a stiff cold breeze clattered the shutters. Athelstan recalled the events of the previous day: the death of Huddle, the arrival of his parishioners and of course the disappearance of the assassin. Athelstan had quietened and comforted his parishioners, stayed the night in the priest's house and led Huddle's requiem early the following morning. Afterwards he had conducted the candle-bearing, funeral procession into God's Acre. The harsh soil had been broken. Huddle, wrapped in his deerskin shroud, was interred in the frozen mud. Athelstan had performed the last rites, praised Huddle's work and declared that an assassin had slain the painter for reasons known only to Satan and, Athelstan grimly added, to God. Then he had issued the general blessing for all the faithful dead but added that he intended to conduct a thorough review of burials in the parish cemetery, beginning with the grave of Watkin's parents. Athelstan had secretly smiled at the consternation this had caused but then left, hurrying across the  bridge to meet Sir John at the appointed time in their chamber at the Tower. Now, at the hour of Christ's passion and death, he had assembled those he wanted to question here in this opulent, warm room.

Athelstan breathed in deeply to control his temper. He had

stomached enough secrecy and malevolence. It was time for the truth to be defined and published. He wanted to shake and disturb some of the certainties behind which these people defended themselves. The friar glared round. Thibault, Cornelius and Lascelles sat along one side of the table; on the other were Rosselyn and the Straw Men: Samuel, Gideon, Samson, Rachael and Judith.

'Brother,' Thibault's voice was almost a drawl, 'break free from your meditations. His Grace the Regent is demanding answers.'

'In which case we do have something in common,' Athelstan retorted. 'So do I. First, however, I do not yet understand what happened during that attack at Saint John's Chapel, how Barak was murdered and thrown from that window or how Eli was slain so feloniously in his chamber. I confess I do not know who slaughtered the bear keeper, released Maximus and opened that postern gate so the Upright Men could enter the Tower. Nor can I fully account for why the spicer and his family were massacred. However, I have discovered, Master Thibault, that you have a spy or spies in the company of the Upright Men.' Thibault smirked. 'And they undoubtedly have a spy close to you.' The Master of Secrets simply flicked his fingers. 'Spies, traitors, Judas men,' Athelstan pointed at Samuel in the Straw Men, 'that's what you are, aren't you? My Lord of Gaunt's spies as you move through the countryside? You stay in this hamlet, you rest at that village, you collect information.' Athelstan raised a hand. 'No, no, please don't deny it.' He glanced swiftly at the other Straw Men: he could tell from their faces that he had hit his mark; they sat heads down, shuffling on their stools.

'Brother Athelstan?' Thibault protested.

'You are Flemish, Master Samuel?' The friar just ignored the interruption.

'What makes you ask that?'

'Nothing at all . . . pure speculation. Well, are you?'

'My mother was.'

'I thought as much. I've noticed how My Lord of Gaunt surrounds himself with people from the country he was born in. I suspect you were born in the same city and your parents had some connection with His Grace's household. You are well versed in the tongue – you must be.'

Samuel nodded warily; his eyes slid to Thibault.

'You travel to Flanders, Master Samuel and no, don't mislead me.' Samuel was now looking directly at Thibault for guidance. They are allies, Athelstan concluded. There is more between them than just miracle plays. Thibault and Samuel, when it comes to their master, think with the same mind and act with the same heart. They are Gaunt's men, body and soul, in peace and war, day and night, totally devoted and loyal to their royal master. Athelstan had met such before – men who accepted the legal concept of the emperor Justinian, '*Voluntas principis habet vigorem legis* – the will of the prince has force of law'. In other words, if Gaunt wanted something done, they would do it within the law or beyond it.

'What are you implying?' Thibault asked testily. He paused at a sudden roar from the royal menagerie. Athelstan recalled that great snow bear bursting into the inner bailey with its blood-flecked paws, gore staining its front.

'I am not implying anything.' Athelstan strove to concentrate on the fog of mystery he was trying to thread through. 'I am saying that Master Samuel and his troupe visited Flanders and travelled the roads of that country. You were looking for something, weren't you, and you found it.'

'Enough!' Thibault shouted, clapping his hands and springing to his feet. The Master of Secrets grasped the silver chain of office around his neck as if it was some sort of talisman. 'Brother Athelstan, it is best,' he indicated with his hands, 'if you all left except . . .' He gestured at the friar and Sir John. The others did. Rosselyn paused to whisper in Thibault's ear but his master, face all grim, shook his head. Once the chamber was cleared, Thibault bolted the door and sat down, patting his stomach, staring at a point above the friar's head. 'Continue, Brother Athelstan.'

'You know what I am going to say. I can't state when, but the Straw Men visited Ghent. They eventually discovered a certain lady sheltering at Saint Bavin. They later discovered, or at least Master Samuel did, that this lady, whoever she really is, had been joined by a former royal nurse or midwife, together with the latter's son, a scrivener. This precious pair were beginning to peddle the story of how this mysterious lady, to whom they had attached themselves, was really the legitimate daughter

of King Edward III of England and his wife Philippa of
Hainault, and how she had been changed at birth and replaced
by the son of a peasant because of some hideous birth defect.
The peasant boy, of course, is now My Lord of Gaunt, Regent
of England.' Athelstan paused. 'I admit this is pure conjecture.
I probably have the sequence of events jumbled or even inac-
curate, but my conclusion is that the Straw Men are your spies.
They, among others, were used to track down your mysterious
prisoner as well as the mother and son who had prepared to
publish, or at least record, what could have been an outrageous
scandal.'

Thibault continued to stare at the point above their heads.

'Master Samuel immediately informed you as well as your
agents in Ghent, the Oudernardes. They seized the former nurse
and her son, tortured them, tore their tongues out and beheaded
them. The woman, your mysterious prisoner, was then taken into
your care and, together with the severed heads of her former
patrons, brought to England. A traitor close to you, whoever that
is, divulged all or some of this to the Upright Men, hence the
attacks at Aldgate and here in the Tower.'

Thibault shifted, lower lip jutting out, a set of ivory Ave beads
now threaded his fingers.

'How did you know?' he demanded.

'I searched.'

'And?' Thibault raised his head. 'If this is all true, what is it
to you, Friar?' He smiled with his lips. 'Should you really know
such information?'

'Don't threaten me, Thibault, just let us visit this woman.'

'Why?'

'Because I am curious to see the cause of so much slaughter.
I also want to question her; she may know something.'

'Such as?'

'I don't know until I question her and if I can't,' Athelstan
shrugged, 'I also speak for Sir John – I would say we are finished
here.'

'You play with fire, Brother Athelstan.'

'I've warned you once,' Athelstan snapped, 'don't threaten
me. I am a Dominican friar. I am here by my own grace and
favour. I cannot be detained by the Crown – you know the law,

so do I. I would plead benefit of clergy.' Thibault, fingering his
Ave beads, rocked backwards and forwards in his chair.

'You are clever, Athelstan,' he lisped. 'Gaunt truly admires
you. He said you would pick up the scent and pursue it ruthlessly.' Thibault blinked. 'He also said that you and Sir John
could be trusted,' he laughed abruptly, 'which is the most rare
of virtues.' Thibault pulled a face. 'Very well,' he pointed to the
leather-bound book of the Gospels on its intricately carved lectern.
'Both of you must take the oath that you will not divulge anything
you see or hear when you visit the prisoner in Beauchamp. Once
I have your oaths, I will take you there.'

Athelstan gazed around the comfortable lower chamber of the
Beauchamp Tower. Thibault had led them through the lines of
hooded and visored archers and men-at-arms down the steps and
into this very cavernous room with its hearth fire and numerous
flickering candles. Thick tapestries cloaked the grey walls; straw
matting and Turkey rugs warmed the flag stones, while the air
was sweet with herb and spice smoke. Cranston was sitting to
his right. Thibault, for his own personal reasons, stood behind
them. Athelstan tensed as a woman came from behind the drapes
which cordoned off the small enclosure that served as the
bedchamber. She was dressed in the simple blue robe of a nun;
a starched white wimple framed her face, which she kept half
hidden behind a gloved hand as if pretending to scratch her
forehead. She sat down on the leather-backed chair, blessed
herself swiftly and glanced up, her hand no longer covering her
face. Athelstan heard Cranston's swift intake of breath. The
woman leaned forward, her small black eyes bright with curiosity
as she stared fully at Athelstan.

'You.' She pointed a long finger. 'A Dominican, an inquisitor?'

Her English was good but the accent was heavy and pronounced.
She blinked furiously, a nervous gesture. Her hand dropped and
she leaned forward again. Athelstan scrutinized her. She was dark
skinned, her eyebrows finely etched, lips pushed together as if
she was ready to kiss. She was comely enough, though the dark
mulberry stain which marked the entire right side of her face
could be clearly seen, emphasized by the starched white wimple.

'Well.' She smiled. 'Are you an inquisitor?' She glanced up at Thibault and the smile faded.

'I am no inquisitor, mistress. I am Athelstan. This is Sir John Cranston, Coroner of the City. And your name?'

'Eleanor,' Thibault answered for her.

'Not Eleanor,' she retorted. 'Call me Mara, for Shaddai has blighted me.' Her answer caught Athelstan unawares yet he was sure she was making some reference to a verse in the Bible.

'Why . . .?'

Mara, as she called herself, raised her hand and stroked the stain on her face. 'A birth mark,' she whispered, 'but when I saw the play . . .'

'The Straw Men?'

'Oh, I've seen theirs but it was at the first staged in the nave of our convent church that I recognized it – my true name. I realized God has struck me, for God knows what reason.'

Athelstan nodded sympathetically. He'd met such people before who identified themselves with individuals in the Bible, be it Mary Magdalene or Job; after all, hadn't he called Huddle a Judas? Wasn't he hunting a child of Cain?

'And your true origins?' he asked.

Mara lifted her tearful eyes, small pools of sadness.

'Brother,' she murmured, 'a curse. I always thought I was a foundling raised in that convent of Saint Bavin by the good nuns. I never gave it a second thought. I always considered my mother to be some poor woman who gave birth to me but could not nurse or support me.' She brushed her eyes with the cuff of her gown. 'That is, until Evangeline and her son arrived. They seemed fairly prosperous and took lodgings in our guest house; once settled she soon singled me out. She claimed to know the truth about me. I promise, I shall be swift.' She glanced hard-eyed at Thibault. 'I am sure the magister has related my story.'

'He hasn't,' Athelstan interposed.

'Evangeline and her son,' the words now came in a rush, 'maintained that I was the true daughter of Edward of England and Philippa his Queen.'

'What proof did they offer?'

'Evangeline claimed to be in the birthing chamber when I was born. She would repeat time and again what she alleged to have seen – how I was replaced by a peasant's son because I was a sickly girl with this mark of God on my face.'

'Did she say why she had delayed for so long in coming forward to tell you?'

'She could not answer that except to say that she had been frightened and, of course, she did not know what had happened to me. Only much later did she discover that nothing, in fact, had happened. I had been raised in the same convent where I had been born, so she waited to summon up enough courage to visit me.'

'But why? And just as importantly, why now?'

'She claimed others in England would be greatly interested in my story. She said she had that on very good authority.'

'Whose authority?'

'She said she couldn't say because she did not know their names, but Gaunt's enemies would be interested in who I really was.'

'Did that interest you?'

'Brother, I will go on oath. I am not greedy or ambitious. I simply wanted to know the truth. Perhaps Gaunt's enemies,' Mara glanced at Thibault, 'might have helped me.' She shrugged. 'Or perhaps even his friends and henchmen. The former nurse did say there were rumours that Gaunt might be illegitimate.'

'Scurrilous tales,' Thibault interrupted. 'Filthy lies about a great prince!'

'But what proof could she offer?' Athelstan insisted.

Mara, hands folded in her lap, bowed her head.

'I mean,' Athelstan added, 'with all due respect, mistress, you do not have the look or colouring of a Plantagenet.'

'I know,' Cranston intervened. Mara lifted her head.

'I know,' Cranston repeated. Athelstan sensed Thibault stiffen behind him.

'They showed me a likeness of Queen Philippa,' Mara murmured. 'Peas in a pod was how Evangeline described both her and me.' Mara glanced coyly at Cranston. 'You met Queen Philippa?'

'I did,' Cranston declared.

'And what further proof?' Athelstan asked. He felt truly frightened for this poor, desolate prisoner. Thibault was, and would be, absolutely ruthless in defence of his master. This woman would not survive another winter.

'Evangeline persuaded me to ask the lady abbess about my origins. I did so. I discovered I was not a poor foundling but left at the convent by a woman of quality.'

'Left?' Athelstan queried. 'Not born there?'

'Brother, that was forty years ago.' She shrugged. 'That's all I was told. No manuscripts or records survived. I cannot tell if I was born there and left or taken there and left.' Mara turned and sipped from a horn-shaped beaker on the side table. 'Evangeline said her son, a scrivener, would relate my origins and later story. Of course, Brother, as you know, abbeys, monasteries, convents and priories are not closed communities – gossip travels faster than a swift over the cloister garth. I began to have other visitors. Evangeline and her son paid to use the convent chancery. I began to tell them what I knew and the son transcribed it. Then one evening, just before vespers, mailed horsemen arrived in the courtyard; the Oudernardes and their henchman, Lettenhove, along with a cohort of mercenaries. They had words with our lady abbess. I believe,' her voice sank to a whisper, 'a great deal of gold and silver changed hands. All documents and possessions were seized. Evangeline and her son were taken up, as was I. I protested. Mother Superior replied that my presence was no longer conducive to the peace of the convent. The Oudernardes would find me a better place.' She spread her hands. 'And I suppose this is it.'

'You've been questioned?'

'*Tace*,' Thibault retorted in Latin. 'Silence, Brother. That is not your business.'

'You are treated well?' Cranston demanded.

'I have every comfort. I have asked Master Thibault to see a play. I know the mummers, the Straw Men, are also here in the Tower. I have heard rumours that two of them have been killed.'

'Murdered!' Athelstan declared. 'And who told you that?'

'Brother Athelstan, I have a window; servants talk. I'm sorry.' She paused as if searching for words. 'I also understand others, whom you call the Upright Men, tried to seize me.'

'Have you ever had dealings with them?'

'Never!'

'Have you ever had any dealings with My Lord of Gaunt's enemies?'

'Never.'

'So how would they know about you?'

'As I have said, Evangeline would know more about that than I . Or at least she did,' she added wearily. 'Until she lost both her tongue and head, or so I was informed.'

Athelstan crossed his arms and stared down at the floor, trying to arrange what he had learnt. He truly believed this woman was an innocent. According to her, the origins of her present misfortune lay with the former nurse Evangeline. Until she'd appeared, this unfortunate had lived in comfortable, safe obscurity. Now Evangeline may have heard rumours, but who prompted her? Had she been approached by Gaunt's powerful enemies at court?

'Brother?'

'I'm sorry,' Athelstan apologized. 'You mention the Straw Men. What do you want with them?'

The woman's face became suffused by a brilliant childlike smile. Athelstan felt a surge of pity. Mara was truly innocent; he sensed she had told him the truth and could say no more. She waved her gloved hands.

'Brother, I love miracle plays – the colour, the pageantry, the make-believe. I could sit and watch them from Matins to Compline. I would love to see the Straw Men.'

Athelstan glanced over his shoulder at Thibault.

'It's possible,' came the clipped reply. 'But, Brother, we are finished here, yes?'

Athelstan and Cranston, wishing the woman well, rose and left, joining Thibault in the freezing cold outside. Thibault led them away from the guards.

'There is a real problem here, Athelstan,' he whispered, 'I am concerned about how many people are getting to know our prisoner.' The friar turned at the sound of laughter which came from the chapel of St Peter ad Vincula, a strange merry sound in this bleak, stone-cold place, the daylight already fading.

'And what will happen to her?' Athelstan turned back to Thibault. Thibault's eyes were as cold, hard and unblinking as those of the giant raven spearing the ground nearby with its beak. The Master of Secrets pulled a face.

'*In media vita*,' he lisped, '*sumus in morte* – in the midst of
life, Brother, we are in death. Well,' he smiled falsely at Cranston.
'Sir John, when you first met our guest, you took a sharp breath
– you gasped. Did you recognize her?'

'Of course. I did see a likeness between her and Queen Philippa
of blessed memory.'

'And?' Thibault's voice was a menacing purr. 'You see a likeness between our guest and My Lord of Gaunt's mother? Which
means?'

'Don't threaten me, Thibault.' Cranston took a step forward.
'Don't put words in my mouth. Queen Philippa was a saint; she
had a better soul than you or I. What I believe, and I truly do
having watched her closely, is that Eleanor – or Mara, whatever
she wants to call herself – is the child of one of the Count of
Hainault's children; certainly not Philippa but one of the men
folk: a brother, an uncle, God knows.' Cranston put on his gauntlets. 'Every ruling family in Europe has its bastard children.
Didn't our own Henry I of blessed memory have over two dozen?
Even today . . .' Cranston's voice trailed away, in itself an
eloquent but gentle reminder to Thibault of Gaunt's own amorous
dealings with Katherine Swynford and others.

'I shall share your thoughts with My Lord.'

'Do what you want, but you have the truth already, Master
Thibault.' Athelstan stamped his feet and glanced over to the
chapel as another burst of laughter rang out.

'The Straw Men,' Thibault explained. 'Life is so gloomy here,
they are staging an impromptu masque. Sir John, you were talking
about the truth?'

'Evangeline and her son confessed, didn't they, before they
died, how their story was a complete fable? How they were arrant
liars who retracted every jot and tittle of what they had said?
Somewhere, Master Thibault, in your secret coffers lie their
confessions sworn on a book of the Gospels, signed, sealed and
witnessed. Everything you and your master need.'

'Sir John,' Thibault mocked back, 'how did you know?'

'It's surprising what a man and woman will say under torture.'

'The truth will out,' Thibault quipped. 'Sir John, Brother
Athelstan,' he wagged a finger, 'remember you are on solemn
oath. You have seen our prisoner. We now look for further light

to be cast on the murderous mayhem which laps around us. We want,' he threatened, 'the slayer of Lettenhove and the wounder of Meister Oudernarde there.' He pointed to the Tower gallows with its frozen cadavers.

'We are not finished,' Athelstan declared. 'We need to talk to Master Cornelius and you know the reason why we do? Either he or Oudernarde, or both, were present when Evangeline and her son were questioned.'

'So?'

'You reminded me that I am under oath, and so I am, but I have decided that I must see Master Cornelius.'

Thibault looked as if he was going to refuse.

'My Lord of Gaunt,' Athelstan persisted, 'demands answers. At this moment in time I can't provide any. I am unable to clear the mist of mystery which cloaks this entire matter. I need to question Cornelius.'

'About what?'

'About Evangeline and her son the scrivener. I'm sure Cornelius was present at their interrogation.'

Athelstan glimpsed a flicker in Thibault's eyes, a fleeting expression. Fear? Apprehension?

'Out of the cold,' the Master of Secrets murmured. 'Let's get out of this damnable cold.'

They adjourned to Thibault's chancery chamber. Servants provided goblets of mulled wine, their fragrance delicious, the hot steam smelling of nutmeg and crushed raisin. Thibault became interested in the manuscripts on his desk until Cornelius, shuffling like a shadow, entered the chamber.

The usual bland courtesies were exchanged then Athelstan came swiftly to the point. 'Master Cornelius, you were present at the convent of Saint Bavin outside Ghent when the Oudernardes took up, arrested, seized or,' Athelstan spread his hands, 'abducted a former royal nurse, a midwife who had served in the retinue of the late Queen Philippa. She and her son, a scrivener, were ruthlessly questioned, yes?'

Cornelius glanced at Thibault, who nodded imperceptibly.

'Yes, Brother, they were questioned. The son was useless, just his mother's mouthpiece.'

'Did she tell the truth?'

'Which is?' Cornelius stared at them in owl-eyed innocence.

'That the prisoner in Beauchamp Tower is the true daughter of King Edward and Queen Philippa.'

'They maintained that but later, under torture, admitted the truth, that she is not.'

'Of course,' Cranston intervened, 'under torture anyone will say anything.'

Cornelius just blinked like some coy girl. 'Sir John, we know the truth. She knew the truth and eventually confessed it. She was a charlatan and a liar.'

'If that was the truth,' Athelstan declared, 'why did you take it so seriously?'

'Brother Athelstan, remember your learning. A lie is a lie and can be the father and mother of even greater lies. Lies can swell like the waters of a river. Evangeline was ready to spread lies about one of Europe's greatest princes; there are those who would seize such an opportunity to create as much mischief as possible. Evangeline had to be taught a lesson, made to confess, confront the truth and be punished for her treason. Evangeline, like all the tribe of counterfeits, was dangerous. She was a filthy little spider ready to spin a cloying, treacherous web.'

'And that's my next question. Why did she lie? Why did she venture on to such a dangerous path?'

'The root of all evil is the love of money.'

'In this case whose?'

'She claimed to have been approached by My Lord of Gaunt's enemies in England, a masked, mysterious messenger who enticed her and her son out. This messenger, this envoy from Hell, promised wealth and guaranteed even more if she sought out a certain woman at Saint Bavin convent and persuaded her that she truly was a royal princess of England.'

'Who was this messenger?'

'She couldn't say. Oh, believe me, Brother, she couldn't. Trust me, we questioned her most closely.'

Athelstan stared into the man's sanctimonious face, nothing but a mask, he thought, for a very cruel soul. Cornelius, he suspected, like some of his kind, did not like women. He would truly relish the opportunity to torture one, to break her will.

'Brother, she told me that the messenger's face was all hooded.

He appeared like Satan and what he offered was too good to resist.'

'Did he say who had sent him?'

'Gaunt's enemies in England.'

'Who?'

'She did not say.'

'And what was she to do?'

'Go to Saint Bavin. Persuade, convince that woman, now our prisoner. Take her confession, write it down and record it. She was instructed to do nothing with it until "her protectors" – that's how she described them – came to visit her.'

'But you came instead?'

Cornelius smiled. 'We cut off her villainy at the very root.' He got to his feet. 'Is there anything else?'

'No.' Athelstan also rose. 'For the moment.' He blessed both Thibault and Cornelius. 'There is nothing else.'

'Well, Athelstan?' Cranston whispered once they were free of the royal lodgings. 'Are we any closer to the truth?'

'No.' Athelstan pulled his hood closer. 'Still I pray, as I always do, that God's grace will hone our wits keen. But, Sir John,' Athelstan pointed at St Peter's, 'it's wonderful to hear laughter in this grim place.'

The nave of St Peter's chapel thronged with garrison people who had assembled to enjoy the Straw Men stage an impromptu play at the foot of the sanctuary steps. Athelstan and Cranston watched from the pillared transept as Rachael, garbed in wig and robes, played the cunning wife of Herod the Great. Samuel, dressed in all the tawdry finery of a makeshift king, acted the role of her husband. Samson and Gideon played his henchmen, though now and again slipping into other minor roles. Judith was a female devil, Rachael's cunning helpmate.

Athelstan watched intently. He recognized the play as the *Slaughter of the Innocents*. The Straw Men were not staging the entire drama but presenting the earthy subplot about Herod being cuckolded by his wife. Dramatic emphasis was laid on contrasting headwear. Herod constantly grasped his crown while his wife kept a pair of horns beneath her dark murrey cloak or handed these to Judith. Samuel acted as the stiff, unbending tyrant though, once again, as he had in St John's Chapel, Athelstan was taken by how the Straw Men could shapeshift into different roles. The two women were extremely skilled at this. Rachael could alternate between an imperious vixen to a sly-eyed tempt-ress in a colourful wig as she twisted and turned like a serpent to bait and confuse her husband. She could change both face and voice, her slim but sinuous body being both regal and then, in the blink of an eye, transform into the arrogant sluttiness of a Cheapside strumpet. Many of the young men in the audience whispered and whistled their admiration as Rachael wrapped herself around the seated Herod only to slip behind him to mock with sly grimaces and the horns she held above his head. She'd then sit submissively at his feet or stand with her back to him while flirting lasciviously with someone else. Judith was equally talented. A merry but foul-mouthed demon, she could imitate the manners of a roaring boy, the mincing gait of a court fop, or the sanctimoniously prim attitude of an arrogant clerk. Athelstan noticed how swift and nimble she could be, darting around Herod's throne or climbing a ladder placed against one of the pillars. She too played the spectators with lascivious looks and gestures but was too agile for any of the men who good-naturedly tried to catch her.

The drama unfolded until somewhere in the Tower a horn wailed and a bell clanged, marking the passing hour. The masque ended. The mummers stripped off their costumes and headdresses. Some of the audience wanted more but Rosselyn, who had been watching the play intently, clapped gauntleted hands, his harsh voice assuring the departing spectators that His Grace's mummers would perform again. Samuel came up to accept Sir John's congratulations and two silver pieces. The master of players looked pale and drawn; he mumbled something about staging another masque then shuffled off, accompanied by Gideon. Cranston was about to follow but Athelstan grabbed his arm.

'I think two of our players want to speak.' He nodded to where Rachael and Samson were squatted at the base of one of the pillars, half hidden by the darkness of the transept. Rachael waved at them. Cranston and Athelstan walked across. The young woman got to her feet, her sleek body tight beneath the shabby green gown.

'Brother Athelstan,' she beckoned him deeper into the dark-ness. Cranston stayed as the friar followed her.

'Rachael, what is this?'

'Father,' she smiled dazzlingly over his shoulder at Cranston, 'Samson and I would like to be shrived. We wish to confess, to be absolved.'

Athelstan raised his eyebrows at the thickset, heavy-limbed young man who came to stand beside Rachael.

'We need to be shrived.' Samson's voice was a thick, rustic burr. 'I have not confessed since Easter, Maundy Thursday.'

'Together?' Athelstan joked, gesturing further up the transept to where the shriving chair and mercy pew stood just before the Lady altar.

'Separately.' Samson's moon-like face broke into a smile.

'Brother,' Cranston declared, 'I shall go elsewhere. I too need to be shriven but, there again,' he wryly added, 'that would take at least a week.'

Athelstan led Samson up to the mercy pew. Athelstan turned the chair slightly; they were now hidden by the creeping darkness and lengthening shadows.

'In the name of the Father and of the Son . . .'

Athelstan began the sacrament with the usual blessing. Samson immediately blurted out his litany of sins: his anger, the fights he'd been involved in, his resentments, drinking too much ale and lecherous doings with certain young ladies. 'I even have very lustful thoughts about Rachael and Judith. Father, they plague my mind both day and night.'

'Along with every other man who meets them.' Athelstan smiled. 'Even priests! Samson, Christ knows our weaknesses, but what have you really come to confess?' Athelstan tried to control his breathing; he sensed both of these young people wanted to unburden their conscience of more than just petty sins.

'The murders, Father,' Samson whispered, 'the killings, the attacks, the hangings and the decapitations.'

'You did not cause them.'

'We had a hand in it, Father! We journeyed to Ghent. We stayed at the convent of Saint Bavin. We heard the rumours. We know Master Samuel was closeted with the Oudernardes. We are not stupid, Father. We may not know the secrets, but we believe that our stay at that convent is an important part of the horrid happenings which dog our days.'

'But that's not on your soul, Samson. Samuel must answer for that.'

'There's more, Father. You were correct: we are Gaunt's spies. We travel the shires. The village people trust us. They take our pledge. We take their money and their secrets, then betray them. We pretend it's Samuel's doing but we are all guilty. That's why Boaz left our company – he was sickened by it all.'

'And where did he go?'

'I don't know, Father; perhaps deeper into Essex to join the Great Community. Father, I am finished with the Straw Men. I want your absolution and, as soon as I am able, I will be gone. These are my sins.'

Athelstan pronounced absolution.

'And my penance, Father?'

'You have punished yourself enough, Samson. Give glory and thanks to God. Do as much good as you can, as often as you can, whenever you can, to as many as you can. Now go, and be at peace.'

Rachael came and knelt at the mercy pew. Athelstan smelt the strong herbal perfume which she must have dabbed on while waiting. She recited the usual benediction in a whisper then paused.

'Rachael?'

'Father, Samson persuaded me to confess, to be shriven. He has probably told you the reason. All these killings, the Warde family, the spicers in your parish.'

'What about them?'

'How gruesome it was, that killer moving from chamber to chamber. I understand you also buried one of your own parishioners this morning. Father,' she continued in a hiss, 'we, me, Samson and the others, had a hand in all of this. We discussed our trip to Ghent, our visit to that convent. Samuel was spying on behalf of his master. I'm sickened by it.'

'As was Boaz?'

'I know nothing of that. Judith was his friend. Father, I am certain that we are all in danger from both the Upright Men as well as My Lord of Gaunt.'

'What!' Athelstan turned in the chair. 'Your own patron?'

'We not only work for him,' she whispered, 'but also for the

Upright Men. Father, think – we are nothing but strolling players. We need licences to wander the roads, to enter towns and villages or seek the help of the local parson.'

'I understand,' Athelstan murmured, 'that without those licences you could be driven from any village, harassed by any sheriff's man or bailiff. Indeed, you'd be nothing but vagrants to be whipped from pillar to post. Gaunt's protection may open many doors,' he didn't wait for an answer, 'but of course you are frightened . . .'

'Not me, not Samson.'

'Very well. Master Samuel,' Athelstan drew in a deep breath, 'like everybody else fears the Great Day of Retribution. Samuel is worried that Gaunt might be toppled so he sits and secretly sups with the Upright Men?'

'More than that, Father,' Rachael murmured, pushing her face closer, 'the Great Community of the Realm is very powerful especially in the shires around London. If the Upright Men want, they can make our life very difficult out on some lonely trackway.'

'And so Master Samuel has reached an accommodation with them. What proof do you have?'

'Father, we know that Samuel was on Gaunt's business in Flanders. I do wonder if he told the Upright Men about this. I have no real proof, Father, just a feeling. Isn't it true that, if you betray one cause, you will betray another? Isn't that why the Crown executes those guilty of treason?' She shifted the Ave beads around her fingers. 'But what does it matter, Father? Perhaps we should be called the "Judas Men" not the Straw Men. There again, we are aptly named, bending to any breeze which blows. Betrayal and treachery are our stage; we mouth words we don't mean. Father, I know Gideon is growing tired, while I'm with Samson on this. Once the Tower gates are open, we shall be gone.' Her voice lightened. 'Father, Samson and I are close. When this business is over we shall become betrothed. I just want to confess the deep resentment I feel. We are mummers, nothing more and nothing less. The games of princes should not concern us. Now, Father, please, your absolution.'

Athelstan replied with the same penance he had given Samson. Both mummers then left the chapel.

Athelstan sat staring at the slender wax taper burning merrily in front of the Virgin's statue. He reflected on the confessions he had heard. He sensed both penitents felt they had become squalid, dirty, polluted by the treachery swirling about them, the brutal deaths of their comrades, their confinement here. Athelstan moved uncomfortably on his chair. Yet something was very wrong here. Undoubtedly traitors flourished in both camps – that was a hard fact of city life. Cranston constantly talked of how the great lords of London were in secret negotiation with this faction or that. When the great revolt did occur, many merchants didn't want to see their beautiful Cheapside mansions pillaged and burnt or, even worse, be hustled out into the street for summary execution. Many of those who fawned upon Gaunt bowed and kissed his ring but kept one hand on their dagger and an eye on the main chance. So, if that was true of the powerful, why not the Straw Men?

'"This is London and everything is up for sale".' Athelstan quoted the famous proverb. '"Even souls. Yet what doth it profit a man if he gain the whole world but suffer the loss of his immortal soul?"' Athelstan gazed at the shadow-wrapped statue of the Virgin. 'Sweet Lady,' he prayed, 'please help me because it is not just as simple as that, is it? There is something else, another play here, something I've missed, something I've glimpsed out of the corner of my eye but cannot recall.'

'Father! Are you well? Is there someone else here?'

Athelstan turned swiftly in his chair. Judith had quietly slipped through the door of St Peter's and was standing cloaked in the shadow of one of the pillars.

'I'm sorry.' Athelstan half laughed. 'I was praying. I forget how nimble and soft-footed you are. I admired you performing. Come.' He gestured. 'Come into the light. Do you also want to be shriven?'

Judith picked up a stool and sat down next to him. 'Father, I don't want to be shriven. Rachael and Samson have spoken to you?'

Athelstan nodded.

'She, Rachael, should lead our troupe, not Samuel.'

'And you, do you want to leave like Boaz?'

Judith simply pulled a face and shook her head.

'I've spoken to Wolkind.' She laughed at Athelstan's puzzlement.

'The servant who looks after you and the fat coroner in the Garden Tower? Well,' Judith continued in a rush, 'he took me to the Leech as my eyes are sore, and he told me about you and your parish. He has a kinsman who lives there. You would like a mummers play? All I can say,' she paused to catch her quickening breath as Athelstan secretly marvelled at this young woman who could chatter more merrily than a spring sparrow, 'is that when this is over, I will leave the Straw Men. Father,' she grasped his arm, 'could I settle in your parish? I have some money and I could arrange my own home. Father, the others are leaving. There'll be no place for me to go. I could help you stage masques. I've served in taverns and workhouses. I am cook to the Straw Men . . .'

'Mistress,' Athelstan smiled. 'I assure you. Once this is over, I shall give your request the most favourable consideration.'

Judith, grinning from ear to ear, jumped to her feet.

'One thing, Judith . . .'

'Father, I cannot speak about my companions.'

'I respect that. You are Gaunt's spies.'

'Master Samuel certainly is.'

'Did you spy for the Upright Men?'

'I don't think so, except for one strange thing.'

'Yes?'

'Father, whatever Samuel is, he's well known as Gaunt's man and . . .' Judith screwed up her eyes. 'Father, isn't it strange? We wander the shire roads, lonely paths where the power of the Upright Men is well known. Now, we have been attacked by wolfsheads, outlaws but the Upright Men . . .'

'Have never accosted you.'

'Yes, Father – at least, not until now. Isn't that strange?'

'Yes, Judith. Yes, it is!'

# PART SEVEN
## 'Celamentum: Secret'

Athelstan crossed himself, rose, genuflected towards the altar and left the chapel. He paused at the roaring from the menagerie which carried clear on the river breeze. Maximus! Athelstan made his way out into the inner bailey, down Red Gulley to St Thomas' Tower. The entrance door was guarded by men-at-arms; one of these, eager to escape the evening cold, said he would fetch the royal beastmaster. The latter soon appeared and, seeing it was Athelstan, beckoned the friar into the cavernous cage chamber now dimly lit by torch light which jumped and spluttered in the wet breeze. Athelstan noticed how the narrow aisle past the bars had been scrubbed clean though the air was fetid. The great snow bear was not active but lay sprawled in one corner. Athelstan walked the full length of the aisle then turned and came back. He paused to examine the bar around which the great clinking chain was secured. He scrutinized it carefully and realized how quickly someone could pull back the clasp and leave it loose.

'It was deliberate, wasn't it?' Athelstan turned to the beastmaster.

'Oh, of course, Brother, we can't understand how the intruder entered.'

'What do you mean?'

The beastmaster pointed to the door leading down to the wharf, then the great gate which Maximus would go through to swim in the moat.

'They are always locked, Brother, lest anyone tries to gain entry from the river. If Artorius left by the way we came in, he always locked the door behind him. When he returned, he'd do the same.'

'But visitors? Artorius allowed Sir John and me to view Maximus.'

'Oh, come, Brother, we all know why you are here.'

Athelstan smiled and turned away. They left the Tower, and Athelstan beckoned at the beastmaster to follow.

'Whoever killed Artorius must have first persuaded him to open that door and allow him inside?'

'Yes, and I reported so to Magister Thibault. Artorius was surly; he didn't take kindly to visitors.'

Athelstan stared back at the door: of course, the bear keeper had no choice but to admit Cranston yet, even then, silver had changed hands.

'There is another problem,' the beastmaster declared. 'Artorius was an old soldier; he served at Poiters. He was quick-witted, swift on his feet and could defend himself.'

'What about some member of the garrison?'

'Artorius despised them as weaklings, while he openly resented Master Thibault and his coven.'

Athelstan thanked him and strolled back into the inner bailey, lost in his thoughts.

'Again there is a mystery,' he murmured and stared up at the darkening sky. How could someone persuade Artorius to take him into that aisle then kill him? Athelstan walked on. If he remembered correctly, Thibault had informed him that a crossbow bolt had been loosed straight into Artorius' forehead so he must have been facing his killer. Athelstan returned to his chamber in the Garden Tower. He fired the brazier, built up the meagre fire then nibbled at the dried bread, meat and fruit left on the platter. He was sure the good coroner would be feasting himself in the Tower refectory. Athelstan washed his hands, sat down at the chancery table and began to list what he termed 'the steps' leading into this mystery. Firstly, the attack on Cranston near Aldgate. Secondly, the assault on the Roundhoop. Thirdly, the murderous assault in Saint John's Chapel. Fourthly, the attack on him outside St Peter's. Fifthly, the murder of Eli. Sixthly, the slaying of the Wardes. Seventhly, the freeing of the great white bear, the murder of Artorius and the Upright Men's assault on the Tower. Eighthly, the attack on himself and Sir John at Saint Erconwald's. Ninthly, the meeting with Eleanor – or Mara – in Beauchamp Tower. Athelstan studied these steps. Was there, he wondered, dipping his quill into the ink, anything to connect all these? Was it the same one person behind all the mayhem, or most of it? Athelstan conceded that he was working on imperfect knowledge and uncertain facts. However, he reasoned, if one person was responsible for the murders, the assaults and the treachery, that person was not only a professional assassin but one who could move freely both in the Tower and outside it. Yet then again, according to what Athelstan knew, Thibault had severely restricted all passage in and out of the Tower; only he and Cranston had been permitted to leave and re-enter the fortress as they wished. Yet who had left the Tower and gained such easy entry into the Warde household to deal out death so silently, so carefully? And had the same person, armed with a war bow, struck down Huddle? If a professional assassin was at work outside the Tower, that would explain everything which had occurred beyond its walls, but Athelstan was sure that the same person was responsible for the attack on him near St Peter's as well as the murder of Eli. Athelstan curbed his annoyance; try as he might, he could make little sense of what had happened. He drank a full goblet of wine, finished the meagre platter food and returned to his scrutiny.

'If I make no progress,' he whispered, 'perhaps I am following the wrong path, but where is the right one?' Athelstan felt himself slacking. He was hungry but also tired and did not want to brave the cold outside. He prepared himself for sleep, wrapped a heavy military coat around him and lay down on the cot bed, murmuring the opening words of the sequence from the Mass of the Holy Spirit. He fell into a deep sleep, disturbed slightly by Sir John returning, but then slipped back into his dreams even as the good coroner wished him goodnight. Both were awakened, just as a greying dawn broke, by the bell booming out the tocsin. He and Cranston hurriedly dressed, stumbling out into the eye-watering, limb-numbing freezing air. Mercifully it had not snowed but what lay on the ground had hardened into a sheet of slippery ice. The sky was crystal clear, the stars beginning to disappear. Somewhere a night bird shrieked, answered by the bell-like howling of a dog. The tocsin continued. The tower buildings emerged out of the mist like brooding monsters. Torches flared. Shouts and cries trailed. An archer, stumbling on the ice, hurried up pointing to his right.

'Bowyer Tower!' he exclaimed, though the rest of his words were muffled and lost. Cranston and Athelstan, clinging on to each other, staggered and stumbled until they reached the circle of cressets clustered near the soaring Bowyer Tower. Cornelius, Lascelles and Thibault were already there. A man-at-arms was pointing up the side of the tower while another was pounding on its locked door. Cranston and Athelstan joined them, staring up through the gloom at Master Samuel, dressed in his robe and cloak, dangling by his neck from a thick rope lashed to some clasp in the chamber window, its shutters wide open, through which Samuel had either been flung or thrown himself. Samuel's corpse exuded its own singular horror, just swaying slightly, the toes of his boots pointed down, hands by his side, fingers slightly curled, his frosted face almost hidden by his hair. The creak of the rope and the clattering of one of the shutters provided a sombre, funereal sound.

'The morning watch found him.' Thibault, shrouded in his cowled cloak, edged his way out of his circle of henchmen. He pointed back to where the man-at-arms still pounded at the door. 'We cannot gain entry. Apparently no one else is within.' He paused as an enterprising archer brought along a close-runged ladder which could reach the window.

'Why not go through the one below?' Cranston pointed to the shuttered window of the ground chamber just beneath the swaying feet of the corpse.

'If we have to,' Thibault rasped. 'But this is swifter. Right.' He gestured at the archer to go up the ladder.

'No,' Athelstan intervened, 'I will go.' And before Cranston could stop him, Athelstan, begging the archer to hold the ladder steady, climbed up. As he passed the corpse he noticed its clothes were stiff with cold, the hands and face deeply frosted; the open shutters were also covered in a white dustiness which showed they'd been open for most of the freezing night. He reached the chamber and clambered in. The braziers had sunk low in the chilly air. Athelstan, murmuring the requiem, found a taper and hastened around the room. He lit the large lantern horn on the table. As he did so he noticed the rumpled bed, the one goblet and food platter on top of a trunk. The lights of the lantern and freshly lit candles strengthened, making the shadows shift. Athelstan scrutinized the goblet and platter but could smell nothing tainted. He swiftly surveyed the rest of the chamber.

'Thibault will sweep through this like the wind,' Athelstan whispered to himself, 'so I must be just as quick.' He examined the clothes hanging from pegs as well as a few lying on the floor. The small treasury casket crammed with coins seemed untouched. The other coffers and chests simply held clothes, belts and hoods. Eventually Athelstan discovered what he was looking for, a small iron-bound chancery coffer. He hastily sifted through its contents: bills of purveyance, indentures, memoranda and a few personal letters, as well as strange jottings on scraps of parchment made against the names of villages, towns and hamlets. 'The fruits of your spying,' Athelstan murmured. He studied these carefully but put them back. At the bottom of the coffer he found a book; it looked like a leather-bound book of hours, but when he undid the clasp he realized it was a master book of plays, masques and dramas. Samuel must have copied these from other manuscripts. He ignored the calls and shouts from below as he continued his search. He realized this was not Samuel's personal chamber, just temporary lodgings in the Tower, so there would be no secret hiding place. Satisfied that he had done what he could, Athelstan crossed to the door and studied the eyelet high in the wood. He pulled this back and peered out – it was very similar to the one in the door of Eli's chamber. Athelstan pushed and pulled back the shutter, noting how smoothly it moved. Athelstan stood staring at it wondering about the possibilities but the continued shouts from below shook him from his reverie. He drew back the bolts and turned the great key in the lock. The stairwell outside was empty and cold, its corners coated with mouldy cobwebs. He returned, took a candle and went down the stone spiral staircase. The door at the bottom was bolted and locked but the key was missing. Athelstan crouched down, holding the candle close to the ground. He caught the glint of metal then looked back at the gap under the outside door, wide enough for a constant draught of icy air. Athelstan ignored the hammering and shouts from outside. He picked up the key and studied the door to the ground floor chamber slightly set back in a narrow recess to his left. He tried the key in its lock but it didn't work. He grasped the iron ring and pushed hard; the door still held firm. From outside Cranston shouted his name.

'My apologies, Sir John,' he murmured. 'You must be worried

– I did not intend that.' He unlocked the outside door and was virtually pushed aside as Thibault rushed in, shouting at his men to search Master Samuel's chamber and cut down the corpse.

'Well,' the Master of Secrets turned on Athelstan, 'you took your time!' Athelstan glanced swiftly at Sir John, who knew exactly what he'd been doing.

'I had to look for the key,' Athelstan shrugged, 'but now you are in. Master Samuel is dead, probably suicide: the door of his chamber was locked and bolted from within. I would like his corpse laid out on the bed – I must examine it.' Thibault nodded and, pushing through the throng, tried the door to the bottom chamber.

'It's locked,' Athelstan declared, 'and there is no sign of any key.'

'Force the shutters,' Thibault shouted over his shoulder, 'and where is Rosselyn, my captain of archers? He should be here!' Thibault, followed by Athelstan and Cranston, walked up the steps. Samuel's frozen corpse had been hauled back through the unshuttered window and laid on the bed. Cornelius, who had been trailing behind them, bustled through to administer Extreme Unction. Athelstan and the rest waited until he had finished, then the friar swiftly inspected the corpse. He established that there were no wounds to the back of the head, no scars or cuts to the hands or wrists. He pulled up the ice-sodden jerkin and scrutinized the dirty white torso marked with old scars but displaying no fresh wound or injury.

'So,' Athelstan declared, straightening up, 'according to the evidence, late last night or very early this morning, Master Samuel, for whatever reason,' Athelstan pointed to the great iron clasp fastened into the wall beneath the window, 'took the rope intended for escape should a fire break out. He secured one end to that clasp; the other he tied around his neck and threw himself out of that window.' Athelstan picked up the sawn-off noose and examined the slipknot.

'Samuel would be skilled in that,' Cranston declared, 'constantly packing, lashing up coffers, baskets and chests.' Athelstan agreed and returned to the corpse to examine the deep weal around Samuel's throat. The wound was a dull red where the coarse rope had tightened and dug deep into the flesh. Turning the head,

Athelstan examined the contusion caused by the bulky knot behind the right ear. The friar knew enough about hangings, be it execution or suicide, to realize all was in order. 'God forgive me,' he whispered, 'if I can call it that.'

'Pardon, Brother?' Thibault tentatively approached the bed, pausing at the crashing which broke out below as the thick shutters on the lower chamber eventually shattered and crashed to the ground. This was followed by a sharp wail and keening.

'The Straw Men,' Cranston declared. 'They must have heard the news.'

'Master Thibault! Master Thibault!' An archer came bounding up the steps, bursting into the chamber. 'Master Thibault!' He paused for breath. '*Domine* – you must come, you must see this! Rosselyn is dead, foully murdered.'

Thibault swept from the chamber, Cranston and Athelstan hastening behind. A crowd had assembled, blocking the entrance to the lower chamber. Thibault screamed at them to stand aside then, followed by Cranston and Athelstan, entered the dark, foul-smelling room. Grey light poured through the now-open window. Two archers stood, torches held high; their juddering glow only made the sight they were guarding even more hideous. Rosselyn, dressed in his leather jacket and leggings, sat on a high stool with his back against the wall. The hood of his jerkin had been pushed back, his face all twisted, his right eye half open. Blood crusted the mouth and nose. The look frozen on his face by death was one of agony at the long rapier dagger which had been thrust deep into his left eye socket.

'Lord and all his angels,' Athelstan breathed, wrinkling his nose at the rank stench. He peered closer: the corpse's face was stained with filth, the slimy dirt on the dead archer's clothing glimmering in the torch light.

'The bucket.' One of the archers leaned down, picked up the leather pail and handed it to Athelstan. He sniffed at the fetid smell then did the same to the corpse.

'The bucket was probably left here,' the archer observed. 'Used to clean up some mess then never emptied. Well,' he shrugged, 'not until now. The assassin must have poured it over Rossleyn – he reeks like a midden heap. Why should someone do that?'

'Sharp of eye and keen of wit,' Athelstan congratulated the

archer. 'I wish I could answer your question.' He took the cresset
torch from the man's hand and paused at the cries and wails
coming from outside. Athelstan pointed at the door. 'Master
Thibault, please ensure that no one goes up to Samuel's chamber.
I would be grateful if the door to this room was closed over.'
Thibault, now clearly frightened, fingers to his lips like a fearful
child, could only nod in agreement. He went to it, shouted his
orders and came back, slamming it behind him.

'What is this?' the Master of Secrets whispered. 'Rosselyn
was My Lord of Gaunt's most trusted henchman, he kept guard
here in the Tower. He was a veteran, a seasoned soldier; how
could he be killed so easily, like some pig in a sty?' He crossed
over to the corpse: staring into the face as if the dead man could
answer. Athelstan carried the torch and crouched, scrutinizing
the corpse: the mire from the bucket had mixed with the blood
which had spouted from the pierced eye, as well as the nose and
mouth, to form a gruesome black mask.

'He certainly died swiftly,' Athelstan observed. 'The dagger
is long and sharp; it would shatter the humours of the brain.
Rosselyn was sitting down. The attack was so swift, so deadly
he'd be shocked, unable to move. Strange.' He lowered the torch
as close as he could, aware of Thibault standing beside him. 'Oh,
yes, very strange,' he mused.

'What is?' Cranston queried.

'Sir John, Master Thibault, the dagger pierced the eyelid – look
at the right eye half open. Now that could just be an effect of
death, but I suspect that Rosselyn had both eyes closed when he
was stabbed. You, sir,' Athelstan beckoned at a second archer,
'bring your torch closer.' The extra light illustrated the full
grotesque horror of Rosselyn's face: the thick veil of dirty blood,
the half-open right eye, and the dagger pushed into the left almost
to the hilt so deep, so violent that the eye had burst like an over-
ripe plum.

'Was he asleep?' Thibault asked. 'Drugged with some opiate?'

'I asked myself the same question about Samuel,' Athelstan
declared, drawing away. 'But there was only one goblet, a small
flagon and a food platter. I detected no taint. Is there anything
here?' Athelstan grasped the second torch and, holding both up,
walked round that dismal, desolate chamber with its flaking walls

and crumbling plaster, a squalid mess underfoot. There was nothing but rubbish, broken pieces of tawdry furniture and a few cracked pots and bowls. 'This hasn't been disturbed for months, perhaps years,' Athelstan commented.

'The chamber was unused,' one of the archers agreed. 'A storeroom for rubbish.'

Athelstan moved to the open window, gratefully breathing in the fresh air. He peered out; night was over but a dense mist had swept in. He examined the shutters, the ruptured clasps and shattered bar.

'I helped to break in,' the archer declared. 'The shutters were firmly clasped.'

'And?'

'We climbed in and saw poor Rosselyn. Who could do that? He would not give up his life easily.'

'What else did you find?' asked Athelstan, moving back to the corpse. He gently moved the head and felt the grizzled hair at the back. 'No blow,' he declared. 'I do believe Rosselyn was conscious and awake when he was murdered. Well?' Athelstan turned back to the archer. 'What else did you find?'

'The chamber key, close to his boot.'

'That was probably slid back under the door.' Athelstan grasped the handle of the rapier dagger, drawing it out, trying to ignore the stomach-churning plopping sound, not to mention the blood and mucus which seeped out. Athelstan felt his robe brush the dead man's right hand; the fingers were curled but Athelstan glimpsed the scrap of parchment pushed there. He pulled this out, beckoning forward the archer now holding both torches.

'Give it to me,' Thibault demanded.

Athelstan ignored him. He unrolled the piece of parchment and loudly recited the doggerel verse scribbled there.

'When Adam delved and Eve span,
Who was then the gentleman?
Now the world is ours and ours alone,
To cut the Lords to heart and bone.'

'The Upright Men!' Thibault rasped, plucking the parchment from Athelstan's fingers. 'But how could they gain entry here? How could they trap and kill a man like Rosselyn? Look around you, Athelstan, there is no disturbance no signs of struggle or any resistance. Rosselyn must have been drunk or drugged.'

'I don't think so.'

'Then how?' Thibault demanded. 'What in God's name was he doing here in the first place? Did he kill Samuel?'

'How could he?' Cranston asked. 'Samuel's chamber was locked and barred from the inside.'

'For the moment,' Athelstan declared, 'I cannot answer these questions. Master Thibault, have both corpses taken to the Tower infirmary – they should be stripped ready for shrouding. I must examine each again before they are coffined. God knows if that might reveal anything more of this mystery.'

Athelstan settled himself comfortably in the chair in Thibault's council chamber in the royal lodgings. Cranston sat to his right, while the rest were grouped around the table. The Straw Men, Samson, Rachael, Judith and Gideon were distraught at the death of Master Samuel, their tear-streaked faces ashen, strips of black mourning cloth tied to their clothes. Thibault, sitting at the far end, appeared distracted. Lascelles, standing behind him, constantly fingered the pommel of his sword. Cornelius threaded Ave beads as if lost in his own devotions. Athelstan sensed some of this must be pretence, people wearing masks to confront others wearing masks. He was utterly convinced that Rosselyn's killer was here in this chamber and, despite appearances, even Master Samuel's. Athelstan was convinced that there was something very wrong with that apparent suicide, though what he couldn't say. He drummed his fingers gently on the leather master book of plays taken from Samuel's chamber. Thibault had allowed that as he had permitted Athelstan to search Rosselyn's narrow chamber. He and Cranston had discovered nothing though that came as no surprise; he suspected that as soon as Rosselyn's corpse had been discovered, Thibault's henchmen would have scrutinized the dead archer's belongings. Knowing what he did of Thibault, Athelstan accepted that the Master of Secret's minions, be it Rosselyn or Samuel, would be under strict instruction to keep as little as possible in writing. After all, what was said in secret could never be traced. The friar had also examined Rosselyn's naked corpse in the Tower infirmary, but apart from that hideous wound to the left eye he could discover nothing to explain the archer's mysterious death. Samuel's naked corpse had also failed to produce any fresh evidence.

'Brother Athelstan,' Thibault called out, 'we are waiting.'

'So is God,' Athelstan retorted, 'for the killer I hunt.' The friar gathered himself, steeling his mind, will and soul to concentrate on the task in hand.

'Master Samuel's chamber,' he began, 'was locked and secured from within. No secret entrances or passageways exist. After apparently securing the door to his chamber and drinking a little wine and eating some food, Samuel took that rope and ended his life. Why?' He turned to the Straw Men, who could only gaze tearfully back.

'Did you meet Master Samuel last night?'

'No.' Rachael shook her head. 'He retired very early. He left Gideon, Samson, Judith and myself playing chequers in the refectory with some of the guards. Eventually, when we retired,' she turned to her companions, 'the chapel bell was tolling the end of the day.'

'And did Samuel betray any dark mood?' Cranston asked.

'No,' Samson replied, lower lip jutting out, 'he was quiet and withdrawn, but then again, so are we.' He waved a hand. 'This business . . .' His voice trailed away.

'Brother Athelstan,' Gideon said forcefully, 'we know nothing.'

'Master Thibault, do you?'

Gaunt's Master of Secrets still seemed profoundly shocked by Rosselyn's brutal murder.

'I hardly spoke to Samuel,' Thibault murmured. 'There was no need. How was all this done?'

'According to the evidence Samuel committed suicide.' Athelstan took a pair of Ave beads from his wallet, fingering the cross. 'Rosselyn, on the other hand, was lured into that chamber by someone close enough, swift enough to drive that rapier blade deep into his left eye. Now,' Athelstan stared round, 'what was Rosselyn doing there?' Nobody replied. 'Why did he have his eyes shut?' Athelstan let the silence hang for a while. 'Was he drunk or drugged with some opiate?' Athelstan cleared his throat. 'How could a veteran warrior be killed so expertly with no sign of any struggle? And why did the assassin abuse Rosselyn's corpse by throwing that bucket of filthy water over him? The murderer came and left like a thief in the night, locking the door behind him, pushing the key under the door. He did the same to the outside entrance.'

'Surely,' Rachael spoke up, 'it's a strange coincidence that both men died in the same tower? Samuel committing suicide in the chamber above, Rosselyn murdered in the room below.'

'Were there guards, sentries?' Cranston asked.

'Sir John,' Thibault beat his fingers against the table, 'the weather is freezing cold, the nights are as dark as pitch . . .'

'And the supervision of the evening watch?' Lascelles spoke up abruptly.

'Was Rosselyn's charge, yes . . .?'

'Yes, Brother.'

'Master Cornelius,' Athelstan asked, 'you will see to the burial of both corpses?'

The chaplain murmured he would. Athelstan picked up the book of plays. 'I think I am finished here for the while.' He made to rise but Thibault gestured at him to sit.

'Brother Athelstan, Sir John, I need to speak to you alone.'

'Wait.' Athelstan held up a hand as the rest rose. 'Tell me now: is there anything anyone knows that will cast even a glow of taper light on these mysteries?' Athelstan stared down at the floor. 'Silence again,' he murmured, lifting his head. 'Ah, well, Master Thibault, you want words with us.'

The Master of Secrets just nodded. He had a hushed conversation with Cornelius about both victims having a requiem Mass in the Tower chapel followed by swift burial in the adjoining God's Acre. Once the luxurious chamber was emptied, Thibault leaned his elbows on the table.

'My Lord of Gaunt will not be pleased.'

'And neither are you,' Athelstan retorted brusquely. 'Your spies among the Upright Men, the painter Huddle and the Wardes lie dead and buried but the traitor close to you remains hidden. That is your concern, is it not?' Thibault raised a hand in agreement.

'I never dreamed,' he breathed, 'to nurture a viper.'

Athelstan felt tempted to reply that those who play above viper holes should not object if they get bitten, but discretion was the better path.

'Master Thibualt,' Athelstan rose to his feet, 'I understand your concerns. I shall do what I can.'

'What can you do?' Cranston asked once they had returned to their own chamber.

'Pray,' Athelstan retorted, 'reflect and think.' The friar was true to his own word. He washed, shaved and changed his robes, then walked over to celebrate Mass in St Peter's chapel. The only congregation was the coroner and a young lady whom Athelstan had glimpsed before because of the brindle-coloured greyhound which followed her everywhere. After they had broken their fast in the refectory, Cranston announced that, despite the freezing weather, he was off to the city. Athelstan accompanied him to a postern gate in the south-east wall, bade him farewell and trudged back across the ice. A group of children were playing 'Hodman Blind', shrieking at the boy who was Hodman not to lower the blindfold and keep his eyes shut. Athelstan watched them for a while then continued on to his own chamber. He made himself comfortable and reviewed the steps he had already constructed, adding two more: Samuel's apparent suicide and Rosselyn's gruesome murder. The friar brooded over his collection of facts but could see no logic or order. He took the book of plays from his chancery satchel and leafed through the pages. He enjoyed reading the transcripts of miracle plays and the plots of the different masques. He paused at one, his eye caught by the word 'gleaning' and the list of characters: Boaz, Mara, Naomi and Ruth. Athelstan crossed himself; his belly tingled with excitement as he studied the short play, ideal for any hamlet square or the nave of its church.

'Of course, the Book of Ruth,' he whispered. 'Oh, Lord, save me.' He scribbled a note on a scrap of parchment, got to his feet, threw a cloak about him and searched out Master Thibault in the royal lodgings. The Master of Secrets caught Athelstan's excitement; his eyes narrowed as he clasped the friar's hands.

'Brother, what is happening?'

'Not for now, not for now, Master Thibault, but I need two favours.' He handed across the scribbled note. 'Please give that to Lady Eleanor, your mysterious guest, and ask for an immediate reply.'

'And secondly?'

'I need a copy of the Bible, the Vulgate as translated by the blessed Jerome.' Thibault took the scrap of parchment, still trying to press Athelstan on what was happening but, when the friar refused to answer, he promised the Bible would be brought immediately to Athelstan. Within the hour both requests had been answered and Athelstan stood before the lectern in his chamber. He hurriedly turned the stiffened leaves of the Bible until he found the Book of Ruth. He swiftly read the story of how Ruth, a Moabite woman, was widowed but when Naomi, her mother-in-law, decided to leave Moab for Judah, Ruth, the loyal daughter, insisted on following. What happened next led to Ruth becoming an ancestor of David from whose line the Messiah came. Athelstan read the story carefully. He listed all the characters and returned to the 'steps' he had drawn up beginning with the attack near Aldgate. He tried to fit into each one a possible assassin but he could not establish a logical development. Frustrated, he tried again and again until he flung the quill pen down, took his cloak and tramped round the Tower. He visited the scene of each murder, hoping to recall who was where and doing what. He stayed sometime in the chapel of St John, sitting at the base of one of the pillars, staring through the cold darkness trying to visualize what had happened. The crossbow bolts whirling so swiftly, the dramatic appearance of those severed heads. He racked his brains as he recalled who was where, who had fled and who had stayed. He stared around the oval-shaped chapel, concentrating on how the top half near the rood screen had so swiftly emptied after the attacks. So how, he thought furiously, had they been carried out? The only logical conclusion he could reach sent him scrambling to his feet. He hurried back to his chamber where Cranston sat toasting his toes before the fire as he savoured what he called, 'the sweetest chicken leg in London with the claret to match'.

'There are two of them!' Athelstan exclaimed, shaking off his cloak and sitting down at his chancery desk.

'Most chickens do have two.'

'No, no, no,' Athelstan laughed, 'two assassins, Sir John, not one. Stupid, stupid friar,' Athelstan continued. 'I did think of this before but dismissed it too soon. I forget my logic: never dismiss a possibility until it's proved to be impossible.'

'Ah, well,' Cranston murmured. 'Perhaps perfection can never be found beyond a well-roasted chicken. Brother, are you sure?'

'Yes,' Athelstan smiled over his shoulder. 'Two killers, but which two?' Athelstan concentrated on building a logical argument based on the syllogism that there were two assassins. He worked late, absent-mindedly informing Cranston that he would eat and drink anything the coroner brought from the Tower buttery. Athelstan did so and returned to his studies, working until his eyes grew so heavy he began to nod off over the scraps of parchment littering his desk. The following morning he celebrated his Jesus Mass, broke his fast and returned to his syllogism. Sir John tried to question him but Athelstan kept bringing the conversation back to the 'steps' he'd constructed, urging Sir John to recall all the details he could.

Eventually, as early evening crept in, Athelstan made his decision. He stared at the names of possible culprits, yet what evidence could he produce? Moreover, he had failed to resolve how Eli and Rosselyn had been murdered or if Master Samuel had truly committed suicide. Athelstan now realized what had happened at the Roundhoop, the attacks on himself both here and St Erconwald's, the massacre of the Wardes, the freeing of the great snow bear and the Upright Men's assault on the Tower. Yet Eli and Rosselyn's murders remained an enigma. How had that young man been killed by a crossbow bolt in a locked, barred chamber? No opening could be found. The eyelet had been fastened shut, stuck hard in an ancient door by the passage of time, the chamber shutters barred so the assassin could not have escaped by the window. Or Samuel's apparent suicide. If he had been murdered, why was there no mark or violence in his chamber or on him? The assassin could have climbed down using both rope and corpse to reach the chamber below but what then? And Rosselyn, found sitting in that lower chamber with a dagger piercing his left eye? The evidence pointed to Rosselyn's eyes being closed. Was he sleeping? Yet as a veteran soldier he would have been very alert to any danger. He could have been drugged with some opiate, yet there wasn't a shred of evidence for this. And why had the assassin drenched him in that filthy water which reeked like a midden heap? Why did Rosselyn close his eyes? When did anyone close their eyes? Athelstan recalled the children playing Hodman's Blind. Athelstan then wrote on a scrap of parchment: When would any adult close his or her eyes outside of sleep? When did he? Athelstan began to list these and abruptly paused at a surge of excitement. He had it! He returned to Eli's murder and that of Rosselyn. Yes, he had it! He was sure. He had unmasked the culprits, the two assassins, except for why they had been killed.

Athelstan waited until Sir John returned from his 'devotions' in the buttery; he asked him to search out the surveyor of the King's works in the Tower and make enquiries about the door to Eli's chamber. Athelstan now concentrated on drawing up what he called his bill of indictment. Cranston returned with the answer Athelstan already expected. He quietly congratulated himself and continued his summation, steeling his will against the heinous consequences of his conclusions. Once finished, Athelstan revised his 'billa'. He did this time and again then turned to the coroner.

'Now,' he said quietly. Cranston, sitting on the edge of his bed, put down the book of plays and stared at the friar.

'Now what, Brother? Soon it will be dark.'

'And we must be gone, Sir John, the sooner the better from this benighted place. Do not cause any alarm or provoke the suspicions of Magister Thibault or his henchmen. Quietly seek out the Straw Men and bring them to me, please.' Cranston dressed and swept out through the door. Athelstan prepared the chamber, placing a stool in the centre of the room between the two beds. He cleared the chancery table, pushing the sheets and scraps into his chancery satchel, and waited. Cranston returned with the four woebegone players. Athelstan could only secretly marvel at the sheer skill of the assassin's acting. He greeted all of them, warmly asking Samson, Gideon and Judith to leave and wait in the refectory until he'd finished asking Rachael a few questions about Master Samuel. All three looked puzzled but shrugged and left. Athelstan waved at the stool, asking Rachael to sit while he took her cloak, offered her wine and complimented her warmly on her fresh gown of dark murrey. The young woman, her glorious red hair falling thickly either side of her lovely white face, watched intently, her green eyes slightly slanted, hard and unblinking despite the smile on her pretty lips.

'Mistress Rachael?'

'Brother Athelstan?'

'When did we first meet?'

'Why, Brother, here in the Tower, Saint John's Chapel.' She rounded her eyes. 'Remember?'

'Oh, I do. As I remember the plump whore in the Roundhoop all dressed, or rather disguised, in her orange wig and tawdry finery. That was you, wasn't it? Yes, that's when we truly first met.'

'Brother, why should I be there?'

'To meet your lover, Boaz.'

The smile on the woman's lips faded.

'Boaz,' Athelstan continued evenly. 'That was his name. Your lover, a former member of the Straw Men who had grown sickened of what he saw and heard. He'd become tired of being Samuel's lackey who, in turn, was that of Magister Thibault, My Lord of Gaunt's Master of Secrets. A true serpent, Thibault, using a troupe of strolling mummers to spy on the villages and communities they entertained.'

'I told you that they also . . .'

'Oh, by the way, I don't believe that Samuel had anything to do with the Upright Men. He was always Gaunt's man; that was your lie to distract me. The Upright Men left your company alone, satisfied to have two of their following in it – you and Boaz.'

'My confession to you,' she glanced sharply at Cranston, 'was under the seal of the Sacrament.'

'And it remains so. I am just commenting on the possibility that Boaz was an Upright Man who slipped away to join his comrades. He and you formed a pact. He would leave while you would remain with the troupe to keep everything under watch. The Upright Men would be pleased with that. You truly loved Boaz, didn't you? He took his name from the Book of Ruth in the Old Testament. In that story Boaz falls deeply in love with the Moabite woman, Ruth, and she with him. They met when Ruth was gleaning Boaz's fields behind his reapers. In both your eyes, their story was being re-enacted in your lives. You were his Ruth, weren't you?' Athelstan stared at this young woman, a true killer, yet her great tragedy was that a fiercely fatal and frustrated love had turned her so.

'You both played your part in a deadly masque even as you

staged the Bible story here and there and, above all, in the convent of Saint Bavin's at Ghent where the woman Eleanor, now Thibault's prisoner in Beauchamp Tower, was sheltering. She had seen the play before but was much taken by your interpretation. Indeed, she identified herself with one of the characters, Naomi, Ruth's mother-in-law. Like Naomi, Eleanor changed her name to Mara, meaning "bitterness" because God,' Athelstan touched the side of his face, 'had marred her skin. She had also become the plaything of those who wished to meddle in My Lord of Gaunt's murky and very dangerous pool of politics.'

'We agree on some things, Brother.' The reply was icy, belying the smiling mouth.

'Once Samuel returned from Flanders,' Athelstan continued, 'he moved to the shires. Your beloved Boaz, however, could tolerate it no longer. He left the company of the Straw Men but not before swearing his love for you. Perhaps he quoted that marvellous hymn of loyalty from the Book of Ruth, how does it go?' Athelstan closed his eyes.

'Wherever you should travel, I shall travel,
Wherever you live so shall I,
Your kin shall be my kin,
Your God shall be my God,
I shall die wherever you shall,
There shall I be buried.
Let Yawheh send all kinds of ills against me,
And more if need be,
If anything but death should separate me from you.'

# PART EIGHT

## *'Dissultus: Severance'*

A thelstan abruptly opened his eyes and caught a look of deep sorrow pass like a shadow across Rachael's face before it hardened again.

'You were his Ruth. She gleaned the fields, gathering ears of corn after the reapers. You did that. Master Samuel would spy on the Upright Men and you would spy on him, collecting what you could and passing it on to Boaz. Now and again he'd return to meet you secretly, as he did that January morning at the Roundhoop; a safe meeting, or so you thought. The Upright Men met. You joined them to provide whatever information you had gleaned as well as meet the love of your life. You went disguised as a city whore, a poor street strumpet, hair covered by a garish wig, face masked by thick, cheap paint, rags pushed up your gown to make you look fat, teeth blackened. You kept your head down and, when you did speak, mouthed the patois of the slums.' Athelstan spread his hands. 'You are, Mistress Rachael, a most skilled mummer, a player who can shift in both substance and shape. You have all the paints and disguises at your disposal. You not only posed as a city whore but as the strumpet of that friar of the sack who, in fact, was an Upright Man. Later that same day they visited me. I wondered why they took such pains to emphasize that you were just a common whore. They were in fact protecting you. All should have gone well except,' Athelstan held a hand up, 'the meeting had been betrayed, probably by spies in Saint Erconwald's. The Roundhoop was surrounded. Thibault was desperate to defeat the Upright Men and retrieve those severed heads seized during the ambush at Aldgate. I was brought in to negotiate. In truth, I was only Thibault's catspaw, a diversion. The Roundhoop was stormed. The Upright Men fought back; in all that carnage who would care for an ugly city whore? One of the Upright Men, I believe it was Boaz, could have killed me but he decided not to – an act of mercy. He was looking for you when he was struck down by an arrow. I tended to him as he died.' Athelstan fought to keep the tremor out of his voice. 'Poor Boaz could only think of his Ruth. In his final fever he talked of "gleaning" – he was referring to you. Even as he died he wanted one last look at his beloved. He searched past me, staring desperately.' Athelstan paused. He was telling the truth. Despite her attempt to remain impassive, Rachael's eyes filled with tears; her lower lip trembled slightly.

'He died of his wounds,' Athelstan added softly. 'In the violent struggle you escaped. Only later did you discover what had actually happened. How your beloved was dead, his corpse further abused by the removal of his head so it could be thrust on a pole over London Bridge.' Athelstan glanced at Cranston who sat on the edge of his bed, watching intently. The coroner was used to Athelstan's ways and waited for the conclusion. 'You were always sympathetic to the Upright Men.' Athelstan sipped from his goblet of watered wine. 'Now you changed. No longer a gleaner but a reaper, and a fearsome one indeed. You wanted revenge on Gaunt and all his ilk, as well as inflict vengeance on your comrades.'

'Mistress,' Cranston spoke up, 'you have nothing to say to counter all of this?'

'The play is not done yet,' she retorted, her eyes never leaving Athelstan. 'Every mummer has his lines.'

'You entered into a solemn compact with the Upright Men,' Athelstan declared. 'They would trust you as Boaz's helpmate, his lover. They would relish your hunger for vengeance, to wreak havoc however, whenever, wherever you could. They decided to bring you into close alliance with their own spy high in the councils of Master Thibault.'

'Who?'

'Why, mistress, you know, you killed him – Rosselyn, captain of archers.'

Rachael threw her head back and laughed. 'Rosselyn!' she exclaimed. 'Thibault's man body and soul. Brother, surely?'

'Oh, yes, surely, mistress. Rosselyn was of peasant stock – he would not find it difficult to be sympathetic to the earthworms. More importantly, like many in this city, he was preparing against the evil day, the hour of reckoning. To put it succinctly, Rosselyn had a foot in either camp. The Upright Men wanted to ensure that he was with them. I suspect Rosselyn informed them about the cavalcade bringing Gaunt's mysterious prisoner to the Tower; at the same time he could act the loyal henchman and advise Thibault to take great care, hence the summons to Sir John here to strengthen the cavalcade as it approached the Tower.'

'If that was so,' Cranston, full of curiosity, spoke before he could stop himself, 'why didn't Rosselyn warn the Upright Men about the impending attack on the Roundhoop?'

'Yes,' Rachael taunted, 'why not, Brother?'

'I shall come to that in a while. Suffice to say that you and Rosselyn met secretly here. Like pieces on a chess board, you checked each other. Neither of you could betray the other without rousing deep suspicions about yourself. As if in a play, Rachael, you would be the principal actor. Rosselyn was your support. You'd like that, wouldn't you? Directing a man such as Rosselyn as you would some lurcher in a hunt? You decided to cause mayhem here at the very heart of Gaunt's power.'

'Why would Rosselyn agree?' Rachael interrupted. 'Surely it would be too dangerous?'

'It would have been dangerous for him not to cooperate. The Upright Men could kill him or, even worse, betray him to his master. You know full well they would demand Rosselyn's complete cooperation or else . . . First came the attack at Saint John's Chapel. I was puzzled by that. How could an assassin strike twice so swiftly as well as leave those severed heads? I first believed the assault was launched from Hell's mouth wedged into the entrance to the rood screen. You are a mummer, mistress, you create illusions, perhaps that's what you intended.'

'I was there being watched . . .'

'Nonsense! Who really cared for you, a strolling player? Above all, you were helped by Rosselyn. I remember him that day in his heavy military cloak.' Athelstan picked up his goblet and offered it to Rachael; she snatched it from his hand and drained it before handing it back. Athelstan carefully refilled the cup.

'The rood screen in front of the sanctuary was a barrier, as were the heavy drapes or arras hanging on either side stretching into the transepts. You and Rosselyn waited until there was no one behind that barrier, an easy enough task on a cold winter's day when everyone was hungry and intent on food and delicious wines. Indeed, it was Rosselyn who came to invite us all to join Gaunt and his guests. I stayed. Rosselyn returned to ensure I also left. He wanted that sanctuary cleared. He was successful and moved to the next step of your plot. Rosselyn provided the arbalest, one of those small hand-sized crossbows. You went behind the arras and waited.'

'I could have been seen.'

'No, you had prepared well. Rosselyn had wedged small pouches of cannon powder into two of those braziers. The confusion caused by the explosions diverted attention. You pulled the curtain aside, took aim and, probably shielded by Rosselyn, released the catch, killing Lettenhove. Again, attention was diverted. All the guests had been distracted by the explosions; now Lettenhove's bleeding corpse was all that mattered. You moved swiftly behind the rood screen to the other side where Rosselyn had hidden another crossbow already primed, like before, a narrow gap between curtain and wall was all you needed. Everything was now in chaos. You loosed again, not as accurately as you would have wished, but Oudernarde was struck.' Athelstan turned to Cranston. 'Sir John, how long does it take to loose a crossbow bolt?'

'I could patter an Ave and not get far.'

'But the chapel was crowded!' Rachael protested.

'No. You had people diverted by explosions then by a bolt being released by you standing in no more than a slit between arras and wall. No one was behind that rood screen – Rosselyn had seen to that. As I have said, who would go there with all the food and wine on offer in the nave? Rosselyn also protected you. Did he stand in front of the gap for a brief while then step aside, providing you with a clear aim? Ah, well.' Athelstan stared across at the window. How much of this, he wondered, could he really prove before the Justices of Oyer and Terminer or King's Bench in Westminster Hall?

'Rosselyn would take care of the small arbalests by hiding them somewhere in the chapel,' Athelstan narrowed his eyes, 'or on those hooks on the war belt beneath his heavy cloak. Who would dream of searching him?'

'And the severed heads?' Cranston asked, brimming with curiosity.

'Oh, they'd been snatched from the care of Master Thibault during the attack at Aldgate. As a taunt to My Lord of Gaunt, the Upright Men handed them to you and Rosselyn to return to him. First a sharp reminder that, during the attack at the Roundhoop, Thibault did not find what he hoped for. Secondly, Rachael, ever the player, the severed heads provided you with a macabre climax to your murderous assault in the chapel.' Athelstan rolled the goblet between his hands. 'I suspect Rosselyn brought the severed heads – that's why he was so valuable. Who would distrust Thibault's captain of archers? Who would dare ask him to open a bag or a chest or even bother to note where he stored something?'

'And how were the heads placed?' Cranston asked.

'During the confusion caused by the attacks, Rosselyn collected the heads, carried them beneath his cloak and walked by the rood screen. Twice he stopped to place a head. Look,' Athelstan rose and swung his own heavy cloak about him; he then took two small cushions from a bench beneath the window, holding both up with his right hand. 'These are about the same size. I grasp these grotesques with that parchment scrap pushed deep into one of those dead mouths, and I hide them beneath my cloak.' Athelstan did so. 'Now I walk, see?' He passed his own bed and swiftly crouched twice, on each occasion releasing a cushion to lie on the floor alongside the bed.

'No more than the blink of an eye,' Cranston murmured.

'And you are watching me,' Athelstan retorted. 'Remember, we are describing a chapel where all attention had been diverted by a man being killed, another seriously wounded. Most of the guests were trying to leave the other way.' Athelstan undid his cloak. 'Of course, it could have been you, mistress, carrying some cloak or costumes, crouching down to leave those heads as if the cloths were difficult to hold or to pick up something from the floor. You could do it just as quickly, just as adroitly. Did Rosselyn screen you, or did you him? I confess I can't be precise except to demonstrate how the positioning of those severed heads would not be difficult either after the explosions or, more probably, immediately after one of the attacks.'

Athelstan fingered the vow knots on his waist cord. 'It was easily done. Attention was on the victims and, after that, the doorway: people wanted to flee. Indeed, Lascelles was ushering them away from the rood screen. I have not asked him yet; I did not wish to rouse his suspicions. However, I am sure Lascelles will confirm that Rosselyn asked him to do just that while he left to ensure all was well in Beauchamp Tower.'

'And Barak?' Cranston asked.

Athelstan stared at Rachael. She sat so composed, eyes unblinking, watching him carefully as if weighing his every word. What was she thinking? Would she have the stubborn courage to deny all this?

'Yes Barak,' she whispered, half smiling. Athelstan felt a stab of pity. Rachael was undoubtedly highly intelligent: she had been as assiduous in plotting murder as any scholar in the schools or halls of Oxford would study his horn book. A talented young woman, but had her wits turned? Had the savage death of her beloved truly twisted her soul?

'You are beautiful, Rachael, fair of form and lovely of face, graceful and lithe. You possess a keen mind and sharp wits. I have watched you play the mummer's part. You shape shift, you become whatever you want to be.'

'Brother, flattery is a perfume: you smell it but you never drink it.'

'Ah, yes, mistress, your perfume. I shall return to that by and by.' Athelstan cleared his throat. 'As for Barak? Well, he was easy for you with your winsome ways. Somehow, very soon after the attack in the chapel, you enticed him down to that long, gloomy crypt beneath Saint John's. You fled with the rest but I can imagine you separating yourself from the others, plucking at Barak's sleeve, telling him to shelter with you in the crypt. Who would notice? Or perhaps you told Barak to go there and you'd join him? Anyway, you lured him into that darkened recess. Rosselyn was lurking there. Again, I cannot say who struck the blow but Barak was hit, probably twice, to ensure he was either truly senseless or dead already. Perhaps you stood on guard while Rosselyn moved swiftly. He put the war belt around Barak. He made a mistake: the quiver for the bolts was on the wrong side, while it didn't make sense for Barak still to be carrying one of the arbalests. Nevertheless, you were intent on making it look as if Barak was the assassin. Once ready, you opened the shutters of that far crypt window. You threw out the fire rope to make it look as if Barak had tried to use it during his abortive escape but, in truth, poor Barak was hurled through that window with great force. He would be depicted as an adherent of the Upright Men, a subtle plan – the flaws in your plot could only be detected through careful scrutiny.'

'Why?' Rachael retorted. 'Why Barak?'

'No real reason. You grew to hate all of them, didn't you? What did it matter? Perhaps Barak was the easiest to persuade, to follow you into that darkened crypt. He was just a sacrifice. The real reason for Barak's murder was to spread terror, cause mayhem, deepen suspicion, proclaim that Gaunt's much-lauded acting group the Straw Men could not be trusted, that no one was safe, even in this grim great fortress. Barak was a sacrificial lamb on your altar of vengeance. Eli was no different. He too was much smitten with you.' Athelstan rose and walked to the door of his chamber. He pulled the eyelet shutter backwards and forwards, 'Strange,' he mused loudly, 'how the shutter in Eli's chamber was stuck and had to be prised loose. This one isn't. The same is true of Master Samuel's chamber. Rosselyn claimed it was a common problem yet it only occurred with Eli's chamber door.'

'But it did!'

'Oh, I agree. Do you remember when we first talked? How Samuel maintained that all members of his troupe were skilled in arms? How you had to be ready with weapons to fend off dangers on the road?' She did not answer. 'And aren't you mistress of the wardrobe? Responsible for the scenery?' Again, there was no reply. 'On the night you visited Eli? Oh, yes,' he stilled her protest, 'oh, yes you did! Just before you entered his chamber, you put in that small recess near the door a pot of glue with a small horsehair brush and another hand-held arbalest already primed. Outside that tower prowled Rosselyn to conceal and protect your coming and going. I am certain he started that fire to divert attention away from you.' Athelstan sat down. 'You visited Eli. You acted the loving wench, flirtatious and coy.'

'Why should I kill Eli?'

'First, he had sheltered beneath a table near the rood screen. Did he see something untowards, Rachael? Something he mentioned to you?' She did not answer.

'Secondly, Eli was a member of the troupe who spied for Thibault and brought about your beloved's death.' Rachael blinked and glanced away. 'I will be brief.' Athelstan hurried on. 'You made sure there was no sign of your being there. You probably drank from the same goblet as Eli, a token of your loving pledges to him. Eli must have been delighted. You were acting the fair damsel in considerable distress, shocked by the hideous death of poor Barak.'

'Eli died in a locked, barred chamber.'

'I agree. You left that chamber like the amorous wench you pretended to be. You told Eli to lock and bolt the door, to take great care; after all, a killer did stalk the Tower. You then drew him into a loving but deadly game. Once outside the chamber, the door secured, you picked up that small arbalest and knocked on the door. Eli would hear your voice and pull back the eyelet shutter – he may have even offered to let you in but you teased and flirted. The hour was late, you'd return soon enough. I do not know what lies you spun but you asked Eli, peering through that shutter at his new-found love, to close his eyes.'

'Why should he do that?'

'Oh, come, Rachael! Lovers often close their eyes when they kiss. Are there not games when you tell the beloved to close his or her eyes to wish and, if they do, you'd tell them a secret, some promised pleasure at the next tryst? Rachael, the possibilities are infinite. Eli was staring through that eyelet at this beautiful young woman who was promising to be his. He'd do anything – certainly some innocent lovers' game, or so he thought. All aflame with the wine he'd drunk and the prospect of impending seduction, of course he agreed. You played the game. You whispered that he should keep his eyes closed, not to open them until you said. You brought up that small crossbow. You released the bolt as fast as a bird across the briefest of distances; it sped through that eyelet, smashing into Eli's face. Stricken, dying on his feet, Eli stumbled away and collapsed to the floor.' Athelstan turned to Sir John. 'My friend, calculate the time it would take: Eli peering out through that squint, eyes firmly closed, the crossbow coming up, the release of the bolt only inches from its victim's face?'

'A few heartbeats,' the coroner agreed. 'Eli would never suspect.'

'Eli died,' Athelstan continued. 'You then took that pot of glue, the same substance you use in creating and setting up scenery. A few drops on the old dusty shutter and, by the time the alarm was raised, the eyelet is stuck fast. The glue had hardened, the shutter just another task waiting to be done, an ancient piece of wood in an ancient door in an ancient place.' Athelstan pointed at Rachael. 'You are not only a very skilled mummer, you are also a weaver of dreams and illusions.' Athelstan sat staring at the young woman's face. 'Very soon afterwards you removed all the evidence, didn't you?'

'What evidence? Brother, what are you talking about?'

'Well, not you precisely – Rosselyn saw to that. I checked with the surveyor of the King's works here in the Tower. Our late departed captain of archers was most insistent that the door to Eli's chamber be mended. He personally supervised it, including the eyelet. He himself freed it with his dagger, thus removing any evidence of what had actually happened.'

'Rosselyn was no friend of mine.'

'Of course he wasn't. You have more than proved that but, while he was alive, he was a useful foil for you.'

'When?' she protested. 'How?'

'I was attacked near Saint Peter's ad Vincula, when you were close by. The same is true when Maximus escaped and the Upright Men attacked the Tower.'

'Are you saying I had a hand in those assaults, that I even freed the bear?'

'Oh, I'm sure you did. Your accomplice, Rosselyn, probably helped you. He had no choice. The Upright Men, as I have said, ordered him to assist you. He had a foot in either camp. The Upright Men probably despised him for that; they wouldn't really trust him. However, for the moment, he was useful to you as well as to them. On one occasion Rosselyn took the lead. That arrow attack on us near St Peter ad Vincula? Rosselyn loosed those bolts from his hiding place near the White Tower then later appeared as the concerned, loyal captain of archers.' Rachael simply glanced away, scratching her brow.

'And the bear?' Rachael peered at him from under her hand.

'Artorius would have nothing to do with the likes of Rosselyn but he'd be very susceptible to your flirtation. I suspect

Rosselyn, in this dark, freezing narrow place, let you slip down Red Gulley to Saint Thomas' Tower. You'd be all simpering and pretty-faced as you knocked on that door. In a matter of seconds your charms and a little silver persuaded Artorius to allow you in to view Maximus. The door closed behind both of you. He would lead you off down the narrow aisle. He'd feel your hand on his shoulder and, when he turned, you loosed that bolt straight into his forehead. You took his keys and opened the cage door. You hastened out but not before you released the bear chain on the bar of the cage and left the door to Red Gulley open.' Athelstan gestured to the bailey outside. 'Maximus would be curious. He'd smell the blood of his keeper. You realized he'd soon find his way to the gore-drenched corpse of his former master then make his way out. The great snow bear Maximus was free to prowl; there was only one way for him to go but, by then, you were busy with the next part of your plan.' Athelstan shrugged. 'Either you, Rosselyn or both, once Maximus was on the loose and the alarm raised, opened the postern gate near Bowyer Tower.'

'But the Upright Men would be vulnerable to a rampaging bear.'

'I don't think so!' Cranston spoke up. 'The royal beastmaster and his retinue had one task: to check and drive back that bear. While all this was going on the Upright Men also had one task: to storm Beauchamp Tower, release the prisoner and, using the mayhem as a shield, withdraw as swiftly as they'd entered.'

Rachael stared down at her feet, tapping her ankle-length boots against the floor.

'Surely,' she glanced up, 'if Rosselyn was a traitor, why didn't he inform the Upright Men that Thibault was bringing down war cogs as a defence against any attack?'

'Very sharp!' Athelstan retorted. 'There are two possibilities. First, as with the assault on the Roundhoop, Rosselyn dare not inform the Upright Men; the number of people who knew about that would be very limited. Rosselyn was frightened that the finger of suspicion might be pointed at him. Secondly, perhaps Thibault decided to inform nobody in his entourage about what he was planning. After all, there was a traitor in his camp. Thibault is no fool; he'd have his own suspicions that something was wrong.'

'Or Rosselyn was just unfortunate,' Cranston declared. 'He was never given the opportunity. Nevertheless, the Upright Men must have been furious.'

'Oh, I suspect they were. Rossleyn's days were numbered.' Athelstan rose to his feet. 'Such is the problem with traitors.' He sighed. 'Judas discovered that, in the end, nobody really trusts you and nobody allows you back. Rosselyn wasn't your concern. You were looking after yourself. How would anyone possibly suspect the fair Rachael, who was always close by, the distressed maiden when these assaults occurred?' Athelstan picked at a loose thread on his robe, rolling it between his fingers, 'And, of course, there were other occasions when you couldn't possibly have been involved, or so you would have everyone believe.'

'What are you talking about, Brother?'

'Huddle the painter was killed leaving Saint Erconwald's Church. You, along with the others, were supposed to be detained here in the Tower. '*Quis Custodiet custodes?*' As the great Augustine said, 'Who will guard the guards?' Rossleyn provided you with the weapons and allowed you secret passage in and out of the Tower. You are a master or mistress of disguise. You followed Sir John and across the bridge and waited. A figure wearing the black and white garb of a Dominican left Saint Erconwald's, you loosed and killed Huddle.'

A smile flittered across Rachael's face.

'Or was it me that you intended to kill? Did you suspect, or were you informed, that Huddle was the real traitor? I cannot be precise about everything in this hideous affair and, to a certain extent, it does not matter now. Huddle lies cold in the soil. However, you did make a mistake over that poor painter's death as well as your other doings in my parish. What did you know of them? You talked about my burying a parishioner. You implied he had been killed – but how did you know that? I never told anyone here, nor did Sir John. None of my parishioners know you or you them. So how?'

'I confessed under the seal.'

'Not as a sin. Are you doing that now? Then your confession must be public.'

Rachael flicked her hair, rubbing her face between her hands.

'Much more serious were the Wardes. You discovered they

were Gaunt's spies in the cell of Saint Erconwald's. The Upright Men must have told you that, or Rosselyn. You'd surely demand the truth about how Boaz and others were so neatly trapped. The finger of suspicion pointed at the Wardes. May God absolve you, Rachael. You did not confess to me, not really. You did not validly take the sacrament; you are not covered by the seal. You seethe with hatred. You have an unslaked thirst, a ravenous hunger for revenge. Did the Upright Men demand the total annihilation of the Wardes? If not, your vengeance certainly did.'

'So I left the Tower, crossed to Southwark and massacred an entire family?'

'In a word, yes! Rosselyn allowed you out. You ensured all was safe, quiet then you moved. You carried out your hideous crime without any sign of resistance or struggle. Why, Rachael?'

She just shrugged.

'Because,' Cranston spoke his thoughts aloud, 'Warde admitted someone he either knew and trusted or someone who appeared to pose no threat.'

'Precisely,' Athelstan agreed. 'On that fateful evening Humphrey Warde opened his door to a delightful young woman who claimed to have a recommendation to visit him. I presume you came in disguise, hooded and cowled. You also gambled on the fact that the Wardes were distrusted – not the type of family to be entertaining in a parish where they were so fiercely resented. If there had been any obstacle to your plan, you'd either wait to come back or visit again.' Athelstan sipped from his goblet. 'Anyway, why should Warde fear a charming young woman? You are well spoken and courteous. He greets you warmly, you respond. The rest of his household hear this and return to their routine. You follow Warde into his small shop and ask for an opiate. He turns away. You bring up the crossbow you've concealed and kill him. Warde, before he died, had prepared a small pouch of opiate for you. You'd also probably learnt that the only people in the house were his family. You intended to deal with all of them, the pretty, smiling young woman who carries death beneath her robe. You moved through that house, swiftly slaying before slipping into the darkness like the demon you've become.' Athelstan took a further sip. 'God forgive you, at least you spared the baby, but you made a mistake.'

'What, what are you talking about?'

'You made a mistake about Huddle's death, but you also described Warde's killer moving from chamber to chamber. How did you know that?'

'I would like a drink,' Rachael declared loudly. 'My throat is dry. Have you finished, Brother?'

'No, because you had not. The Upright Men did not really concern you. They could plot whatever they wanted against Gaunt. At the same time Thibault and his coven were growing more vigilant. So you turned back to easier quarry. You regarded the Straw Men as a coven of traitors, not so much to the Common Good but to the ideals your beloved Boaz died for.'

Athelstan leaned forward, offering her the goblet which she took. 'I truly believe that you put the entire company under the ban. Samuel was your next victim.'

'He committed suicide.'

'No, you made it appear so. Once again with Rosselyn, now much smitten with you. Oh, yes, he was! I saw him watch you play that masque in Saint Peter's ad Vincula. He, as with so many men you have dealt with, followed you like a dog guarding your ways. You slipped through the dark and into Bowyer Tower. You knocked at Samuel's chamber. Only the good Lord knows what part you played then: worried, anxious, coy, timid or flirtatious. You also brought along a wine skin and a goblet. I'm sure the wine was laced with the opiate that you had taken from Warde's shop. You pretended to drink. Samuel certainly did and fell into a dead swoon. You summoned up Rosselyn. You took the fire rope, fastened it around the senseless Samuel's throat and thrust him out of the window to strangle. You then cleared the room and put anything you'd brought back into a sack. You leave. Rosselyn locks and bolts the door behind you and climbs out of the window. He uses the rope then the corpse to reach the chamber directly below. You were waiting for him. You opened the shutters and Rosselyn climbed through. You then close and bar the window. You would wipe away any wet, perhaps even sprinkle a little dust, but who would really notice in that darkened chamber? Moreover, those same shutters were violently disturbed – broken – when Thibault decided to force the chamber. What evidence could they offer? You hoped that would happen, which

is why you locked that chamber and slid the key under the door.'
Athelstan paused and went to stand over her. She gazed coolly
back.

'Samuel was not your only victim. Rosselyn was much taken
with you but you, unbeknown to our captain of archers, had
unfinished business with him. Rosselyn constantly played the
two-faced Janus, acting as Thibault's henchman yet also spying
for the Upright Men. In your eyes he could have informed the
Upright Men about the trap being planned at the Roundhoop,
but he didn't.' Athelstan chewed the corner of his lip. 'As I have
said, I could understand why: that would have been too dangerous
for Rosselyn.' Athelstan bent down, holding Rachael's strange,
green-eyed stare. 'But to you, Rosselyn was just another traitor,
a coward who could have saved Boaz but didn't. In that darkened
chamber in Bowyer Tower, lit only by a scrap of candle, you
decided on both judgement and punishment.' Athelstan returned
to sit on his bed. 'We men are easy to scrutinize, Rachael. Our
lusts are our weaknesses. Rosselyn must have been full of his
own prowess. He viewed himself as your partner with hopes of
becoming your paramour. He'd flirt and demand a kiss. You sat
him on that stool. You bestrode his lap like any tavern wench,
pressing yourself up against him, moving backwards and forwards
to excite his crotch. You caressed him. You put one hand behind
the back of his head, the other, hanging by your side, carried a
long Italianate poignard. Once again you act the lover, telling
him to close his eyes. Rosselyn did. You struck, a swift killing
blow pushing the dagger deep into his left eye while keeping
him pressed against the wall. He would jerk and struggle but
only for a few heartbeats; you would have two hands on that
dagger handle, pushing with all your strength.'

'True,' Cranston declared. 'A blow to the brain like that would
be deadly. I have seen the same happen in battle. The shock
alone would kill a man.'

'Once Rosselyn was dead,' Athelstan continued, 'you pushed
the acclamation into his lifeless hand. You also did something
else. Before your visit to Master Samuel, you doused yourself
in perfume. Now you had cleared his chamber and the shutters
were left open. You certainly didn't want your fragrance being
detected on Rosselyn's corpse. Help was at hand, a bucket of

filthy water full of slime and rottenness. You doused Rosselyn's corpse; the rank smell would kill any scent of perfume on him or in the chamber. To any observer, the killer would be depicted as abusing his victim's pathetic remains. Once done, you collected what you had to. You left, locking the chamber and the main door of the tower. On each occasion you pushed the key beneath the door to delay, to mystify, to deepen the confusion.' Athelstan breathed out. 'I wonder who was next. Samson? Gideon? Judith?'

'How say you, mistress?' Cranston leaned forward. 'The case presses heavily against you.'

Rachael glanced up, eyes crinkling into a smile. 'What can I say, Brother, except that you have much to say and even more to prove.' She moved restlessly on the stool. 'What about Judith? She is also a player, a mummer, a mistress of disguise?'

'*Concedo*,' Athelstan replied. 'I concede. I did speculate about Judith. She could have done this and she could have done that. She could have been here or there yet she flies against all logic as the killer. Firstly, she is not as courageous as you. She has a mortal fear of bears. Secondly, she suffers an affliction of the eyes, and so finds it difficult to calculate distances. I noticed that when she stares at people some distance away. How could she release a bolt, an arrow shaft? Finally and most importantly, and you know this, Rachael.'

'Know what?'

'Judith is very much in awe of you. She has very little time, if any, for men. She can act the role of a braggart in a tavern but such parts only help her express the contempt she has for men in general. I cannot see her seducing Barak, Eli, Master Samuel or Rosselyn. When you asked me to shrive you, you implied that Boaz and Judith had been close friends. I am sure if we brought her in here and questioned her closely, she would strongly deny this and perhaps point the finger at you. Nor would Samson describe himself as your betrothed, another fiction to confuse me.'

'Still, you have little evidence against me.'

'Oh, I can obtain that; as I said, you made mistakes.' Athelstan gestured at her gown. 'We will search your chamber. We'll find, among other things, a green gown heavy with perfume but stained here high in the chest with thick blood – Rossleyn's blood. It must have spurted from his eye like juice from a pressed grape. I doubt if you've had time to wash it. We would also be able to trace the stains left from that bucket of filthy water.' Athelstan shook his head. 'I'm sure Thibault's interrogators will discover more.' He spread his hands. 'Mistress, you are young and fair yet you have the blood of many on your hands. You can expect little or no mercy from Thibault. There is nothing I can do to save you. They will spend days, if not weeks, torturing you and, if you survive that, it will not be a swift hanging at Smithfield. You are a woman: they will burn you before the gates of Saint Bartholomew's. Knowing Thibault, the wood will be green and the executioner will not move through the smoke to strangle you swiftly. You could confess. I could take you into sanctuary, I could . . .'

Rachael moved with the speed of a lunging cat. She threw the goblet at Sir John as she rose, clutched the stool and hurled it at Athelstan, then she was at the door fumbling with the latch before they could recover. Athelstan immediately sensed what Rachael was going to do. But, by the time he had reached the door, she was already racing up the steps to the top of the Tower. Athelstan, with Cranston lumbering behind, climbed as fast as he could but it was fruitless. Rachael was young, energetic, nimble on her feet and, by the time a breathless Athelstan burst through on to the icy windswept tower top, she was already standing between two of the crenellations, the wind tossing her beautiful hair and fanning out her thick murrey robe. Dusk was sweeping in, grey and freezing cold. Sounds from below echoed up. Athelstan, fighting for breath, walked carefully around the beacon brazier.

'Please?' He extended a hand.

'Brother, do not be foolish. You are correct – what can you do? Save me from Thibault's demons? They will strip me naked, rape me and abuse me before they even start their questions. You know that.'

Athelstan sensed she was smiling through the murk.

'You will find evidence in my chamber. I never had time to hide everything. Your indictment is sound.' She waved a hand. 'Some details are wrong but, in the main,' she fought for breath, 'Boaz was the only person I ever loved. Samuel and the rest are

Thibault's creatures, body and soul despite their protests. They are what they are, Straw Men. Their words mere mumbling, they were weasel people who serve a weasel lord. All of them.' Her voice turned hard and defiant. 'Rosselyn was no better, a turncoat to the heart. The Upright Men despised him. Thibault would have discovered his treachery sooner or later. Rosselyn was weak, uncertain. He tried to stride either side only to blunder. He did not inform the Upright Men about the Roundhoop. He failed to reveal the plot to trap the Upright Men in the Tower. Once that happened, I received notice: Rosselyn, the Wardes and Huddle your painter were placed under the ban. Grindcobbe personally decided that.'

'You were given permission to slay at will?'

'Oh, yes, and I enjoyed it. Ah, well, I won't see Thibault smirk. I won't burn at Smithfield. I don't want to spend weeks in a filthy cell in this ghastly place.'

'Please?' Athelstan begged, even though he knew it was fruitless.

'Remember, Brother, those lines from the book of Ruth? "Wherever you go I shall follow",' then she was gone, slipping back into the gathering darkness, red hair flaring, gown billowing, her body plummeting to smash on the cobbles below.

Athelstan sat in Master Thibault's warm, luxurious council chamber. Lascelles was there, standing behind his master's chair like the shadow he was.

'So?' Thibault picked up a stick of sealing wax, weighing it in his hands. 'Rachael the vixen, the treasonable bitch! What a pity she escaped, to fall like that. She could have told us so much but,' he smiled, 'now you can do that, Brother Athelstan.'

'No, I shall not,' Athelstan retorted.

Cranston stiffened, breathing in noisily.

'Cannot, shall not?' Thibault queried. 'I can make you.'

'Do not threaten us,' Athelstan murmured. 'Please, Thibault, don't be so stupid. You have powerful friends, but so do I. I am a Dominican priest, a cleric protected by the full power of Holy Mother Church. I will tell you in return for four favours. Firstly, Rachael is to be given honourable burial here in God's Acre. I do not want her corpse dismembered.'

'I see no problem with that.'

'Secondly,' Athelstan dipped into his chancery satchel and brought out the book of plays, 'I keep this as a gift. My parishioners would benefit from it.'

'Sic habes,' Thibault quoted. 'You have it. And thirdly?'

'The woman Judith is allowed to settle in Saint Erconwald's.'

Thibault shrugged. 'And finally?'

'You take a solemn oath,' Athelstan indicated the Book of the Gospel on the lectern, 'here in the presence of Sir John Cranston, Coroner of the City of London, that Mistress Eleanor, who calls herself Mara, your prisoner in Beauchamp Tower, will be kept safe and sent to the Domincan convent of Saint Frideswide outside Oxford. I know the Mother Superior, a Scottish lady, Isabella Urquhart. You will swear that Eleanor will be kept safe, lodged most comfortably and given a pension for as long as she lives.'

Thibault looked as if he was going to object.

'Do so,' Athelstan urged. 'She is religious, protected by the church. She has committed no crime. She is innocent of any wrongdoing and I know she will pose no threat. Saint Frideswide lies near the palace of Woodstock. She can be, in a most careful manner, watched without being bothered.'

Thibault sucked on his lips and smiled. 'Brother Athelstan, Sir John, I agree. You have in fact solved a problem. Can you assure me your order will guarantee the Lady Eleanor will cause no trouble?'

'Believe me,' Athelstan grinned. 'The Lady Urquhart will see to that.'

Thibault rose and took the oath, his right hand planted firmly on the Book of the Gospel, and returned to his seat. Athelstan then described what had happened, moving swiftly through the evidence and citing the proof he had found in Rachael's chamber: certain scraps of parchment, an arbalest, a pouch of opiate and that blood-soaked gown.

Once he had finished, Thibault, his face contorted in fury as Rosselyn's treachery was described, sat head down. Eventually he glanced up. 'I heard about the business in Flanders. I sent the Straw Men and other agents to hunt the rumours down – the rest is as you describe it, Athelstan. As for Rosselyn, he must have been suborned very recently, possibly in the early winter but, there again,' Thibault blinked and glanced away, 'I wonder how many of those who eat My Lord of Gaunt's bread act the Judas once darkness falls. I did wonder about the attack near Aldgate; perhaps that was Rosselyn's offering, a guarantee of his word to the Upright Men.'

'That business in Flanders,' Athelstan retorted. 'Master Thibault, you have been very honest in taking the oath. I accept your assurances about the Lady Eleanor but there is one thing you haven't told me. And I swear, if you keep your oath, so will I.'

'What do you mean?'

'Evangeline was a former midwife, a royal nurse or whatever she called herself. I have no doubt that the tales she spun were based on rumour, lie, wishful thinking,' Athelstan shrugged, 'or court gossip. Well, you can take your choice.' Athelstan could feel the rise in tension. Thibault pulled himself up in his chair; Lascelles' hand slipped to the hilt of his dagger.

'When I was a boy,' Athelstan continued softly, 'my father had a small holding. Most of our summers were dry and I always remember my father being anxious lest a fire be started in the wheat field. He and other villagers hired Machlin, a former mercenary, to guard against this. Machlin was given a small hut on top of a hill. He was provided with food and drink and accepted into our community.'

'And?' Thibault asked.

'Machlin was very good, extremely vigilant in reporting the outbreak of fires until, of course, my father became suspicious. He discovered that Machlin was starting the very fires he was reporting. Machlin wanted to be a hero, a saviour.'

'The business in Flanders?' Lascelles rasped.

'Now I think,' Athelstan continued, holding Thibault's gaze, 'that Evangeline would have gone to her grave and kept to herself the farrago of lies about My Lord of Gaunt. But someone approached her posing as Gaunt's great enemy, enticing her greed with the prospect of fat profit.'

'My Lord of Gaunt has many enemies.'

'I just wonder,' Athelstan replied, 'if this mysterious messenger was sent by Gaunt's friends, someone who wanted to depict himself as a saviour, the man who crushed filthy lies and rumours about our glorious Plantagenet Prince. Someone who started the fire then posed as the saviour who extinguished it.'

'And whoever could that be?'

'Oh I would have to prove that, but Sir John here could help. We would go through the licences issued to those who have travelled to Flanders. We would make careful enquiries about why they went, where they went and what they did.' Athelstan now stared at Lascelles, who moved uncomfortably.

'I don't think that would be necessary,' Thibault remarked.

'No, neither do I,' Athelstan smiled. 'I'm sure the Lady Eleanor will remain safe. I am also confident, Master Thibault, that you will always hold the parish of Saint Erconwald's in tender respect, and that you will regard my flock as more misled than malevolent.' Thibault smiled and nodded. Cranston bit his lip to stop laughing.

'In which case . . .' Athelstan pushed back the chair and raised his hand in blessing. Thibault opened the small coffer on his right. He took out a small purse of clinking silver which he tied securely and pushed across the desk for Athelstan to take.

'Please distribute that among the poor of your parish, Brother Athelstan.' He gestured at the coroner. 'Sir John, you have done my master a great service – it shall not be forgotten. Now, it's best if you go.'

Within the hour Cranston and Athelstan had left the Tower and joined the noisy, colourful throng on the approaches to the bridge.

'Athelstan!' Cranston paused and pointed to the severed heads displayed above the gatehouse.

'Do you ever despair at the sheer, squalid wickedness, the weariness and waste of it all?'

'Isaiah, twenty-six,' Athelstan replied. 'God's promise that one day he will wipe away the tears from every eye. I truly believe that, Sir John. In the end, time will run backwards and full justice will be done.' Athelstan closed his eyes. He shivered as he recalled that beautiful young woman falling against the coming night, tumbling into the hands of God and those other souls cruelly snatched from life and dispatched to judgement.

'I must not despair,' he whispered. He opened his eyes and tugged at Cranston's cloak. 'For the moment, Sir John, let me wipe away a few tears and what better place than the Holy Lamb of God!'